A ROMAN SMILE

by

Gilly Beckett

Published by New Generation Publishing in 2016

First Edition

www.newgeneration-publishing.com

New Generation Publishing

The Island of Vectis - Winter Solstice

Hora Quarta (approximately – I am a wealthy man but not wealthy enough to possess a clock)

My eyes were dazzled by ever-changing patterns of early morning light that contrasted vividly with the more typical gloom of the Britannic winter. The god Sol poured luminescent rays through grey cloud strata causing a million golden flecks to ripple the surface of the sea.

Memories of Rome and the elaborate splendour of forums, basilicas, colonnades are rapidly fading after eighteen years' absence. Nevertheless, today the translucence emanating from sky and sea prompted me to remember the fine hues embodied in marble.

A startling commotion of sea birds swooped past, weaving, rising, falling; and then they were gone. Beyond the wide courtyard, blue green foliage nestled between twisted trees and bare branches where small birds twittered and shivered. I shivered too, in my woollen tunic guaranteed by optimistic manufacturers to combat the extremes of the unpredictable Britannic climate. If I could not recall the exact hues of Parian marble I could certainly remember warmer winters.

I do not often indulge in reminiscences, but this morning I was transported irresistibly back to Rome. I again heard my father recounting the whole astounding episode when Constantine gathered his government and nobility and marched the lot off to the New Rome. I recalled my father's description of how vulnerable and abandoned everyone felt, left behind. He stubbornly refused to follow many of his medical colleagues to the new centre of power, later insisting that I took up his profession. Physician's skills will always be needed no matter how uncertain the Empire's future, he portended. Rome went downhill of course, slowly. Rome was not built in a day; it could not disintegrate in a day.

Flaccilla and I had become betrothed when the Januarius *familia* approached my then ailing father, to suggest marriage terms, and I was happily bewitched by her coy, flirtatious manner and the little smirk playing around thin lips that concealed early warning signs of bad temper and sulkiness. Flaccilla never bestowed an affectionate smile to warm my disenchanted passion. Flaccilla's younger sister, Galatia, was a miserable woman if ever there was one and I felt an earlier misplaced pity for her husband Egnatius, irrevocably tied to the Januarius bunch. But later I needed the pity for myself. I recalled their ridiculous address in Rome, if you could call it such, 'near the place going down from the Palatine to the Forum' and completely misleading. I know that in Rome the street directions can border on the haphazard. But I remember my own. On the 'Quirinal Hill'. And very pleasant it was too. All the windows of the *domus* faced inwards towards flower beds and pools; the *peristylium* my particular pride and joy, surrounded by a two storeyed colonnade. It was perhaps somewhat ostentatious. But wealthy people like to consult surgeons rather than irresponsible street doctors and a showy house immediately gained the confidence of new clients. And Flaccilla needed to impress her snooty sister Galatia. But mostly she wanted to astound her beloved father. And he was effectively struck by the contrived grandeur as he lounged heavily on a specially reinforced bench, knocking back my favourite (hideously expensive) falernian, his belly ashake under swathes of wine-stained toga as he laughed immoderately at his own fatuous jokes. After our marriage, Flaccilla clearly preferred her widowed father's company to mine. He and I quickly grew to dislike each other. He despised my profession preferring to make his money through unrevealed shady deals that provided endless embellishments for his garish villa and his spoilt daughters.

I made the decision to go to Britannia as I pondered over the increasing uncertainties of life in Rome, even allowing for Flaccilla's familia. Violent crime was spreading from the Urbs and into the very heart of the city, fed by acquisitiveness encouraged through fear of poverty and brutality in a society that felt aggrieved and abandoned by its leader. Of course no city can be crime-free but there seemed a complete lack of interest by the magistri or anyone else to enforce the laws of Rome. People were jumpy. There were always murmurs of barbarian invasions about to happen just around the next corner, although I knew of no-one who heard or saw anything to bear out the rumours and I dismissed the fears as unfounded, mostly to placate my wife. Except that Flaccilla never seemed to desire any sort of attention from me after the early, heady days of our marriage were too quickly over.

What I cannot deny however is witnessing the Forum gradually stripped of its magnificent statuary and even whole columns and blocks of marble, hauled away by order of the Emperor, to beautify the New Rome. Such perturbing exercises were difficult to come to terms with, for the citizens who remained. We could not all relocate to New Rome along with the monuments. Many Romans did not want to leave. Most could not afford to forsake the former heart of the Roman Empire that threatened to become a vandalised wasteland.

I had been supplied with reliable information by Galatia's husband, who worked in the praefectus praetorio that seemed to have a hotline extending from New Rome to Britannia. His reports revealed that as the victorious Empire extended to ever widening territories, colonies like Britannia had become well-established. This Northern corner of the Empire seemed to me to offer stability for a young family. The important civiti, and the smaller towns, the *burgi*, rendered safe from marauders by strong fortifications and connected by well constructed roads. The people of Britannia were enjoying the benefits of a civilised society, not least the hitherto unheard of luxury of public baths and urinals. They were allowed to continue the worship of their own gods and to pursue their own cultures. Recognition by our Empire of a conquered peoples' right to homegrown religions seemed a particularly wise formula.

The Britons, displaying guileless confidence in their victors, also seemed keen to adopt Roman fashions. They were welcome to the toga, a wearisome garment to put on, complicated to adjust once it was on, the heavy pleats impossible to manipulate without help from a loving wife, or a disinterested bodyslave. (In my experience the choice was either a bodyslave or struggle alone.) The conquered people were also introduced to the doubtful recreation of amphitheatre spectacles, a pastime I firmly avoided. The sight of blood, spilt during gladiatorial contests for the pleasure of a rapacious audience, was impossible for me to contemplate. '…What good is armour, what good is swordsmanship? All these things only put off death a little…' I quote from an equally disgusted Seneca. Men against animals in the morning, men against men in the afternoons. Enjoyment derived through the agony of the dying can surely only inflame a culture of heartless violence. My father described turning away in bitter tears as Christians, men and women were dragged into the Colosseum to suffer the most terrible tortures, but that's another story. I had heard that there was an abundance of slave labour in Britannia, but that they consisted of those natives foolish enough to flout the benevolence of their conquerors. I have strong reservations over the use of slaves. Like my father, I too question the accepted ethics behind the often brutal, unrewarded employment of men, women and children too. That's how it is here in the Roman Empire of course, but I have always toed my own philosophical line where my slaves are concerned.

I heard that it was cold and it was wet most of the time in Britannia. Nothing is perfect. I went anyway. My insatiable urge to travel forced me, regretfully, to sell my beautiful house by the park but, gladly, wave goodbye to Flaccilla's surprised father. After the long uncomfortable journey over land and across the sea, in search of a better future, everything that I had heard about Britannia, including the weather, was true.

We settled in Durovernum, a large fortressed civitas, a big river nearby and excellent roads constructed by our armies. I established my practice as eye surgeon to the citizens of Durovernum, which provided a very comfortable income.

Flaccilla hated Britannia from the moment we set foot on its cold muddy banks. She never intended to make the slightest effort to examine the advantages of a civilised life in this chilly but green and pleasant land. Her sour demeanor told me all. I should have recognised that turned-down mouth on our Betrothal Day. The sacrificial pig had a prettier grin. Her displeasure at being forced to live in Britannia was not appeased by her pregnancy. Fannia was born, to lighten my life, although not that of her unimpressed mother. I thank the gods that it was my prerogative as husband and father to make the decision to keep the baby. Statistics prove that there are fewer children born nowadays and women are no longer interested in being mothers. Flaccilla whined that if our daughter had been a son she would have been happier and tried to enjoy Britannia, which could have been a show of sibling rivalry because Galatia had successfully reared a son. But I knew that 'happy' was not on either woman's itinerary. Once before we moved away, I shared furtive comments with Galatia's husband. Egnatius was obviously disaffected with his lot back in Rome. Here in Britannia, I grew pretty disconsolate too. My marriage was dwindling away.

There were other factors. Many Curiales were unwillingly abandoning their professional careers, forced out by escalating demands for rapidly increasing taxes, and mandatory participation in onerous official duties. The future of the Northern Empire looked bleaker when Emperor Theodosius I died and the Empire was divided and the Western portion of the Roman Empire left to his son Honorius who was only10 years old! A child Emperor could only weaken the throne. Murmurs abounded in bars and during dinners and at the Baths. Who knew the identities of the real leaders, hidden behind a little boy figurehead?

Mucius, an unmarried architect acquaintance, unexpectedly provided the opportunity for me to divert from the city to a quiet rural existence. He was selling his villa and farm and he wanted a quick sale. Why he chose to return to Rome when the news from there seemed so depressing, Jupiter only knows. Besides, the Roman Empire encouraged self-sufficiency in a country estate, however modest. Living from the land meant availability of local produce and provision of much needed local employment. I was tempted.

I remember well the showdown with Flaccilla, one unusually balmy summer night in Durovernum, as I laid out my neat plan to extract us from the rat race. I tried unsuccessfully to interest her in my description obtained from Mucius, of the pretty villa facing the sea on a small green island. Flaccilla had no intention of being wooed by my logical arguments for the move to the country, any more than the balmy evening.

'You never consider me and how I feel. You know how much I hate Britannia, tied to a girl child, no social life, and no news from Home.'

She slammed down chicken in a clay dish to the table with such force that I slopped my drinking cup of mulsum. All down one of my best togas, donned with much irritation (I have explained about toga trauma) to look my best for the occasion of the discussion. I kept my temper, despite my irritation. That honeyed wine was my favourite, not to mention the toga, once it was properly adjusted. I raised myself on my couch, dabbed ineffectually at the mess, ignoring the nasty comment about our 'girl child'.

'We have a very efficient postal system here. Your family could perhaps be persuaded to occasionally send you news?' I suggested.

But Flaccilla hadn't finished.

'You may not have noticed that I am very ill!'

I was mildly surprised. She had a lively spirit for a person declaring herself to be sick. Eyes tell me a lot. I turned my attention to Flaccilla's, but she kept her lids drooped, her face turned away, towards the untouched chicken lying soggily in its clay coffin.

'And do you want to discuss the symptoms of your illness?'

'As if you care! If you are set upon purchasing a villa buried on some unknown island, then go without me. I want to return home, immediately, to Rome and my father. I am ill. If I stay in Britannia I shall die.'

She added her last pathetic excuse in an undisguised attempt to remove the emphasis from her beloved father. She knew that I detested him.

Whilst doling out portions of the unappetising chicken, because for sure she would not, I told her that the journey back to Rome would finish her off, if she were as ill as she would have me believe. She refused my invitation of an examination by an excellent physician, also a good friend of mine. So that, it seemed, was that. I did not believe for one moment that Flaccilla was mortally ill as she insisted she was; her behaviour seemed normal, except towards her daughter, and except where I was concerned, and when she was at home, which wasn't often.

Which was why I had indulged in my liaison with Flaccilla's body slave, the beautiful silent Quinctia. I didn't care one cold night when Dionysus must have been hovering close, and she offered to pour my wine and murmured a gentle song deep into my ear. I didn't care that she was as silent in her lovemaking as when she performed more mundane household duties. I didn't care that her passionate kisses set my nerves tingling. I certainly didn't care as we moved rhythmically together to the sounds of a lyre being played badly across the street. At first, we were very discreet but I got careless. And one dark rainy day when Flaccilla returned home within a short time of going out to retrieve her bright green umbrella, the unpredictable Brittonic weather forecasted the end of our gloomy marriage.

Flaccilla's father was welcome to her. She had exercised her right not to relinquish her ties to her familia. She was the doted elder daughter and her father was wealthy, wealthier by far than me. But at least her decision meant that our daughter would inherit everything that I owned. Everything.

The night before her departure, Flaccilla had appeared unexpectedly in my bed and involve me in uncharacteristically passionate behaviour that left me breathless and confused. As she fussily rearranged her tunic for her return to her own bedroom, she reiterated that no one, certainly not me, could have ever persuaded her to stay in Britannia. I was left knowing it was my fault. All of it. Taking her away from Rome in the first place, making her pregnant with a daughter she did not want, using her slave as my concubine.

I try very hard and mostly unsuccessfully to forget that night. There was little pleasure involved and for sure no love, especially after her swaggering exit when I realised how thoroughly she was wreaking her revenge. I was helpless. A nasty feeling. Flaccilla was no fool. She took my silent concubine with her.

After months of missing Quinctia and not missing Flaccilla, I became convinced that I had made a serious error in considering Flaccilla to be in good health, although the *familia* couldn't be bothered to send news of her, good or bad, not even to little Fannia who constantly persuaded me to despatch her imploring messages to Rome for news of her mother. That was cruel of Flaccilla and the familia, but am I surprised?

Watching my daughter Fannia, on this chilly Vectis morning, I shrugged away the undesirable and unproductive thoughts. I was entranced by her silhouette outlined against the marbled sky and her loosened black hair lifting in harmony with the morning breeze, the fine folds of her long morning *stolla* drifted by the adulating zephyr, revealing a provocative glimpse of her lithe form. Her expressive hands fluttered, the gold and amber beaded armilae slithering around her wrists with a bell-like resonance. She called to me.

'I can see tiny black dancing objects dancing before my eyes. Why are they bothering me, those strange specks? If I shut my eyes, they are still swimming about!'

The bands of armilae tinkled urgently again, as she shrugged her pretty shoulders in exasperation at my silence.

'You are an eye surgeon. Why cannot you answer my question?'

I basked in her admiration of my expertise, although it was now more than ten years since I ceased practise as a surgeon and carried my little daughter Fannia away to the tranquil island of Vectis and the peaceful villa near to the sea.

But now the statuesque 16 year old was impatient for my learned reply. How quickly she had grown up, enjoying her role as domina of our household, planning our menus, chastising our domestic attendants over badly executed tasks. But at times I was uncomfortably aware that the quietness of our island existence undoubtedly held its own disadvantages. Fannia had inherited my own love of travel. She yearned to see Rome. But not to see her mother. I eventually told her that Flaccilla was dead. She took it surprisingly well.

But her fascination for Rome lingered. Fannia knew that Rome was warm and exciting. It was certainly warmer than this small island off the coast of Britannia. But in Rome the colourful concept of excitement had taken a different, menacing hue. My two oldest slaves talked as much as Fannia willingly listened, of the city they had loved, of the winding Tiber, the Palantine of Rome, the splendours of the marble statuary (though I wonder how much marble is left in Rome these days?). Fannia loved to hear about the sancturies of the gods. She could describe, as though she had seen it for herself, every aspect of the Temple of the Divine Julius in the Forum even the detail of his star of godhood. She honoured the goddess Vesta by throwing pieces of salt cake in the hearth for good luck, and dancing around in a childish Vestal Virgin fantasy, ignoring my reminders that she would have been taken away to serve the goddess at six years old until she was the grand old age of thirty. I left out the more sinister duties, probably nasty rumours but not what you'd want for your daughter. Tending to the sacred fire was the easy bit.

I didn't begrudge the men their reminiscences; they never encouraged Fannia's Roman dream. 'They tell me that Rome has changed. Bad things are happening there. They say that the city is threatened by the Goths - whoever they are! They say we are much safer here.'

Too true. They know what side of their bread has olive oil in abundance.

I remembered her demand for my optical knowledge.

'There are tiny objects in your eyes that hate sunlight. Forget them and they will go away.'

I clenched my fingers in the folds of my tunic. I often wondered what these entities were myself. Fannia's smile melted my heart. I made a mental note to discover which goddess possessed such an entrancing smile. She had certainly not inherited her mother's petulant demeanor.

Satisfied with my expert response, Fannia ran lightly towards the edge of the parapet and paused there, like a pacified muse, gazing out to sea. What an adorable creature she was, entirely unaware of her natural grace. Any man would quickly fall under her innocent spell and claim the provocative maiden for his wife. I knew that sometime soon she needed to find a husband. I dreaded that time. My anguish at parting with my daughter would be difficult to contain. For all the years we had lived on the island, she and I had shared our lives, her tantrums, nightmares and childhood illnesses; her education, but the less said about that the better, and now Fannia had suddenly grown up. Yes, my thoughts were selfish. My daughter had become my reason for living. And one day I would have to overcome my egotistic argument for keeping her to myself, and present a brave, even delighted face before an eager suitor. But hopefully not yet.

Our separate morning reveries were interrupted by a slave advancing nervously through the vestibulum. I was grateful for his intrusion. I was conscious of my inadequate tunic and my toes turning blue in my ancient skimpy sandals as I shivered in a breeze that was changing from balmy to biting. Fannia had discovered a tiny kitten and was enticingly calling to it whilst the pathetic creature cringed beneath a naked rose bush.

'Come I'll find you something to eat' Fannia told it as the animal eventually scampered after her.

Hmm. The kitten might have been warmer in Rome but it wouldn't have been fussed over; more likely hurled into the Tiber like a rat. But at least Fannia had forgotten about the tiny black objects in her eyes. I got it right sometimes.

This slave had a serious stutter. He obviously wasn't used to introducing guests but I remembered that I had granted Fidus leave to go to the postal station as he anxiously awaited news of his ailing mother in Byzantium. I had written a message on his behalf to the family she worked for. I happened to know them, before they settled there and I settled here. Fidus' concern left a lot to be desired by my wife's family who had never bothered to reply to messages from me or from Fannia. But that was then. My wife was a distant, unhappy memory though I had to take care to hide my feelings from Fannia. I have overheard Fannia's whispered prayers to the Lar in the niche near the triclinium, pleading him to send her love to whereever her mother might be. I doubt the Lar listened with too much enthusiasm. The foppish icon that purports to represent my ancestors in the form of our Household God seems completely self-absorbed to me.

All my patience was required not to get too irritable at the length of time it took to glean the identity of my visitor, from Fidus's jabbering underdog.

It seemed that the visitor was my near neighbour, Melania Luperca. According to local rumour, the lady was a devout Christian with considerable estates that she sold to distribute her wealth amongst the poor. I have to confess that despite the spreading popularity of Christianity, I am undecided, although my father, a good and just man, converted and became a devout follower of this religion. He whole-heartedly embraced the faith, and the way Christians unreservedly loved and helped each other. Also there was no longer any ban on Christian worship as in earlier times that prevented Roman citizens converting to Christianity. Septimus Severus comes to mind, although my father in defence of Severus once told me that he merely enforced long-established laws and employed Christians in his household and was known to protect Christians from onerous hostilities. I remember the triumphal arch in Rome erected by Severus and somewhere amongst my possessions I have an aureus minted to celebrate his legion XIIII *Gemina Martia Victrix.* I only remember the detail so well because it represents an exceptionally fine featured man, the black Emperor, born I believe in Leptus Magna, popular with the citizens of Rome for his tough stand against corruption; not so well liked by the Roman Senate because he seized power with the help of the military. And significantly for me as I now lived in Britannia, Septimus Severus, after many notable achievements, restoring the ageing Wall of Hadrian and successfully keeping the Gauls away from Britannia, died in Eboracum, in the Province of Britannia Inferior. That was over 200 years ago when some Christian saints, Piran and Patrick and Andrew passed through Gaul to Britannia and over to an island beyond.

But I only know this much because my father once told me.

Regretfully, young people neglect to pay sufficient attention about matters that do not immediately affect them. I was guilty of this myself, as I was to discover.

Constantine effectively established Christianity as the favoured religion. Only Jupiter knows if that bodes well for the Roman State, if indeed anything bodes well for the Roman State these days. I wondered idly what Jupiter thought. But there were many rumbles of change for Jupiter to ruminate about nowadays besides Christianity. Even here in Britannia, the rumbles of change echoed, including stories circulating of a larger army to handle the increasing disorder in the Empire particularly in Rome. Where can they start, I asked myself a little smugly, not being in Rome, if everything has become out of control. Central economic planning, expanding bureaucracy for tax collection and increased regulations was another rumble, or three. Administration of new laws in this far-flung place, would be an interesting exercise. (It didn't do to be too complacent Marcus Cassius. The news hadn't yet reached Vectis that individual military and civil administrators were to be set up to enforce the new regulations.)

Perhaps Jupiter should intervene, but he probably can't be bothered. And I was getting side-tracked.

I left the courtyard and walked through the aisle around the inner garden. I inspected the nymphaeum. I was convinced from certain tests I had performed, one using a sick pet mouse of Fannia's, without telling her, that this walled pond might contain curative water. I can never completely put aside the discipline of ophthalmic training, but I am also intrigued by the concept of votive remedies, and curative water. And the mouse recovered.

As I entered the triclinium I slowed down to admire my mosaics, I never tire of this occupation. The finest craftsman I could find, and he is a local man, created the imagery of peacocks that are also echoed on wall paintings both here and in other rooms of my villa. I take enormous pleasure in those haughty magnificent creatures. I have a breeding pair in the grounds of my villa, but Fidus keeps them in a separate protected area during winter for I believe they are rather delicate until they are fully adult.

I discerned a movement ahead of me in the shadows. My visitor came forward to greet me, Melania Lupurca, an extremely handsome woman wearing a palla of dazzling blue that swirled about her as she moved. A focale was knotted about her neck and a mappa dangled from her arm, to wipe her face in case of dust I assumed, for there was no heat in the weather in this part of the Empire now or ever that could lead to excessive perspiration.

She smiled. A noble controlled smile. But a smile nonetheless.

'Marcus Cassius. Thank you for receiving me without prior appointment.'

'You are always welcome here, Melania Lupurca. How may I assist you?'

She did not answer immediately. She turned away and glided towards a figure hunched on the stone bench who rose shakily as she took his arm.

'May I introduce my husband Pinianus. We desperately seek your knowledge and expertise.'

VECTIS - Later the same day

Fannia was in one of her chatty moods. It was the twelth hour – approximately. (I believe I have made the point that I am not wealthy enough to possess a clock, and sundials in Britannia are about as useless as sandals.)

We remained together companionably after dinner. I lounged upon my favourite couch (embroidered with peacocks of course). I was very grateful for the suspensurae that ensured a continuous flow of warmth through the villa, because I detected a distinct bite of frostiness outside in the black night air when I locked up as I always did myself. Fannia of course had never known life without central heating,

Fannia sat upon a stool at my feet, hugging her knees, telling me about her two old women. They lived alone without servants or slaves, but they cultivated and cooked everything they needed for themselves having no help of any kind. Fannia was describing their small and simply furnished, thatched house. It had been built, the furniture too apparently, by the old ladies' brother who had long since died. Of hard work I should think, though I kept my thoughts to myself as Fannia prattled on, telling me of her journey along the hazardous path that led to her finding the hovel, close to the cliffs where the force of the wind almost blew her into the raging sea.

Her graphic description of her near disaster caught my wandering attention and I chastised Fannia who laughed.

'It wasn't really as bad as that and the women gave me a delicious warm drink that tasted like your mulsum; one of them makes it herself! I shall visit them again. We talked and talked. Do you know, they are Britons, they have never been married and they have never left the island! And they say they don't want to…'

My daughter's prattle faded into the intricate imagery of the wall mosaics, as I mused over the problem caused by the visit of Melania Lupurca and her husband. The problem was in the eyes of Pinianus, thick with cataracts, both of them, the worst case I had ever encountered. He had not told her when it all began, but as he stumbled about and crashed into everything, worse and worse over the years, and refused to be interested in going out or looking closely at anything, it became obvious that this was not just carelessness or laziness as he insisted. Melania Lupurca was appalled by her failure to recognise the symptoms. To compound the problem Pinianus was a very old man. Thirty years his wife's senior. And I calculated that the lady was at least 50 years old and I was being generous, but I am a gentleman, even in my private thoughts, most of the time.

I warned Pinianus that the treatment to remove the cataracts would be uncomfortable. He was quite obviously frightened to death, and I did not want to be responsible for despatching him to that particular finality. For one thing his wife gave the impression of being inordinately fond of him, he being a fractious little man. Loss of one's precious sight could certainly be blamed for making one crabby. Not that his irritable manner was directed at me; though I abhorred the rough ill-mannered tone he reserved for his patient wife. And Melania Lupurca accepted it calmly with her noble smile, merely pleading with him to be brave and with me to perform the operation. I had sent them away to discuss the matter in the privacy of their own villa. They departed in a raeda, a surprisingly sturdy four-wheeled carriage. It appeared that the lady had retained some degree of luxury considering her rumoured over-generosity to the poor. However upon reflection I decided that the carriage was more likely to be the property of Pinianus. I would have not taken him for a Christian willingly giving away his wealth. Whereas compassion shone like a lamp from the lady who was his long-suffering wife.

I realised that Fannia had wearied of chatting and was excusing herself, and her affectionate bedtime kiss warmed me more than the suspensurae.

In the small cubiculum where I kept the accessories and instruments of my former profession, I located my collection of fine needles that were necessary to push through the eye and then break up the offending opaque growth; and the small piece of equipment to suction it out. The operation was guaranteed to improve most people's sight moderately although there would undoubtedly remain blurriness thereafter. But I would remember to suggest a medallion of polished amber that assists impaired vision considerably.

I slept badly that night. The old and dreaded visions of Flaccilla haunted me. I saw her cruel smile. I thought I heard Quinctia calling me; a desperate sound that woke me fearfully. When I fell asleep again I dreamed of Melania Lupurca begging me to perform the operation and I was refusing. And it was my fault. All of it.

The next day there was an unusual event, weatherwise. Snow. The Villa gardens and trees looked uncommonly pretty in their layers of sparkling winter finery. I wasn't in the mood to appreciate it. I was cold. I sent for Fidus.

'Is the slave checking the hypocausis regularly enough?'

'I will check that the slave is checking. It is unusually cold today Marcus Cassius.'

'I am very aware of that.'

He hesitated.

'Yes?'

I barked at the man who unusually trembled and not from the cold. By Jupiter, I was bad tempered today.

'One of the peacocks… She looks poor. Not good at all. I am sorry…'

'The female! Well she had better not die. You are supposed to check her regularly too.'

Fidus shuffled out. I was instantly repentant. I must be getting old, feeling regret at bellowing at a servant. But Fidus was always reliable. Unlike the weather. If the peahen died it would be despite his attention not because of his inattention. I heard a distant roar from the charcol fed hypocausis in the bowels of the villa. I knew that the slave had been found to be not been checking. I would soon be warm. But my temper did not improve. Fannia appeared wrapped warmly against the snow, asking my permission to visit her ladies in their hovel along the cliffs. I refused.

'The weather is too unpredictable for such an expedition. And your tutor should be here by now.'

'Oh he won't come out in unpredictable weather. Why is everyone so afraid of the weather?'

She left me alone. Although to be truthful, she flounced out, but she did it beautifully.

Melania Lupurca with or without her distasteful husband did not make an appearance nor deliver a message. I was distinctly relieved. But the snow showed no signs of abating. It would be advisable not to venture out on such a day. Unless the journey was really necessary.

When Fidus aroused me from an unfortunate doze, I realised that I was snoring loudly with my jaws fully opened, somewhere around mid day, he looked both pleased and apologetic.

I yawned and stretched and did not bark at him.

'The female peacock…'

'Peahen!' I barked.

'Yes, she seems a little improved.'

'That is good new Fidus. Thank you.'

'And… there is a messenger waiting.'

I stood up too quickly and the cubiculum spun.

'What messenger? What news? Is it from the Empire?'

I was being indiscreet before Fidus, showing over-concern at the possibility of unwelcome official bulletins. But I was hardly awake. Moreover I had again endured bad dreams, almost a continuation of the night before. My eyes were sore. I might have to resort to using one of my own remedies, the amber eyeglass, if there were something to read.

'He brings the message in person.'

'I will see him in the triclinium. Give me a few moments.'

'He says his news is confidential.'

Much later I showed the man out into the whirling white storm and returned shivering uncontrollably to pace the floors of the villa. My weary eyes followed the wall designs that depicted painted ravens, such ugly birds, imagery I had since regretted allowing, merely because they are similar to the local choughs. Ravens or choughs, in my present mood they loomed over me threateningly. Their ominous brooding shapes hovered within my hideous dream. Except that it was not a dream. The news brought by the messenger filled my heart with every emotion it was possible to experience. I returned to my cubiculum where we had talked in privacy, I shuffled through the documents he had left. My head reeled. My heart thudded with such intensity that I thought I would drop dead. But dropping dead was not an option. The timing was wrong.

I realised that Fidus had returned. By Jupiter! I had seen more of Fidus lately than I could cope with. Fidus coughed and fidgeted edgily. Perhaps Fidus felt the same about me.

'The lady Melania Lupurca is waiting with her husband. They wish that you perform the operation on his eyes - in all haste the lady says.'

VECTIS – almost Summer Solstice

Actually it was only early Spring. But Winter Solstice was passing quietly, the weather had improved, mostly and with it my composure, mostly. It was the Day of the Sun, by Constantine's decree a long time ago. The important religious day for the Christians that could also be enjoyed by everyone else. This particular Day of the Sun was important for me too except that I knew that it wouldn't be the relaxing Day that it should be. Now that the damaging winter storms were over, boats would be sailing again. And I had ordained privately that this was the Day to talk to my daughter – about one particular Boat.

I found Fannia sitting in the garden, near to the walled pool, nursing the kitten, grown fat and affectionate under her personal supervision.

'Look how big she is; how soft her fur is.'

'She is a She?'

'Of course. I call her Juno.'

'Hmm. Fannia I have to talk to you. Concerning a serious matter. Not about cats.'

'All right.'

Fannia obediently tipped the furry creature from her lap and it slunk away stealthily. More of a stealthy roll really. I feared the worst. But I hastily kicked the cat from my nervous mind.

'Fannia, the matter that I need to discuss with you - it concerns your mother.'

I knew it was a bad opening.

Fannia jumped up clasping her hands together.

'Oh she is not dead?'

'Dear child, your mother is dead. Make sure that you understand that. You came to terms with the fact a long time ago.'

Bright tears were forming in her bright brown eyes. This was going to be very difficult.

'If she is dead, why do you talk of her now?'

‘During the winter, a messenger arrived here at the Villa. He brought some incredible news from Rome. I have taken all this time to find words to tell you.’

Fannia opened her mouth to interrupt with a question but I held up my hand.

‘No, let me talk. Before she left Britannia, your m… Flaccilla told me that she was ill. I doubted it was so. She refused to have medical attention. But I let her go. She was not a good mother to you my dear. And our marriage was all but over. We were no longer husband and wife; there was no love. She loved only Rome. And her own father. I had no power in law to prevent her departure. But in Rome, she was delivered of a baby. She never wrote to tell me she was pregnant. And not one member of the family told me of her death. But the birth killed her.’

‘And they never told us! Not even Aunt Galatia? How could they be so cruel…’

Fannia dissolved into tears and I let her cry. She could at last mourn, for strangely when I told her years before that Flaccilla was dead, when I was so unsure of the truth, she shed not a tear.

Eventually she calmed herself. I sighed quietly with relief.

‘The baby. Did the baby live?’

‘It did and is alive today. You have a brother, now ten years of age. His name is Philippus. And he may be crossing the water now, to see us.’

‘A brother’ she repeated slowly. ‘You say he is coming to visit us? That will be - pleasant.’

Fannia sounded uncertain of the pleasantness of such a visit. But sweet thoughtful little person that she is, Fannia turned her attention to me.

‘It must have been a great shock for you, dearest father. But the boy will surely stay in the patria potestas of my mother’s familia since your marriage is dissolved?’

I ignored her surmises. For now.

‘Fannia. Let us go for a walk. We need some air.’

I was glad that Fannia did not seem immediately keen for further information.

'Come with me to visit the old women. The weather is pleasant. Please come with me!'

I had no excuse. Fannia needed normality to settle her down. If Fannia thought the old crones represented normality, I had failed as her father.

I was still puffing from the exertions of the cliff walk, when we sat in the dark hovel on a hard wooden bench, drinking some quite acceptable imitation mulsum from small earthenware bowls. Fannia interpreted the old girls' words as they slurped the mulsum and mumbled their tale and nodded in agreement. The women had been the daughters of escaped slaves. Their parents were captured during one of many small local rebellions and worked in a palace on the mainland. I believe I know the one built by Claudius well over three centuries ago. But the plucky pair had somehow got away and landed up on Vectis where their three children were born. The women had a tooth each and one had only one eye. Their sparse hair dangled like hanks of greasy uncombed wool either side of their brown wrinkled faces. But their long robes were clean and the hovel only smelled slightly of an elderly yellow dog lying comatose at the feet of the woman with one eye. I would have been interested tohear how she lost the other eye. I was halted from making my medical enquiry when Fannia whispered to me that they hated the Romans.

The walls of the crudely devised cottage had been roughly plastered at some time, no doubt by the hard working, long dead brother. One wall boasted a well preserved painting of a female who even I could recognise as the image of Boudicca.

'They think that Britannia is now in the hands of the Britons. Aren't they funny.'

'Hilarious. I think I should go.'

I stood up nearly colliding with the low mud-packed ceiling. The yellow dog glanced at me and then lowered his shaggy head again. He obviously hadn't been trained to smell out Roman chiefs – or surgeons.

'Don't be long' I said to Fannia sternly, but inwardly I groaned. I had handled my talk with her very badly. I still had things to tell her. Important things. I stumbled back along the cliff path, amazed by my daughter's friendship with the strange old crones, dazed by the strength of their wine, worried at how out of breath I was, anxious as to how to tackle my next talk with Fannia.

The raeda standing at the entrance to my villa, and the stately figure descending from it, wearing a heavy overcloak, were not difficult to identify. My heart's heavy thudding subsided to a nervous flutter. Perhaps I should get my pal Nonius, the physician whose services my wife had rejected all those years ago, to give me a once over.

The stately figure moved gracefully towards me as I panted in somewhat ungainly fashion up the wide stone steps.

'Marcus Cassius.'

I held my hands towards her in greeting. The gesture saved me speaking. An attempt at that moment would have emerged as an undignified gasp, but with a big effort disguising my shortness of breath I guided her into the villa. I looked down at her as we moved inside.

The oval face was serene. But something was missing. The noble smile.

VECTIS – late that night

Fannia and I sat in our usual after-dinner places, I reclining; she perching upon her little cross-legged stool. She was not chatting tonight. I belched and it was painful. Yes I would definitely call on Nonius. But I nursed the suspicion that the malaise was not in my chest but in my head. My brain seemed to spin like a child's top, whirling around with all that had occurred in so short a time. First one problem burned for my attention, to be quickly supplanted by the flaring agony of the next.

Fannia, sensitive as always to my moods, leaned towards me gently touching my knee as I jumped edgily.

'What is worrying you father? You ate nothing of your dinner. You drank too much wine. Are you angry with me?'

I patted her hair. How could I be angry with my beautiful and devoted daughter?

'When I returned home today, there was a visitor. Melania Lupurca. Do you recall the lady?'

'Yes of course. I remember when you operated on her husband's eyes. You sent me out because you knew it would not be an easy task. I went to visit my old ladies. They have an adorable little goat and they showed me how to milk her.'

'Her husband has died.'

'Oh! The operation…'

I confess to having had exactly the same concern at first hearing the sad news, although I reckoned it to be highly unlikely to have been the cause. If Pinianus had snuffed it immediately following my performance of the treatment to clear his eye condition, it would have been a heart attack brought on by shock. No doubts could have been claimed. I suppressed a shudder as I recalled the gory event. The poor old chap had screamed and kicked, refusing the opium poppy compound (I had carefully dried and transported the seeds from Rome). I blessed the ferocious strength of Fidus. But it was a good job despite the fight. And I had heard nothing from them since that time.

Melania Lupurca, such a thoughtful lady whilst suffering her own distress, hastened to reassure me that Pinianus had made a good recovery in the time following the eye surgery although he complained that his sight was not fully restored. I meticulously explained the prognosis to him but obviously he decided not to remember. They had, at my advice, purchased an amber medallion and Melania Lupurca thought he enjoyed peering through it. No, he had collapsed at dinner, choking on a fish bone. A nasty end for the old boy but I felt much more compassion for his widow. She looked almost beautiful through her sadness, and we shared a glass of wine by the pool in surprisingly warm sunshine, before she departed.

'I have a request to make of you Marcus Cassius' she said as I walked her to her carriage.

'Any help I can offer' I replied.

Her small hand resting upon my arm looked so vulnerable. All my own problems deserted me, for the moment.

'Will you accompany me to the funeral? There is no-one I would rather ask.'

'I will be taking Melania Lupurca to the funeral' I told Fannia.

VECTIS – And another fine mess

I suppose I am not alone in hating funerals. All that horrendous hair renting and garment tearing and beating of breasts. The air sickly with oil and smoke from too many lamps and candles. The gruesome procession with out-of-tune pipes and tubae. Those ridiculous hired mourners screaming their staged grief.

At the funeral of Pinianus, there were only half a dozen or so guests, nobody I recognised, and they were obviously friends of Melania Lupurca. No one made the slightest attempt at noisy mourning of the passing of Pinianus. I should have guessed that Melania Lupurca would display more taste than to engage professional clowns, and to concern herself less about outmoded tradition.

Instead, we all walked silently behind the bier to a field near to Pinianus's villa. I was amazed to see the unadorned pyre. Something of a shock when one has witnessed the lavish altar-like ustrinae back in Rome. And there was no official service. No *hominem mortuum in urbe ne sepelito neve urito* and all that da-di-da. Nothing. Instead, one of Melania Lupurca's friends quietly spoke some words that I could not catch, while the others lowered their heads reverently; as the corpse of Pinianus was placed upon the pyre. The guests must be Christians, I thought with interest but I would have to choose another time and certainly another place to enquire of the elegantly grieving widow. In accordance with Roman funeral ceremonies I have been more accustomed to, she bent near to her husband, gently opened and closed his eyelids and kissed him. And that appeared to be that.

I felt a great relief flood over me. After all I was a man with serious troubles of my own. This uniquely simplistic handling of funeral rites came as a refreshing change. Except for one aspect so unexpected that it almost threw my composure. She indicated that I was to set light to the pyre.

Melania asked me to remain with her during the conflagration. She sprinkled sweet-smelling herbs and threw aromatic oils as the flames gripped and sucked at the unpretentious pyre and thick smoke mercifully disguised its morbid shroud. Melania's friends moved away. I really didn't know whether they thought I was a relative, or someone else, and this worried me slightly but they all nodded at me respectfully which was pleasant of them. Perhaps they knew of my (former) profession. Surgeons always command deference.

Melania adhered to Roman tradition by staying near the pyre until its destruction. We waited in silence during this tiring procedure. Once she seemed unsteady and breathless, reaching up to grasp the heavily draped material at the shoulder of my voluminous toga. I did not mind at all as I gently took her arm, refraining although I very much wanted to, from holding that fragile hand. It was dark when we returned to her villa. A servant had gone ahead carrying the urn.

We were alone.

'Where will you place your husband's ashes?'

The important finality of the funeral had to be clarified and I was too involved by now not to ask the question.

'Here in the garden' was the almost frivolous reply as I stared amazed, at her calm countenance in the light of the torches that threatened to be extinguished. A lively sea breeze had suddenly erupted, catching the flames and tossing them excitedly hither and thither.

'Pinianus told me I must never sell his villa. But if I find it impossible to keep his last wish… then he will always be here.'

A strange answer. And something even stranger. Her controlled grieving and superlative dignity throughout the day were dispelled as Melania threw back her head. She let out a strange sound, not a keening, not a cry, but more like tinkling laughter. She immediately recovered her noble demeanor leaving me gawping like a servant, uncertain if I had imagined her astonishing outburst. She clapped her hands. A young serving girl appeared gracefully skirting the stone path, almost as if waiting off-stage for her cue. She vanished as quickly, leaving us alone with wine that neither of us wanted.

Later, much later, I staggered home gazing around. Nothing looked any different, but everything was different and would never be the same again. The tensions of the day had dissolved like the cooling of sacrificial embers. I had comforted a beautiful bereaved lady, unable to recall caressing a woman so warmly captivating. My eager arms had displaced her cloak as we searched frenziedly to find unfettered comfort, and amongst swan feather pillows our inflamed passions soared and my hitherto sagging confidence achieved a proud revival.

The crescent moon smiled knowingly at me as stars burned through the silken sky.

The torches outside my villa welcomed me through the evening gloom flaring with cheery yellow tongues.

Fannia was waiting for me.

'You are very late. How was the funeral? How is Melania Lupurca?'

She might well ask. But I could not supply anything but an innocuous answer.

'Melania…Lupurca is coming to dinner with us tomorrow.'

Melania Lupurca coming to dinner became a regular rather than an occasional event. These nightly repasts proved very enjoyable both to both myself and Fannia who like me, loved the sociability of Melania's presence. Fannia meticulously planned the menus with Fidus, I made sure that the wine was absolutely right. We waited with anticipation each evening for the sound of the carriage. I felt important again. Prouder and stronger. Two women, my beautiful daughter and my noble friend, happy to be entertained by me in my villa. I bought two new evening togas from a disreputable salesman who looked as though he and his boat had been dredged from the Styx. He assured me the togas had come all the way from Rome but accepted an inadequate handful of denarius eagerly enough and rowed energetically away. My calculated guess was that the togas had fallen from the back of a wagon. Was I bothered? They were immaculate.

After delightful dinner one evening, I was forced to remind Fannia that she would need to get some sleep to be bright and responsive for her lessons. She had taken a dislike to the young tutor and Greek and Latin seemed to bore her. She informed me that she wanted to learn to dance and play the lyre. Who could I ask? I turned to the noble Melania Lupurca who directed her full attention to Fannia always willing to hang happily upon her words.

'If you and your father have no objection, I recommend my servant Claudia. She is an excellent dancer and she also plays the lyre. 'Oh yes!' cried Fannia delighted at the prospect and expressing curiousity as to what else the talented Claudia could do.

'Claudia could also instruct you in the art of carding, weaving, dying cloths in fresh jewel colours...'

Fannia's face fell just a little but enough to be noticed by me, if not Melania. My minx of a daughter may have enjoyed exercising a degree of power, organising the running of the household, but the more onerous domestic activities that some women still accepted as their duties did not impress Fannia.

'We will see…' I enjoined and Fannia looked relieved. She might not have fancied spindles, but she could certainly weave me around her little finger.

'Thank you Melania Lupurca. Fannia, we wish you a sound sleep.'

And now I had to relieve the enthusiastic young tutor of his post. I do not enjoy such chores. He was Greek, olive-skinned, black haired, with a long snooty nose and heavy-lidded eyes that regarded me with the cynicism of youth. He knew I couldn't stand up to my daughter. 'I trust that

Fannia pays more attention to the lyre than to lyric poetry' he sneered. And that was after I had written him a glowing testimony and a recommendation to a family I know in Durovernum. And paid his transport. Perhaps I am really getting soft.

Witnessing Fannia and Claudia dancing together, whirling charmingly, filled my heart with joy. Fannia seemed happy again and that was what mattered. Claudia was the same age as Fannia. I recognised her as the girl who had swiftly and gracefully served wine that fateful night after the funeral of Pinianus.

As the Summer Solstice wove warmer weather into our lives, my heart no longer thudded and my painful indigestion settled down. Melania Lupurca was entirely responsible. It was gratifying to watch Melania spending time with us, and enjoying her wine, as I do.

One particularly congenial evening, we dined upon apricots (apparently imported from Armenia) with chopped ham, followed by a white fish, of which I am very fond, served with a sweet and sour sauce. The bread was good, rather like the panis candidus that I remember from Rome. Fidus's wife is responsible for the bread and it is always excellent in texture and freshness. For the record, I mention here that my delight in peacocks does not include their use as a gastronomic delicacy. An acquaintance registered surprise that I rear my birds purely to appreciate their beauty and elegance. Flamingo is quite delicious but there are none hereabouts. I never eat chicken, not any more. After Fannia had reluctantly retired, we removed to the garden by my nymphaeum and discussed the increasing bureaucracy forced on the Western Empire and agreed that it was worrying. I had heard that people were being forced to pursue their original careers. Did this mean that I would have to return to eye surgery because my farming activities would be seen as work? She did not think it would be the case.

'You are providing employment and food. The economy of the land is important. I admire you very much Marcus Cassius.'

'Admire me? Why?'

This lady was not only pleasing to look upon, she possessed the aptitude to make me feel good about myself. She had been directly responsible for the restoration of my self-esteem because that particular section of my psyche had suffered quite severely of late. Lazy with the effects of a large after-dinner mulsum, I wondered idly as to the reason, whisking away the unanswered question like a worrying fly. Instead I turned my attention back eagerly to my adorable guest.

'Because you chanied your profession after many years, to one full of uncertainty. The unreliable climate makes farming a difficult occupation. And employing labour has problems of its own. I congratulate you on your tenacity. It could not have been an easy transition from city life to rural Vectis.'

'It wasn't quite like that' I admitted honestly whilst enjoying her admiration.

'The villa farm was already profitable and run by good reliable workers well able to make decisions. All I had to do – was oversee and acquaint myself with country skills.'

'You're being pompous now Cassius' the fly reminded me. 'What country skills have you actually taken on board? Mmm?'

I had also escaped onerous taxes and compulsory civic responsibilities by officially 'retiring'. I had not told Melania Lupurca about this, nor had I mentioned ducking out of my miserable marriage. I felt sure she would disapprove; being a Christian.

We sat on, as stars dotted the sky, and the invisible sea in the distance swished and rolled. Melania was endeavouring to explain to me the essential intricacies of Christianity but after plentiful food and cups of wine I experienced problems concentrating. She seemed to understand because she carefully changed the subject to her observations of Romans living in Britannia. They always wanted to be more cognizant with the Britonnic language than their Roman neighbours, they constantly complained about the weather, Britonnic workers, Britonnic cooking. She on the other hand, liked the people and the changeable weather, and was happy to embrace different cultural habits and food.

But then she had been a perfect wife...

I observed my elegant guest, so animated in her talk, so alive after the short time since the demise of her husband. My flagging concentration leapt like tapers catching a sudden swirl of draught. I needed to confess to Melania Lupurca of the demise of my marriage. I genuinely desired her wise judgement and more importantly her understanding. I genuinely admired her elegant stature as she earlier reclined on the matching couch adjacent to my own, her flowing robe the colours of peacock's wings, complimenting the magical images surrounding us. Tonight she wore unusually, intricately coiled gold earrings. Her wide disarming eyes watched me, and her noble smile touched me.

And here by the pool, I genuinely desired Melania Lupurca.

Jupiter! It was the fly again. An urgent buzzing, not to be ignored.

And then everything leapt up and hit me. Violent chest pains erupted in a disgusting belch. What was I doing? What was I thinking of? Where had I been since the funeral of Pinianus?

Melania, not a little agitated at my sudden onset of malaise, arose from the cushioned bench by the pool, clapping her hands in that noble manner, for Fidus. She said that she would call tomorrow with herbal draughts that would ease my discomfort. Easing my discomfort would take a lot more than a herbal draught. But I thanked her. She held out her hand and I kissed it. It was the most exquisite hand. But I gave it back to its owner.

I managed to see Melania into her coach, with Fidus' help, and I heard her whisper to him to take care of me. She didn't smile her noble smile nor return the airy wave I managed, before her coach moved off, horses loudly snorting, and I staggered on my buckling legs into the *triclinium*, painfully belching. I had some serious thinking to do. I yelled for Fidus. I had some serious drinking to do.

JUPITER! What do I tell Fannia?

I sent Fidus to bed. He didn't want to leave me. He is one in a million. His concern mercifully had the effect of sobering me up. I told him to leave the lamps and he daringly reminded me to take care. Everyone took notice of Melania Lupurca's advice.

I recalled my last talk with Fannia. She understood her brother would arrive on Vectis; some time. The messenger on that fateful snowy day assured me that a message would reach me before the arrival of Philippus. How could I be certain that the messenger reached Rome safely? I had received no message and I had almost forgotten the likelihood of a message arriving. The death of Pinianus and my ensuing delight in the company of his widow had erased the whole disquieting business from my mind.

But Fannia had to be told. It was going to be extremely difficult. Everything was going to be extremely difficult. Because when Philippus arrived, he was here to stay. For ever.

Ironically, Flaccilla, who in life never knowingly helped anyone, had unwittingly relieved her father of a serious financial burden, by dying. Egnatius's clearly etched words upon his wax tablet revealed that the repugnant man I disliked so intensely, had fallen on very hard times. Rampant corruption within the government system meant officials extracting bribes for any transaction however small. Escalating expenses had the old rogue into crime. Egnatius described the scene involving rival groups of the army; our father-in-law received a serious beating, left for dead on the doorstep of his house, but escaping harsher sentence by the skin of his black teeth. He was practically without funds. Egnatius and Galatia and their son were moving to Egypt. They could do worse. The Eastern portion of the Empire remained stable; its wealthy cities reported to be prospering. Meanwhile my son had been put out almost on the streets, together with loyal Quinctia. They were staying in temporary and probably unsavoury accommodation if Galatia had anything to do with it which she apparently had.

Via the messenger, who seemed so far as I could tell, a reliable type, I had instructed Egnatius to arrange for the child to be despatched to me. And I could not leave Quinctia in danger alone in Rome when she had obviously been caring for Philippus.

Travelling somewhere upon the dangerous seas was the son I had never seen, and the woman I had once imagined that I loved. But how did I feel about my former concubine? I could scarcely remember her face.

And I had become seriously enamoured of Melania Lupurca.

I staggered out of the dining room, forgetting the lamps until I saw the illuminated Lar posed in his wall niche, pampered with a posy of rosebuds in a silver holder, no doubt a gift from Fannia, fixing me with his irritatingly supercilious smile.

A thudding headache woke me. And something else. Laughter and a lyre. Claudia's dancing could not be improved upon, but her lyre playing often set my teeth shrieking in their sockets. A couple were a bit wobbly, I admit, and shaming though it might be, I am terrified of tooth doctors. One frequented the Baths at Durovernum. I tried to avoid him, often unsuccessfully. Curius always caught up with me in the caldarium where I forced myself to plunge into the overheated water, but mostly I sat on the stone bench, musing and sweating. His high mocking laugh would jerk me unwillingly out of my meditations. I hated his crooked meaningful smirk at the young slave applying the strigil along arms that bulged with well developed muscles, and his amusement at my obvious discomfort when he insisted relating his tooth drawing technique in gory disgusting detail. In his unwanted presence, I had once laughed immoderately at someone else's ribald joke, my head thrown back.

'You've got gum disease, Marcus' he said with obvious relish. 'Come and see me and I'll sort it. Otherwise your teeth will all drop out by the time you're 40!'

But I smiled as I left the Baths. He had unwittingly made my day, despite the gum disease comment. (I started scrubbing my gums regularly after that day with much improvement.)

He might just possibly be a good dentist. He was a lousy assessor of age. He'd got mine wrong by around ten years. I am not a vain man, but the wall mirror of which I am very proud, it was almost as expensive as a water clock would have been, but Fannia loves it, reveals my image as pleasing, good strong facial bones accentuated by my clean-shaven chin, thanks to Fidus again. I consider myself to be handsome, when I judge myself against others. And taller than most. But as I say, I am not a vain man. Thank the Gods I look a lot younger than my 50 years. But I am not a…And I am getting sidetracked.

I pulled on my heavy endromida, the mornings were chilly. The shrugging movement disturbed my thudding brain. No matter. Action was needed; now. As I approached the triclinium, the two girls were sitting at rest after their frolics, deep in halting conversation. I believe Claudia was originally from somewhere near Gaul and her knowledge of the Roman tongue therefore scanty. I also believe that Fannia was teaching her; an exchange of enlightenment that I had no problem with. Claudia would doubtless be freed some time; society seemed to be relaxing in cultural terms, at least here in Britannia where there were fewer Roman citizens by a long way than other ethnic groups. And we all needed to rely on support from those around us, because for sure there was not a lot of trust around in Rome nowadays.

'You have finished your lessons?' I said, more a statement than a question and they both looked up, recognising it as such.

'Claudia is just leaving.'

The girl picked up her lyre and bobbed in deference to me, and grinned at Fannia.

'What did you learn today?' I asked as Fannia followed me to my *cubiculum* inquiringly.

'I danced, and Claudia played the lyre.'

I winced at the memory but resisted comment.

'Fannia. Do you recall our talk when I told you of your brother Philippus?'

She looked less than enthusiastic, and nodded.

'Fidus regularly enquires at the postal centre for news of the boat. News may arrive at any time.'

I clenched my hidden fists to eradicate the lie. But it served to remind me that Fidus must be told to carry out the mission. Why I had never thought to instruct him before? A fly buzzed innocently past my ear. Because of my growing obsession with Melania Lupurca, that's why.

'When Philippus arrives, Fannia, he will be staying with us. He will be staying here in the villa and he will not return to Rome.'

'Yes' she said slowly and to my surprise. 'Yes I have thought about it and I know he won't go back to Rome. It is not a safe place any more.'

'I am glad that you are such an understanding daughter. We will all live in harmony here.'

'Until I get married.'

'Married? What in Jupiter's name do you mean?'

'One day' Fannia said slowly. 'One day, my brother will arrive. And one day…' she paused.

'I will meet the man I am to marry and I will leave.'

'Yes, of course, one day…' I stuttered as she walked out of the room.

Well at least she was prepared for her brother's arrival. And a girl is entitled to her own dreams.

Oh Gods, I still hadn't mentioned Quinctia.

And Fidus appeared to announce that Melania Lupurca was here.

'How are you feeling today' she asked as we seated ourselves comfortably by the pool. The day had warmed up quickly and my endromida was making me sweat. By contrast, Melania Lupurca looked cool and elegant in her long light-coloured palla. She wore no gold earrings, nothing decorative at all and the simple effect lent a fascinating purity to her appearance. She seemed slightly thinner since her widowhood, younger, and more alluring than I had ever seen her. Her immaculate appearance reminded me that I ought to take some exercise; I had grudgingly noticed a thickening around my belly. But my headache was fading, I realised.

I realised something else. Fannia was not the only woman I needed to talk to.

'Much better. I apologise for last night. Apricots sometimes have adverse effects on my stomach.'

She nodded sympathetically.

'Best to avoid them then.'

'Yes.'

'I have brought a potion. Keep it by you – in case of a re-occurence.'

I took the tiny pottery phial and our fingers touched in the process. My nerve endings tingled dramatically.

She rose elegantly from the stone bench.

'I must not delay your activities. But I wanted to see for myself that you were well again. I spent a sleepless night, I confess, worrying – and praying.'

My guilt rose too, with her devout confession. I was hardly worthy of her prayers, especially Christian ones.

'Dear lady…' I got up, ignoring the signal from my head that told me to move more slowly.

'You are well, Marcus Cassius. That is all I needed to know. I can return to my own duties happily.'

'Stay here a while.'

She looked surprised at my impetuous demand but she sat down again, arranging her *palla*, folding her hands, and smiling at me. Oh that smile.

But I was sweating. I had to change. I clapped my hands hoping someone was nearby to attend and fetch Melania something to drink whilst I disappeared to improve my attire.

Right on cue, Fannia appeared, obviously delighted to see Melania. She ran forward and happily greeted her.

'Oh what a pleasant surprise! You are at our villa so often, you should come and stay here all the time.'

She paused as she registered the shock on both our faces.

'I mean… it would be wonderful if you did…come here…to stay.'

Fannia prattled on.

'You must be very lonely, now that… you are widowed. And Claudia could come too. Couldn't she?'

She turned her gaze to me, knowing she had gone too far, and she blushed. But Fannia needed a resolution.

'When my brother arrives here, we would be like a real family…'

Fannia's voice trailed off.

'Your brother?' said Melania Lupurca.

Daughters can be difficult

I have never been fortunate enough or perhaps unfortunate enough to attend a Greek tragedy or the readings of Horatian Odes. My garden was suddenly transformed into a theatrical setting. Our two faces resembled frozen masks of horror, as the 'Greek Chorus' in the form of my daughter prattled and sang her story. Actually she did it far better than I would have done.

'...My mother cared nothing for us
She gave us no love
I suffered with tears on my cheek before she left us
To return to Rome she lay

In the cold night with my abandoned father and she carried away
His son in her womb
To Rome where she died as punishment
From the Gods for her deceit.

And he knew no hope to smooth his troubled brow
Now through stormy seas
And across the lush grass comes the worthless heir
Favoured by the Gods...'

And Fannia led me to believe that she hated the classical poets, Odes and all. Her luckless tutor would have been surprised. Perhaps even Horace himself. But Fannia was my daughter and I was entitled to be impressed. Although I was worried by the reference to the worthless heir.

Melania Lupurca sat, hands folded.

'I did not know how to tell you' I said to her lamely, shifting from foot to foot, head pounding, body perspiring.

Perhaps somewhat over-dramatically, Fannia ran and kneeled at her feet touching the cloth of her palla. She didn't move.

After what seemed a very long time, Melania Lupurca gently held Fannia's shoulders, encouraging her to rise, indicating that she sat beside her. Tears rolled down Fannia's pale face. They were real tears.

'My dear friends' said Melania Lupurca.

'Are you still our friend?'

She smiled up at me.

'I love you both as my own family. Fannia, run and find your servant to bring us some refreshments.'

Fannia ran willingly.

Melania Lupurca turned her full attention to me.

'You could have told me yourself. Am I so fierce a woman that you feared to tell me?'

'As Fannia explained...' (so lyrically, the minx) ...'I only learned of the child recently'

Lying again!

I swatted the fly and killed it. I don't know whether the fly or I was more surprised.

'I therefore only recently explained the situation to Fannia. I think she is rather bemused.'

'Of course she is. Her world has turned upside down. She is no longer the only person in your life. You cannot blame her for over-reacting.'

Then Melania Lupurca smiled. 'She did it with style. She is a lovely girl. You must be very proud of her.'

'She wants to get married and leave home.'

'What?'

'She told me, but fortunately there aren't any suitable – suitors – hereabouts.'

'When does your son arrive?'

'He is on the way from Rome. Who can tell?'

We paused as Fannia and the stuttering slave returned with the requested refreshments. Water, and a sweet imported wine and two-handled silver drinking cups, also imported. Melania Lupurca and I exchanged mutual glances of relief. We were both in need of a cup of wine.

Melania Lupurca did not seem to want to go home for which I felt grateful. We stayed in the garden, until rain pattered down and the wind got up, when we removed to the triclinium. Fannia had departed hurriedly to find the kitten, that the stuttering one reported helpfully had just given birth. Gods, I need kittens like a pain in the head. Incidentally that particular irritation had gone.

Unusually, we two were silent, listening to the whispering rain and the caressing wind.

Melania Lupurca sat elegantly on the high-backed cushioned cathedra and I opposite on an uncomfortable *sella.* My favourite table, I'd brought it from Rome, the broad polished orbis turned from citrus wood, the metal trapezophorus fashioned like crouching sphinxes, separated us, but not our thoughts.

'We seem to be growing closer all the time' she mused almost to herself.

'I think we are, growing closer' I agreed, but louder because I wanted to be certain that she heard me. She was wearing some kind of oil or perfume, and now that we were cosily within the villa, heavy oak beams above us, the sweet scent wrapped itself around me.

I breathed her intoxicating aroma and sighed. There are some signs one cannot deny.

'Will you excuse me, I really have to go and change this garment, too warm, too warm.'

I stood up and so did Melania Lupurca.

As I hopped nimbly, despite my earlier inertia, around the table and we moved together. There was no hesitation. She seemed to melt into my arms. The nearness of her aroused my highly erotic thoughts, as transparent as her own. Through the uncomfortable garment I regretted donning so hurriedly, I sensed her heart leaping passionately as my own desire swelled with amazing ferocity. We moved almost as one towards my room and as we passed through, I firmly closed the door.

I need the mercy of the whole Pantheon of Gods to get me out of this one

She turned towards me sighing sweetly. Her dark hair lay tumbled across the cushion. Her luminous eyes opened and she smiled a smile that nearly broke my heart.

'Marcus Cassius...'

'We have slept' I said unnecessarily, my head propped by my elbow the better to watch her.

'I think that a sleep was probably necessary. Oh Marcus Cassius!'

'Oh Melania Lupurca!'

'Do you know? I think the feelings of – older – people for each other are stronger and deeper than anything that the young can possibly experience.'

I knew what she meant. The only downside was – that I was one of the older people. Our delicious activities had left me so weak that I flopped back onto the cushion we shared, and stretched and groaned. I ached. All over. But there was happiness and contentment in the aches. I was glad to tolerate them because I knew the delectable causes. She laughed. I recognised the laugh, the light, tinkling giggle on the day of the funeral of Pinianus all those weeks ago.

Melania Lupurca nestled into my shoulder and kissed the giant mole that has sat there since I was a child.

'Questions' she whispered.

I groaned again. Now what did she want to know? But fortunately there was one question that she could not know to ask.

'What questions?'

'Why did you decide to settle here in Britannia with all the uncertainties that lurk in this land? Why Britannia?'

That was easy.

'I wanted a new life for myself – my wife – my family. Britannia seemed in better shape than Rome. The Western Empire attracted me, more than the East. For one reason, I like the cooler climate now that I am... not young.'

'But Britannia is not in good shape. We discussed the problems only the other evening. Workers are becoming expensive and leave at a moment's notice or none at all.

And there is always the fear of an invasion by barbarian hordes…'

'Oh not you too! Dearest, in Rome we expected them at any hour. At best the streets at night were not safe. Crime is uncontrollable, since Rome was abandoned. And it's getting a whole lot worse in Rome now.'

I thought of Flaccilla's father bloody and beaten lying in the gutter by his own door. A nasty business even if the victim was an unsavoury character.

'…It looked a better life here. And I have found it so, especially of late…'

I kissed her noble nose. But Melania wanted to talk.

'Pinianus brought me to Britannia. That was thirty years ago, just after Barbarians had swept through most of the country. It took two years to bring matters under control. Thanks to Valentinian's Government. It could happen again. Since then the Visigoths have been beaten back from Italy, just. But you must have heard of the troubles in Gaul. My servant Claudia's family managed to get here. In a small boat, taking no possessions, landing here exhausted. I took the girl for them. Doesn't the whole situation worry you?'

My face reddened. In my ignorance I imagined that my father's hero, the black Emperor Septimus Severus had quashed all the troubles besetting Britannia from invaders over two hundred years ago. I had no recollection of any news reaching us in Rome thirty years ago, concerning the marauding Goths and Visigoths in the Northern Empire. I had obviously been guilty of paying insufficient attention to matters of importance because they did not seem to concern me. Neither could I tell, lying there next to my beautiful lady, whether such information would have deterred me from leaving Rome when I did. I would really have to make an all out effort to be better informed. The problem was that hardworking Fidus was the only man I saw daily. And how could he be expected to obtain important news? I thought of something else.

'Why did your husband bring you here if it seemed so dangerous?'

'The Government sent him. We were settled in Constantinople. It was there that I became converted to Christianity. But I believe that coming to Britannia had to happen to me. I have been able to help so many poor and unfortunate people here, just as Constantine gave his wealth to the Christians. It helped me live through my marriage to Pinianus...'

What a woman. Turning the upheaval of moving across the Empire into a personal challenge, and coping with an unpleasant husband at the same time. But her involvement with Christianity seemed to be our sticking point. I wanted to ask her more about it, how she felt while eating the symbolic flesh and blood of a son of God. Privately I am not a particularly pious man but I prefer to keep my options open. How could a sane man – or woman for that matter, behave impiously, causing as many still say, the old gods' anger, and we all know what angering the gods leads to. Natural disasters. The Great Fire of Rome in 64 comes to mind. But in fairness the origins of that particular catastrophe haven't been explained to everyone's satisfaction. Even to the present day, one can hear discussions in bars anywhere in the Empire. We all know that Nero blamed the Christians but who in hindsight would have trusted anything that came from those sloppy lips and that addled brain. I really should ask Melania to give me some insight into the faith that had obviously inspired her. I regard myself as an intelligent man. I should be more open-minded. And I longed to understand everything about this wonderful person. I held her close to me.

'I love you Melania Lupurca.'

Her reply, if indeed she was about to make one, never came.

My door shook as a great hammering rent the air.

Fidus was shouting. Somebody was demanding to see me. Now.

‘Stay here’ I commanded the delectable creature, as I stumbled down the steps of my bed, grabbing the heavy robe where it lay in an unsavoury heap on my beautiful mosaic floor. I left the room, shutting the door firmly.

It was the first time I had issued a command to Melania Lupurca. I think I was as surprised as her but I didn’t pause to see her reaction.

‘Who wants to see me?’

Fidus looked pale. He had obviously lost his Roman glow in the years we had been here, but his pallor was positively unsightly.

His expression informed me I looked far from appetising myself. We know each other too well.

‘Who is it?’ I demanded.

I knew it had to be a messenger with news of my son.

‘He says he is from the Government.’

I do not know what twist of imagination led me to expect a large intimidating, even brutish man waiting to greet me. I staggered towards the triclinium, realising too late that my feet were bare, the height of rudeness. I clung desperately to my original assumption, that the man who stood there might be a mere messenger.

The bearing of my visitor quickly belied my hope. His very slightness of build, thin waspish features and glittering eyes, drew one’s attention, and held it. He was clean shaven, and very expensively clothed in a long dark tunic of fine cloth with a glimpse of close fitting trousers, and his enviously smart black leather shoes decorated with an ivory buckle showed him to be a man of substance. I noticed that he held important-looking wax tablets, presumably for jotting down his notes. No. He could not possibly be a messenger.

I shuffled forward, feeling more unkempt than ever in the presence of the forbidding character.

‘Marcus Cassius? I am Marcellus Fronto.’

I muttered some words indicating that I was pleased to make his acquaintance. I doubted he heard yet alone believed them.

'I have taken the liberty of sending my slave with yours to their quarters.'

His voice echoed thinly around the colonnades.

I ignored his comment, mostly because I did not know how to reply without sounding disparaging. I felt an instinctive feeling that that this would be a stressful scenario and I should watch my choice of expressions during any ensuing dialogue. I indicated politely that he should sit upon the nearest bench with cushions. He remained standing. Where did we go from here? I swept my hands down my shabby endromida apologetically.

'Ha! I was about to go to the bath.'

Quick thinking! That would account for my ill-manners in having exposed feet. He revealed no regard for my dishevelled appearance but worryingly no apologies for his unexpected arrival.

'Your slave indicated to me that you were unwell?'

'My servant got it wrong. I got up late.'

I laughed to make a joke of my slothfulness. It fell as flat as my pointed correction of his assumption that Fidus was a slave. I harboured an uncomfortable feeling that I should not have indulged in the modification. But the only way forward was to get to the point.

'How may I assist you?' I asked with a courteousness I certainly did not feel.

'I am here in my capacity as an administrator from the Government Centre at Venta Belgarum. We are visiting some of our citizens in this part of Britannia. You, Marcus Cassius, are the first on my itinerary. Fortunately, you are also the only person I have to visit on Vectis. I confess to finding the countryside very attractive, but it is too far removed from the mainland for my liking. You have lived here on Vectis for ten years I believe?'

I felt angry. He'd been here a few moments and he was criticizing my home. I also felt uneasy. What else did the weasel know?

He told me.

'You bought this villa and its farm from Mucius Minicius?'

'I was retiring and wanted to leave Durovernum. He was returning to Rome'

'I have to correct you there. Mucius Minicius did not return to Rome. He is a civil servant at our central office.'

'Why the gods did he change his plans?'

Jupiter! I had dropped my guard. I had spoken my startled thought aloud.

'I suppose there is no great harm in you knowing. It does not directly affect you. Mucius Minicius is an officer in the secret police network.'

My gasp of disbelief resulted in his thin triumphant smile.

My mind was in turmoil. Mucius was an architect, a damned good one. The secret police? Here in Britannia? How did he get caught up in that line? My calculated retirement to Vectis, shirking high taxes and civic duties loomed real and frightening before me. Surely Mucius had not grassed on me? No of course not. We had only talked on amiable and relaxed terms. He was such a nice chap. Very quiet, no women friends. A good listener...

'Mucius asked me to convey his greetings by the way. We drink in a bar close to the office occasionally.'

The weasel smiled at the memory; there was an implied intimacy about that particular smile. It resurrected social evenings at our Durovernum home and memories of Mucius who accepted our hospitality when passing through the city. Flaccilla called him effeminate, because of his slim dapper appearance. He wore gloriously coloured silk tunics at the time that I rather admired, although I'm rather too heavy in build for such flamboyance. But Flaccilla pointedly remarked more than once that Mucius was not attractive to women. Flaccilla had it seemed got that one right.

'Very nice villa you have here' remarked Marcellus Fronto almost frivolously. 'Did you have to do much work on it or was it ready for occupation? Although I can't see Mucius living in squalor. He is fastidious in the extreme. Like me really.'

I hated the man more and more.

'I had to replace the baths, and floors' I said hesitantly. He had already taken on board the modern style and craftsmanship that could hardly be denied.

'Some were very worn and I have a great liking for mosaics. And I spruced up the servants quarters…'

'Fine workmanship, this tiling. I doubt Mucius could have afforded such expense.'

'He is a comparatively young man' I said defensively. 'whereas I retired after a lifetime's work.'

'You mentioned the villa has baths.'

'Nothing out of the ordinary. Not large. The usual arrangement in a villa of this size; caldarium, tepidarium, frigidarium and of course the system is adapted to supply heating to the villa. Pretty necessary on the island. The winters can be chilly. I believe that many Britons themselves have adopted our heating schemes.'

'These arrangements were in place when you took over the villa?'

'It needed quite a bit of renovation if we were to live in reasonable comfort.'

'We?'

'My daughter and I.'

'Not your wife?'

'My wife left me, and her daughter who was then a baby.'

Fannia got downgraded by a couple of years and I decided continue with the useful theme of abandonment.

'I could no longer work. I was devastated. And my little daughter needed a parent constantly. The loss of her mother… I had no choice but to take retirement and the villa seemed the best place to bring up my daughter.'

Marcellus Fronto ignored my unspoken plea for commiseration.

'You say you retired. But this villa has a farm. Therefore surely you are still working. A farm cannot run itself. We all know that slaves are a big problem these days. Unreliable, thieving wretches. I repeat that I am confused as to how you run your farm. How does the farm pay for itself? If it does not, how do you feed yourself and your slaves? If it does, what happens to the surplus; where are the profits?'

I took an inward deep breath. Watch your step Cassius. Slowly, slowly.

'I must crave your indulgence while answering your many questions.'

'Carry on.'

The man at last sat down, flopped down. He yawned. I noticed his slitty eyes drooping. The long journey across the mainland and over by boat to Vectis must be taking its toll. I decided to take my time with my explanations.

'The men are from farming stock. Mucius would vouch for that.'

I saw the twist of a snarl snaking over his mouth.

'They know their individual jobs well. They understand the seasons, the changeable weather, when to plant and harvest. I am very fortunate in having such reliable workers. Their families depend upon their labours. And so the men value their work here. On such a small island, jobs are not easy to come by. These men are not shipbuilders like the ones you probably saw when you left the harbour; they are men of the soil. They are proud of their expertise. They are pleased to explain when I enquire as to whatever seasonal work is in progress …'

Was he nodding off? The twisted mouth had slackened, the sly eyes no longer glittered. I could only hope.

As I related my description of the simple farming fraternity, I felt a certain pride swelling my chest under the sweaty robe. Gods, I needed a bath. I was proud that I treated the men well. I never ever indulged in punishments for minor annoyances on the horrific scale I saw occasionally in Rome. Even there, my house slaves were treated fairly. It always paid off. Here on Vectis it paid off even better. The farm was yielding a lot more than we needed to feed ourselves and the workers' families. I had recently drawn up a contract with a very grateful distribution company of Britons, on the mainland, arranging for quantities of crops, vegetables and animal fodder to be shipped over. The contract was worth a fairly substantial sum in these depleted days when I had heard talk of farmers opting out, often because they treated their slaves so badly that the men turned to crime or simply ran away. An increasing circle of failure brought about by bad management, greed, and cruelty to people who in many cases were indigent Britons and as such surely deserved fairer treatment. I was probably getting soft. But times were changing. Slaves would not be slaves forever.

What I really hadn't taken on board was the fact that as a farmer, even as a Roman citizen retired/gentleman farmer, I was making good money, increasingly so. And the Government would want a share in my profits, a generous share. Not the token amount I dispatched somewhat grudgingly when my part-time bookkeeper insisted. I had paid enough to the Government in my professional life, more than enough. Jupiter, it was one of the reasons I had retired!

'We are pretty well self-sufficient here…'

'Are you a Christian by any chance?' He smirked as he spoke the word Christian. He had woken up, the gods help me.

'No' I said.

'Well, at least that is something in your favour.'

He smirked again and spat, disgustingly onto the stones at my feet.

'However the fact remains, that your status has all the appearance of a working man, a farmer. As such you are liable for a whole lot more taxes than are on record as being paid to the Empire. I would go so far as to comment that you appear to have been playing games with the Government. I believe that farming was not even your original profession? What was your father's profession?'

I had dreaded this question.

'I was an eye surgeon and my father before me.'

'HA!'

He was honing in for the kill.

'Under the laws that the Empire has recently and I might add, regrettably been forced to put in place, this property and the farm can be seized. You may be forced to revert to your former profession or if you cannot, to be drafted into a Government unit, in other words you will be found useful duties authorised by the Western Empire. I would emphasize, this is for the public good. It is in everyone's interests. Those are the rules.'

Like a revealing flash of lighting, I saw my villa, my farm, my assets, pulled from under me. I wanted to argue. To challenge his absurd statements. But I was terrified.

'I have a young son, born in Rome after my wife deserted me. She died in childbirth. And at this moment he is being returned to me from Rome. How will I provide for his future? To start again in my former profession will be impossible if the Empire takes all my assets…'

'Not my concern' he said.

I sank to the bench adjacent to his, my head in my hands. I was a ruined man.

I was aware of a movement in the air as he shifted and coughed importantly. I smelled his fetid breath. I smelled his perspiration, unpleasantly musky, like a fox.

'There might be a way…'

Had I heard him correctly through my hands stuffed over my ears?

But the thick cloud of despair that shrouded me had miraculously thinned. I made a big effort to calm my agitation by looking him straight in his weasly eyes. I took my time, not instantly rising to what could have, or not, been a bait.

'The new laws have obviously been something of a shock particularly as I had no prior knowledge of them. But I can see that you are very weary. The journey to Vectis, as you rightly say, from Venta Belgarum'… (Jupiter! Where was that anyway?) '…must have been exceptionally tiring. Would you allow me time for a bath. Please join me if you wish…'

He shook his head.

'…then we will relax and have some refreshments… and we can discuss… further?'

I thought he would stand up and leave. I waited as still as one of the statues in my garden. Time seemed to have no meaning. I had probably completely misunderstood him. In the stillness I heard one of my beloved peacocks scream. I focussed my waving attention to stare through the rippled green glass of the nearest window but the sunlight tricked my intent eyes until the glass seemed to waver and melt.

'Sounds good to me' said Marcellus Fronto the man from the Government.

As if on cue for another of her mock-up Tragedies, Fannia appeared like one of those nymphs renowned for their power to be visible or invisible. I could have danced with joy. Except that I make it a rule to never dance. I know my limitations, most of the time. I called her.

'Fannia dearest. Will you escort this gentleman to the garden – no on second thoughts, it will be very warm out there…'

It was I who needed to go into the garden.

And the man from the Government who must be as unsavoury as me at the moment, for very different reasons, had refused to take up my offer of the bath. My repugnance towards him increased.

Fannia looking delightful, her hair braided, her light palla flowing, advanced towards

Marcellus Fronto who stood up. He was charmed. Who could not be?

'...the triclinium will be cooler. I shall not be too long.'

I left them. Marcellus Fronto knew I wouldn't do a runner. He had my daughter. I hated the thought of them alone together. But I had pressing business and very little time. And if he laid a skinny finger of his nasty white hand on Fannia he would be a dead man.

Fannia had run back to me, she was excited about something.

'Don't like him much...'

'Shhh...Be nice to him Fannia. Our future depends upon it. I'll explain later. Off you go!'

'But I had to tell you, Finn has found some valuable stone in the grounds of the villa.'

'Stone?'

'Yes, old altars, centuries old, long before we came here. From the beginning of time itself. He says they are very valuable. He says he is going to sell them for you at a great big profit. He says...'

'Go and do as I say. And don't mention the altars. Understand?'

I waved airily over her pretty shoulders at Fronto, as much as to say 'daughters can be difficult!'

Gardener's World

I walked away nonchalantly until I knew they could no longer see me, and Fannia's high voice chatting about anything and everything faded. Good girl. She was sharp. Then I increased my pace through to the back entrance to the garden. I was looking for a particular person. I desperately hoped he was around.

I have hardly mentioned Finnius Volucius. A serious omission. Strange how one tends to take for granted people in the background of one's life. And there he was, thank the gods. Examining his roses. And there were my preening peacocks. What a glorious sight, crimson roses and golden blue peacocks. But it was the wrong time for admiration. They could be in danger. We could all be in danger. I crept up on him because I dared not raise my voice.

'Finnius…'

He wheeled round with guarded surprise at my untimely appearance and dishevelled state, before his fine features and enquiring eyes settled into their usual disdainful pattern. Finnius had been on the estate prior to arrival; working for the now discredited, as far as I was concerned, Mucius Minicius. Finnius had been head gardener, green fingered, a marvel at all things horticultural. But in recent years I had discovered that the young man had a murky secret. Finnius Volucius had been involved in an accounts fraud scandal in Londinium and sacked although he protested that he was made a scapegoat. Escaping from the accountancy world, unable to find another job, he found Vectis, where he was not known and was fortunate enough to be able to quietly pursue his love of gardening. Since his confession to me, Finnius, glad to be able to keep his hand in, became my sumptuarius, re-organised my book-keeping, scolded me when I didn't supply all the information he needed, paid the tradesmen and the workers, and generally kept the keys to the coffers. I trusted him entirely. Fortunately for him, he never confided his past to Mucius. I must ask him why one day. But not today.

Breathlessly I related my story. Finnius listened with detachment, without comment.

'So Finnius. What do I do?'

'What specific advice do you want?'

'It's obvious surely, I want to know if he will take a bribe? Or do you think that I mis-interpreted his reaction?'

'The man is an official. All officials take bribes.'

Finnius stared at the proud peacocks strutting across the lawns. In his intelligent face I detected an expression of undisguised cynicism.

'They are all corrupt. The important question – how high is his price. The important action - not to offer too low a price.'

'How the gods do I work that one out?'

Finnius rocked slowly on his heels, rubbing his long chin, looking more like a mature lawyer than a young accountant. I wished at that moment I had his knowledge, and his experience of corruption in high places. But instead I had Finnius. My own secret advisor. I should be grateful. But I was getting very jittery. The man who held my future in the palm of his thin white hand, sat in my dining room with my daughter. Waiting for my proposal, no doubt making devastating notes on his wax block.

'A difficult one. You cannot afford to misjudge your offer.'

'Tell me Finnius. Tell me the amount you suggest that I should offer.'

The Importance of knowing who your Friends are

It was the quickest bath I had ever taken since I was an impatient, and probably unclean lad. Lingering luxuriously in the tepidarium a few moments longer than I intended, I experienced the strangest sensation. I knew I was being observed. I turned suddenly causing lazy waves to drift around me as my eyes scanned the length of the room. The hairs on my neck shivered, but I detected no one.

I had almost forgotten as I swiftly left the bathhouse, hair wet, but feet respectfully clad. I gave Fidus who lingered there, instructions on refreshments. I couldn't resist asking him.

'Did you come down to the baths to find me?'

He shook his fuzzy head, confused. But I bet he had seen me earlier, escape outside to find Finnius. Fidus misses nothing.

Evening shadows fell over the villa. Sol was sinking fast after contributing brightness and warmth to a difficult day. My thanks to you Sol. How much worse the day would have been if it had rained.

Voices echoed from the triclinium. And occasional laughter. But there were more than two voices.

Melania Lupurca sat comfortably, near to my daughter. Marcellus Fronto lounged on my favourite *cathedra*. I did not begrudge it. If the advice Finnius had whispered didn't work, Marcellus Fronto would probably be sleeping in my bed.

Cool as ever, Melania stood and moved towards me. She smiled graciously.

'Marcus Cassius! I just called in, and was received by dearest Fannia and this gentleman who has kept us amused with his talk of life in the city.'

I never was so pleased to see Melania. But how she managed to move undetected from my bed to the triclinium, looking so immaculate was a mystery. Perhaps both my ladies were descended from the nymphs with the evanescent reputation. Nice thought.

The refreshments were laid in the garden upon a stone table specially hewn for the purpose of dining outdoors, not that we get much chance here, the exception being today. Herbs and spices blooming in profusion nearby diffused the warm evening air with heady scents. Fidus laid my red Samian pottery bowls of salads, all produce from the farm, laced with a dressing of vinegar, mint and honey, and platters containing small fried fishes, eggs in garum, and other delicacies but the eggs and fishes were the ones I liked best, and of course some of Fidus's wife's wonderful bread. Preserved walnuts and cherries were also on display.

Marcellus Fronto tucked into everything greedily. He seemed to be feeling worryingly at home.

All that was missing was musical entertainment. But remembering Claudia's torturous strumming, perhaps conversation was sufficient. Unfortunately, Fidus had put out my favourite expensive silver drinking cups and Marcellus Fronto's sharp eyes were appraising them. The nice thing was that the ladies were on form. Fannia seemed to be enjoying the impromptu party. Melania paid considerable attention to our guest who responded, between mouthfuls, with interested glittering eyes like a hawk. I was the observer. My frayed nerves prevented me from eating and I did not dare drink any wine. I needed a clear head. Marcellus Fronto on the other hand, drank freely and often. He was completely at ease. I observed him closely.

'Where is your home?' He asked Melania.

'Very close. A short walk. Marcus Cassius is my nearest neighbour.'

'Where is your husband?'

'My husband is dead.'

He stopped chewing and hastily gulped some wine instead.

'Dead? Accept my pardon... I feel sertain that he held a prominent position in our glorious Empire? May I say you look too young to be a widow.'

His eyes flirted with Melania. And not a thing I could do.

'My husband held a position in the Government, yes, but he was an elderly man when he died and had been retired for some considerable years. His name was Pinianus...'

He interrupted.

'Ha! I have met him. Fine fellow. Shrewd... But as you say, elderly. You on the other hand...'

Melania set to replenishing our wine, although she could not dribble a drop more into my untouched cup. She smiled her cool smile to Marcellus Fronto. He spoke no more on the subject of age or anything else for a while. But he continued watching her.

It was Melania who decided that the evening was drawing to a close. She ushered an amazingly uncomplaining Fannia off to bed. Upon her return, Melania expressed a wish to speak to my servants about the preparation of a certain dish and departed. I thought that was very strange. I made no comment. I was a man of few words tonight.

Fidus lit some torches.

I was alone with Marcellus Fronto.

He saved me struggling for an opening. But his tongue, unlike mine that felt dry and parched with fear, was loosened by wine.

'We have unfinished business, you and I.'

I refilled his cup.

He picked it up, examined it, took a gulp, turned it around in his thin well-manicured fingers.

'Very good silver. You have some fine acquisitions.'

'Thank you.'

'During your absence, and in between talking with your delightful daughter, and of course your noble neighbour...'

Not only did I dislike his use of that particular adjective, I was livid at his undisguised approval of my lover. It was very hard to handle.

'…I jotted some notes on my findings pertaining to my visit here. I used two wax tablets.'

The tablets lay on the seat beside him. He watched me with his hawk-like glittering stare. I breathed silently and deeply without flinching.

'On the first I have recommended the following procedures. That your occupation, and your farm, both require careful investigation. There is no doubt in my mind that a vast sum of taxes remains outstanding and due. Cheating the system these days is not an option. The penalties are severe, whether you were aware of your discrepancies or not. You of course consult an accountant?'

'I never imagined at the time I retired and moved to Vectis that an accountant would be necessary.'

Neatly put. But I knew it was not going to help me.

'Never leave things to your imagination. You are an educated man. After a 'lifetime', your word, in business, keeping and submitting tax statements should surely be second nature – to an educated man.'

He may have over-indulged in my wine, but his head was remarkably clear.

'You are right' I answered contritely. 'It was very remiss of me.'

As I spoke, my eyes caught a movement behind a statue under the shadows of the villa. A silent fluttering, a nymph transformed to visibility, Melania Lupurca stood silently, out of the man's line of vision, listening. I was comforted and didn't know why. Not then. I felt a little braver.

'You have two wax tablets? The first you describe seems to outline my fate, if harshly. Am I allowed to know the objective of the second.'

He drank slowly and deeply. He laid the cup down. It made an expensive clink on the stone table.

‘Very good silver’ he repeated. ‘Oh... the second tablet. It is merely imprinted with my idle reflections. For my own amusement you understand, I described an opposite recommendation.’

I raised my eyebrows indicating my interest.

‘On the second tablet, I reported meeting a retired professional man, living frugally from his land. A man who worked hard all his life, saving the sight of his patients. I recommended that Marcus Cassius be wiped from the tax records. It was quicker to note down than the first. It is much neater in appearance. I enjoyed annotating those words. It amused me.’

I was transfixed with something akin to stupification. But the next move had to be mine. My move brought us perilously near the climax of this grotesque game.

‘Might the first tablet be available for sale? To me?’

‘Ho. That’s a laugh. My wax tablets are Government property. How could I possibly sell such a valuable piece of evidence?’

‘Perhaps we all have our price’ I said.

‘Perhaps we do.’

Marcellus Fronto rose from his seat. I glanced nervously at the statue concealing Melania. No movement betrayed her presence.

‘What sum do you consider such a wax tablet to be worth? Considering the observations I have proposed to the Government.’

This was the dreaded moment. I lowered my voice.

‘Four hundred thousand denarii. Equal as I am sure you know to one pound of gold?’

The man was shaken. I could almost see his mind whiring like those strange locust creatures that inhabit olive groves. His eyes flashed. But I sensed his greed was not satisfied. At any moment he could take up the second slate and smash it, regardless of it being Government property.

‘I think you have to try harder’ he said ominously.

‘At risk of crippling me and my young family...Five hundred thousand.’

There was no more than a brief silence.

'I think we have a deal' he said. 'Oh one more thing? These silver cups... They have taken my fancy particularly...'

'They are yours' I said.

Across the gloomy shadows of the garden, charmingly lit by the flaring torches, appeared Melania Lupurca.

'I hope I am not interrupting anything' she said gaily.

'Just men's talk' I joked, my knees threatening to give way as I stood to greet her.

She looked at us sharply.

'You both seem very tired.'

She addressed the scheming Government official, who had also taken his seat again, with an uncharacteristic grunt.

'You are not intending travelling to the harbour tonight? No boats leave for the mainland this late. It is dark, the road is far from good.'

'I will manage...'

'I do not think so' she retorted firmly. 'I have a spare room in my villa. Come and stay in comfort and return here for your luggage at sunrise when you are refreshed.'

He thought the offer over surprisingly quickly.

'If there will be no inconvenience. Thank you.'

He turned to me, glittering scavenger's eyes catching the torch flames.

'My slave can stay here. I will return early. Perhaps you will have ready my 'gift' for collection.'

His eyes fastened greedily on the silver cups.

'Gifts' he amended.

He lifted up his precious wax tablets. I watched them both leave, Fidus leading the way holding up a torch. I heard Melania laugh her tinkling laugh. If he lays a finger on her, I thought, he's a dead man.

I did not sleep that night. Finnius and I counted and re-counted my precious hoard, emptying the coffers. I groaned and moaned at what I was losing.

‘It could be worse. You stand to recoup a good deal of this money, the food contract alone is worth a lot. And I have discovered some stone on your land that will be greatly prized.’

‘Oh yes the stones. Altars from the beginning of time, Fannia hinted.’

‘Not quite the beginning of time. But an amazing find nevertheless. If they are sold for building material, as I fear will be the case, it is a crime that they probably won’t be valued for what they represented, but they will be worth a tidy sum to you.’

Finnius surprised me, he of all people getting emotional over a pile of old stones that had been used for impious purposes. Not like him at all. But everyone had surprised me tonight.

I would have to look at these valuable stones before they were hauled away.

At the end of our labours, as Sol made his early tentative appearance, Finnius told me firmly. ‘Make certain that you obtain the wax tablet. Remember. Do not trust him.’

Marcellus Fronto’s slave, skinny and cowering, obviously scared witless of his master, was already waiting outside my villa with the carriage. He didn’t look as if he’d slept either.

The bag containing my precious coins weighed heavily on my mind and also in my arms. As the slave fiddled with the harness of a rather restless horse, Fidus took the bag from me, nearly crumpling up, unprepared for the weight, and placed it on the floor of the carriage.

Along the lane from Melania’s villa, Marcellus Fronto approached me. He looked terrible. His attired was crumpled. His eyes were slits in a face resembling grey pummelled pastry.

‘Are you well?’

I marvelled how I could bother to ask him.

‘I feel wretched. I fell from the bed! My head aches beyond belief. The thought of the sea crossing…Ugh.’

He shook himself visibly.

'The money is in the carriage?'

I nodded.

'And the amount is correct? It will be bad for you if it is not. But you will know that.'

'Be assured. It is correct.'

I handed him another slightly smaller leather bag.

'Ha the silver cups!' His eyes shone greedily as he positively snatched it.

'The tablet?'

He thrust a package at me, tied up in a short length of rough woven material. An unfastened corner revealed the red wax of the note block.

Fronto's slave emerged from the far side of the carriage, cringing as though he expected to be thumped at any moment. The horse snorted uneasily.

Marcellus Fronto climbed unsteadily onto the carriage. He raised his arm in a salute, thought it couldn't be described as a friendly salute, more of a dismissive gesture. His arm jerked down to steady himself as the carriage pulled away.

I turned to my villa. I offered a silent prayer to anyone up there in Sol's bright blue heaven who might be concerned enough to listen.

'He has gone?'

Melania Lupurca appeared like a reconstituted nymph. How did she do that?

'Hopefully for good.'

I stared after the cloud of receding dust.

'He was a very unsatisfactory house guest' she commented.

'Did he behave?'

'Oh he didn't want to. He insisted on more wine when we got back. I showed firmly him to his room. I knew there was no chance of him staying in there. Sure enough, as I stood hidden behind a statue…'

'Like you do…'

She laughed the tinkling laugh.

'You saw me.'

'Of course. Go on. I have to say I knew he would be trouble. But I hoped the rumours I had heard about him might be true, I heard that he was a fop. That he was not interested in women. But why in Jupiter's name did you offer him a bed?'

She winced but I was in no mood to apologise for impiety or anything else. Not even to her.

'I had my reasons. As to your rumours, I think that Marcellus Fronto seizes the moment. He's an opportunist. But I took no chances. I saw him sidling towards the door he thought to be leading to my room. I appeared from behind the statue and startled him. He said he was trying to find me because he felt unwell. So I gave him one of my potions.'

'Oh like the one you gave to me in the tiny pottery phial?'

'The phial was the same. The contents were stronger. But he tipped it down his throat eagerly enough as though it was some form of aphrodisiac judging by the way his eyes rolled at me. Fortunately it acted very quickly. Claudia and I had a difficult task dragging him into his own room. We did not even try to mount the bed stairs. Just covered him where he lay. I was quite worried he would not wake up.'

I wouldn't have worried if the overdose had finished him off. Melania's beautifully clear conscience had to remain that way, while I nursed revengeful thoughts without a qualm. I stopped Melania in her graceful tracks and kissed her.

'What a gem of a woman you are. Ah a small detail, did the man absent himself from your company, whilst I was bathing?'

She thought a moment, head provocatively on one side.

'He did leave us, to find the lavatory.'

'He found my baths. He refused to join me. He preferred to creep around like a spy. The sly *versipelles*!'

Melania laughed, but it was a serious laugh.

'Yes he is something of a wolf!'

She smelled so fresh, moved so easily. I was ready to drop from exhaustion. We continued to walk slowly around the villa, as I took in the surroundings that gave me so much pleasure, and could have easily been wrenched away from me by a greedy Government official. The warning signs that I had first noticed in Rome all those years ago, and Melania and then Finnius had attempted to explain to me, about the problems facing the Empire, now made sickening sense. Economic disintegration, breakdown of public order, corrupt civil servants, secret police. How could anything else derive from a Government that provided less and less services and little protection for its citizens? Understandably, there would be always problems in maintaining the vast administration structure. But controlled settlement was giving way to uncontrolled, spreading through Gaul, according to Melania, at an alarming speed and it was spreading to Britannia.

We paused, my arm draped easily around her shoulders, breathing in the aroma of nectar that seemed to emanate from her skin. We both looked down at Medusa, my most prized and intricate of the new mosaics.

'She leaps out at you.'

'I wish she had leapt out at Marcellus Fronto.'

'You would not have wanted his demise on your property. It would be a bit difficult to explain. Better this way. He has won, but you have won far more. Be grateful.'

More or less what Finnius had told me. But I didn't feel any more at ease. The world beyond Vectis was suddenly a frightening place. And for the first time I recognised that Vectis was not immune.

A tumultuous commotion tore into our silence, echoing around the walls.

Proof that the roads on Vectis are far from adequate

Fidus, his strange spiky hair standing even more on end, his tunic awry, stomped lopsidedly towards us. I marvelled at his turn of speed for a man who had not been able to run for some years.

'An accident. An accident!'

As we hastened to follow him, I mentally ticked off the possible problems. Had I seen Fannia today? No it was too early, she was not an early riser. Some crisis concerning my peacocks? A calamity on the farm?

Outside, in misty sunshine, a shaking figure crouched by the roadway, alternately screaming and groaning.

'Who is that? What's happened Fidus?'

Fidus did not immediately reply. He hauled the unfortunate form from the stones. The shrieks were increasing to a blood-curdling intensity, but obviously not from pain, it wasn't that kind of noise. I know all about screams of pain.

Fidus saved me the exertion of slapping his face. One resounding thwack across the cheek brought about blessed silence and it was then that I recognised the panting, terrified man.

Marcellus Fronto's slave cowered before me. He wasn't quiet for long. A stream of gibberish issued from his blubbering mouth. His eyes were wide with fear. Although he was a Briton, and I pride myself on understanding a fair amount of useful phrases, he was completely unintelligible.

Fidus, who puts me to shame, knows the language like the back of his horny hand.

'The official's carriage has overturned. It is some distance from here. Shall I fetch your carriage?'

I nodded incredulously as Fidus loped away.

The slave had sunk to the ground again. He had after all, run all the way back to us, after apparently surviving an accident although he seemed unharmed except for his brain.

Melania approached the slavering man.

She asked him a question. Her interpretation was perfect, as I would have expected. He gabbled an answer, and obviously relieved that we didn't beat him, he lowered his arms from their protective angles over his head.

'I think he is saying that his master fell into a ditch and would not get up. The horse is badly injured. I understood that. I think he also says that he is frightened that his master will punish him for crashing the carriage.'

That sounded in character. Melania and I waited silently, each attempting to imagine what might await us down the road to the harbour. A few moments more and Fidus and a gardener returned with my carriage, and we piled in. I insisted the slave came too. He was crying again. Sobbing like a child, pitiful to hear.

'Shut up!' I told him sharply.

He did.

Once we were out of sight of the villa, a chill sea mist descended. Its impenetrable whiteness made it impossible to proceed at more than walking pace. Through the dense cloud-like mass, we saw the carriage turned on its side like an abandoned toy. It was half in a ditch, the wheels had left the ruts on the road and one had sheered off. The horse lay twisted unnaturally, eyes bulging, mouth foaming, in the shafts and I judged its back to be broken. Fidus and the man he had brought along approached the animal that neighed softly, beseechingly. With a swift deadly action, the man thrust his knife into the chest of the animal. It jerked hideously a few times and was still.

I glanced at Melania worried about how she would react to such a horrible sight. I needn't have worried. She was made of strong stuff. She smiled gently at me.

'You have good kind men' she said.

So where was the infamous Government official.

The cold air created an unnatural stifling silence, except for an occasional choke from the slave cowering in the carriage.

Fidus had been clambering around the wreckage, awkward but determined. I heard his shout. I knew he had found Marcellus Fronto.

To be accurate, it was Marcellus Fronto's body.

He was lucky not to be suffering from the headache to end all headaches. A gruesome dent in his forehead announced the cause of his demise. Blood had oozed from nostrils and ears. But being the good doctor, I made certain that there was no heartbeat. It was sickening to crouch there in the ditch beside him, thrusting my hand inside his soiled tunic. Marcellus Fronto was very dead.

I stood up. The swirling sea mist upset my balance, that and the lack of sleep. That and the realisation that a nasty crooked member of the Empire Government lay dead a ditch near my home. No sensible plan of action to deal with the disaster presented itself. Then I remembered my bag of gold. My precious solidus!

'Fidus!'

Vectis on a balmy Summer's Evening

There we all sat again, around the stone table in the garden. Fidus's wife laying out the refreshments. I had given Fidus the night off. The new member of our party, replacing the old dead one, was Finnius Volucius.

He had proved himself to be invaluable in replacing me and my inability to make a decision, as he worked out what to do about the corrupt Government official whose body lay in a ditch along the road to the harbour. Reluctantly, I agreed to have it brought it back to the villa. But we left horse and carriage as evidence, gruesome scenario, though they made. I wrote an urgent wax tablet to the Government office at Venta Belgarum, a place that Finnius knew and not, he said, a tremendous distance once the boat reached the mainland. In my wax tablet I described the official's unannounced visit, and the accident in the fog. I could not resist adding that the roads on Vectis were in dire need of repair but there were no funds available to the island to carry out the urgent work. We removed the body from the ditch to my villa. (I would have happily left it for the carrion but agreed with Finnius it wouldn't have looked good when the men from the Government arrived.)

The red wax note pad had survived the accident intact; Fidus tucked it in the torn muddy cloak and consigned the body of Marcellus Fronto to a large iron clad lidded chest in a stable.

The slavering slave told Fidus that he would be beaten and dragged through the streets. I doubted that sort of brutish behaviour happened here; however I had led a sheltered life of late, and he would not be consoled. He related something Marcellous had told him, while beating him for some crime. 'You have to work harder now, because you will be the only bread winner in your family'. Melania Lupurca listened carefully and translated the message to me.

'The Great Defence Wall in the north of Britannia , has been abandoned by the Roman Army which is very bad news on many counts. And the family of this man relied on building repairs and other essential services connected to the maintenance of the Wall for their livelihood.'

I had heard of the Wall of course. Erected long ago during Hadrian's highly successful rule. The impenetrable barrier against the Marauding Northerners. Were there no Marauding Northerners any more? Or didn't the Empire care about Britannia being attacked by Marauding Northerners any more? In view of what I had been told, the latter reason seemed likely. It didn't make sense. Nothing made sense.

One thing was certain, the slave would have to disappear. Fidus gave him food and a few old secterces from me, proof again that I was getting soft, and an ancient mangy horse that we had decided to put down. If it carried the wretch to the harbour, he would be lucky. Once he was on the mainland, with more luck he might meet ex slaves only too happy to help him in return for his labours. And if he was exceptionally lucky, he could work his way up to the North again and be reunited with his family. I didn't want to think about what might happen if the poor wetch didn't have at least one god on his side. But he had been the slave of Marcellus Fronto. Only one sort of luck about that. Bad luck.

We were all subdued in the garden that evening. Unaware of the body in the stable, Fannia snuggled affectionately next to Melania, obviously confused by the sombre atmosphere. I drank my wine, slowly but steadily, glad to be able to, after the previous night's enforced abstinence. Restless Fannia grew impatient at the lack of conversation.

'How is Claudia? Where is Claudia? I haven't seen her.'

Melania straightened up from some vague examination of the murky contents of the *nymphaeum*, but Fannia was looking straight across the stone table with its untouched refreshments, at Finnius.

He was a cool character, I gave him full marks for his self-control in the face of my daughter's forthright question as he addressed Melania Lupurca.

'Yes how is Claudia?'

Unusually, Melania seemed puzzled by this sudden interest in her servant. Her mind, like my own, was concentrated on more diverse matters. I hoped she had detected my own train of thought. It ran something like 'How do I entice you to stay the night?' I needed her comfort, to feel her voluptuousness. I obviously hadn't got through, because she answered Fannia.

'Claudia has been a little unwell. Just one of these annoying colds. She should be recovered within a short time. Thank you for your enquiry and Finnius thank you too.'

'Finn would have liked to ask you himself…'

'I think Finnius can speak for himself if he wishes…' I said sharply.

'Tell them Finn. Come on. Tell them.'

I intervened again, though I would rather have given up and retired to bed. But I still clung onto my hope of the delectable company of Melania.

'Fannia, be quiet. What is all this nonsense?'

'Not nonsense. Finn and Claudia are… in love!'

Thoroughly chastising Fannia and ordering her to her room, I apologised to Melania and Finnius.

'We have all had a long tiring day.'

'Don't be hard on her' said Finnius unexpectedly. 'Fannia knows our secret. She is absolutely right.'

Melania Lupurca laughed her tinkling laugh.

'My little servant is a pet and no mistake. You both have my good wishes. We shall talk about this some time, when Claudia is well again, and when everything has calmed down again.'

'Thank you Melania Lupurca' said Finnius politely and bade us goodnight. Visiting infectious persons was clearly not on his to-do list, despite the person being Claudia.

We were alone. I was so weary that I couldn't find the right words to tell Melania that I needed her; I couldn't even feel exhilarated about the return of my money. And I certainly couldn't get excited over the revelation of the love affair between Finnius and Claudia.

The world had turned upside down. And it wasn't through with me yet.

'You do have the right wax tablet, I mean by that the one that the Government must never see?'

Melania Lupurca keen eyes sparkled as brightly as the shiny fastening at the shoulder of her palla. Her mind was always a couple of paces in front of my own.

'I shall destroy it tomorrow. Thank you for reminding me, my dearest lady.'

'You have examined it' she persisted.

I frowned.

'He gave it to me - before he – got into his coach.'

She looked at me hard. I immediately knew what the look meant. With the energy of a 20 year old I dashed almost the length of my villa to retrieve the wretched package. I returned, frantically tearing off the wrappings.

'Oh Jupiter. He was out to take my money, and ruin me too. How could I be so naive.'

The wax tablet recommending immediate investigation of Marcus Cassius and his farm, was stuffed down the deceased's trousers.

Melania Lupurca did not seem surprised.

'Come along' she said firmly.

And we went together, across the darkened garden, making our way stealthily to the stables and the gruesome iron chest.

Vectis - Winter Solstice 404AD

The year was closing. The first frosts had hardened the ground, and painted the landscape with an icy black pigment. The animals were safely in wintering sheds feeding on precious hay, their bleating and lowing could be heard resonating across the sharp air. The short dark days hemmed everything in, stifling attempts to work on the farm or to venture out at all.

Melania Lupurca had gone to Londinium. I thought this a very dangerous expedition and told her so, but Melania was of course undeterred. She needed to see for herself, she explained, how women were living and coping in these unsettled times. She intended to sell her deceased husband's effects comprising, she hinted, of some considerable value in gold, silver, bronze as well as books and clocks. Clocks? Selling her clocks? I didn't dare ask the prices. But proceeds were towards helping the needy. Unsuccessful in dissuading the stubborn lady from her venture and too cowardly to ask the price of her clocks, I helped in the only way I knew how. I got Fidus to locate a reliable man, one Fabatus, laid off the farm for the duration of the winter solstice. Melania (sensibly for a change) took my advice on the necessary issue of property protection, agreeing that he and his wife lodged in the kitchen area of the premises, and daily patrolled the house. Claudia, her only resident servant, would stay on and assist Fabatus's wife, and I promised to keep an eye on Claudia. An unnecessary pledge as it transpired.

Melania and I spent an alternately blissful and sorrowful night together before her departure. I craved her sweet responses again as sadly I accompanied her to the harbour and watched her leave on the mainland boat. It was a grey showery day, the sea choppy and uninviting. We waved frantically to each other until the misty spray hid the boat.

I had since heard nothing of her. No news of the outside world had filtered through to Vectis, good or bad.

Kittens scrabbled and fought, skidding along the mosaics, hiding and pouncing on my long warm cloak, posing prettily on the stone seats, furry heads on one side, before pulling out the threads of the cushions. Six of the little horrors. Black ones, tawny ones, and not so little now. But Fannia decreed that it was too cold for them outside. And I replied, in my sternest tone that nevertheless they would have to go out, today. That was last week, and the week before.

'Fannia! These animals must go!'

'It's too cold' she pleaded again. 'When it gets warmer.'

'It won't get warmer. They go outside. Now! Or shall I get a servant to take them away?'

A nasty threat. And she understood the message.

'Oh all right. Can I put them in that old stable? The one where…'

I nodded and firmly dismissed her. The memory was not so easily dismissed of the day when the men from the Government came.

They had arrived within a week of my communication reporting the untimely death of Marcellus Fronto. The road was efficiently cleared by a group of slaves, but the dangerous ruts and holes in the road were left unrepaired. The gory debris of the fatal accident was removed whilst I watched in fascination and revulsion. Then under the command of two soldiers they marched to the old stable to retrieve the body of Marcellus Fronto. The official hardly glanced distastefully at the macabre remains. The iron chest was carried away, in tact. I was asked if I wanted it returned. Amazed at their surprising concern for my property, I had indicated with an impressive show of reluctance that they could take it. And was rewarded with a generous sum for my inconvenience to include the loss of the iron chest.

Initially I had felt intimidated by the unsmiling official, Aquilinus Drusus, a giant of a fellow. Despite his outward generosity, I knew that he was likely to pounce on me at any moment with awkward questions about anything and everything. However over a cup or two of my best falernian, we discovered that our families had lived almost next door to each other in Rome. And he thought he knew my old house. That broke any reserves and we talked about the state of the Empire. Nothing I had heard from various sources had, it seemed, been exaggerated.

'The barbarians are sweeping over the whole of the Northern Empire. Stilicho's efforts in beating them out of Italy were effective at the time, when was that? Three years ago. Yes. My guess is they are reforming to attack again. They're unstoppable. They've got leaders experienced in strategic warfare. There's this Visigoth called Alaric. He's the dangerous one. But our armies haven't managed to hunt him down. He keeps well his movements hidden. He must have a lot of support. Next time the target will be Rome. Our armies just aren't up to it. There was that army revolt in Gaul twenty years ago. I personally think that was the start…'

'What about the Barbarians' invasion of Britannia? Wasn't that about 30 odd years ago? We recovered from that.'

I remembered Melania's story, handy at that moment to be able to supply some informative political history. This man was no more than in his forties.

'The invasion that Valentinian got under control?' I hinted to help him. No reaction.

I tried again.

'And what's that about the Great Northern Wall. Emperor Hadrian's Wall? Been abandoned I heard recently.'

He thought about that too. But he didn't supply any input.

'Personally I think Britannia is safe. Sea all round us for one thing. But ask me about Rome? Rome's finished. Ruined.'

He seemed to be better informed about the rest of the Northern Empire, and Rome, than about the place he was based at. I wondered why.

With a sinking heart, I doubted during that unsettling conversation, that I would ever see the son I had never known. And we sat in the garden, safe and relaxed; dragonflies lazily dancing over the nymphaeum, swallows dipping and swooping through the columns of the peristylum, endless glorious sunshine. It seemed inconceivable that in lands beyond the hazy line where sea met sky, bands of roaming barbarians plotted and attacked. And Rome was dying.

With my beloved daughter dancing attendance on us and refilling our wine, Aquilinus Drusus the official from Venta Belgarum (and I still didn't know where that was) lounging unconcerned, Rome seemed another world. But we fell silent. Perhaps he too remembered people who were still there, desperately trying to exist, in fear and poverty. And then I saw Aquilinus Drusus's eyes following Fannia as she sauntered away.

'A pretty girl your daughter. I have this sensation…that I have seen her somewhere. You have found her a husband?'

'Not yet.' I felt a bit angry at his impetuous question, but perhaps a bit worried too. Was he about to say that he was interested? A possible suitor? And what was the future for Fannia?

His next question was another shock.

'What did you think of our Marcellus Fronto then?'

I decided to tread very warily.

'I never really knew him.'

'Found you by accident did he?'

A strange question. I did not answer it. But Aquilinus Drusus was happy to relax in my garden and drink my wine and talk. Talk too much as it turned out, and to my benefit.

'Whenever he went off on one of his 'holidays' we never knew where he was. Not that we cared much' he added, frowning at the doubtful pond life mouldering in the *nymphaeum*. Glutinous quantities of algae spread an interesting slimy green cloak during the summer. But it was curious how that small circumference of water captured so much attention. It was I suppose another dimension; one could get lost in the liquid depths. I'd done it myself. Though I had for some time decided that its curative powers were a figment of illusion. Shame that. I always liked the theories of the mystical and unknown. Unorthodox cures should never be disregarded. But if I, a medical man, hadn't made the effort to explore alternatives, I had only myself to blame. I could be missing something world shaking although perhaps the world was shaken enough.

Aquilinus Drusus was still talking about the deceased.

'He just took off. On his own.'

'Was he married?'

'Ho you really didn't know him, did you. Liked the company of men. Know what I mean?'

He lifted his huge elbow, bending his wrist in a ridiculously effeminate gesture that I ignored.

'No women friends at all?'

'Occasionally, if he was bored.'

Melania knew a thing or two. But then I knew she did. And where the gods was Melania?

'So he just showed up here on Vectis?'

'Perhaps he wanted to see what a Britonnic island looked like. As I said, I didn't know him.'

I felt unnecessarily hot and bothered. Was this a trap? Drusus surely knew the official's duties.

'Fronto had this weird fascination in all things Britonnic, outside of his government position. He went up to the Northern Wall not so long ago and now it's abandoned, as you said, it's hardly a safe zone. He went to talk to the 'locals'. Can you believe it? Wonder he didn't get bumped off.'

A wonder indeed. They must have been very frightened, those 'locals'. He obviously hoaxed them too. So the man was scouring Britannia, stealing peoples' livelihoods. Using the power of the Government as his protection.

'What was his position in the Government exactly?'

'Oh…transcribed the new Regulations as they came in…'

A lowly pen pusher? I had to reach further. I had to be sure.

'He mentioned the secret police once. Just a vague hint… I assumed perhaps…'

Aquilinus Drusus almost fell off the stone bench.

'Secret police? Here on Vectis? Whatever gave you that idea? They wouldn't waste manpower on a place like this. I heard that Fronto fancied a career underground – suited him in the end, too.' (He laughed unkindly at his jibe). 'No, they wouldn't consider him. He had a chip on his shoulder because promotion passed him by, every time. And to make things worse, his boyfriend was called into the Service.'

My hackles shivered in fear. Fronto's boyfriend. He must know where Fronto went and for what nasty purpose. And I knew Fronto's boyfriend. Worse still, he knew me.

'Does his …friend know what has happened to Fronto?'

The answer struck me like a knife.

'Mucius Minicius is dead. Just a few days ago. Got caught up in a nasty brawl or so they say. He was a fool. He was warned to stay clear of action. His work was surveillance only. Naming rich blokes living off the Empire – for the Government Special Investigation Branch to investigate. Other rumours suggest that it was more of an assassination. We'll probably never know the truth.'

I gripped the cushion of my seat, forcing my face to relax. It was all horribly clear. Fronto nobbled Mucius, and went after the prey himself. Fronto in all likelihood arranged to have Mucius killed.

'I'll tell you something else. This place is pretty remote. You're very out of touch out here. And because you are so isolated …'

Another clever so and so, being deprecating about Vectis. But I stayed low key. Everyone was a traitor. Was Aquilinus Drusus any different?

'If the Government think I'm taking that smelly box of rubbish all the way back to Venta, they are wrong.'

He stood up with a grunt, knocking back the last drops of his wine, and looked out to sea. Calm and blue. An immaculate setting that belied the devious deadly mess I had become involved in.

'You're quite right. That road is bad. Nothing but dust and mud. But it will do nicely for another accident.'

'What do you mean?' I cried. Was he going to kill me?

'I think we might just dispose of your trunk and its contents at a convenient deserted spot. You will have to get your slaves to follow our convoy, and when it falls, they must tip it over into the water? Oh and better get them to put a few rocks in first? Weigh it down? Don't want him floating. A blight on the scenery.'

He laughed.

'What about me?' I jabbered. 'I was responsible for the body.'

'Don't fret, old man.'

Old man? Nobody called me an old man. Except Aquilinus Drusus. He was suddenly allowed as it happened, as he explained.

'I will make out a report that we had a similar accident to the first. We couldn't retrieve the trunk when we had a near accident ourselves. That suit you?'

'I suppose so…'

Making bogus reports was obviously second nature in the new improved Government.

'Do your slaves ever have reason to leave the island? Wouldn't want gossip reaching the mainland, would we.'

'No problem there…They do as I tell them.' (Mostly.)

'Let's not waste time then. If your lot follow the carriage, they can carry on with the messy business when we push Marcellus Fronto into the Styx. Metaphorically speaking. Then Charon can take over and everyone will be happy.'

Dizzy with the swiftness of the man's decision, I summoned Fidus and instructed him as to the procedure.

'The Government men are leaving, they will travel too fast and tip the iron chest over the side. You know the condition of the road…'

Fidus smiled, a crooked ancient smile. Fidus had seen everything.

'The men must dispose of the iron chest so that it will not float. Remember. The body is that of a scoundrel. He tried to cheat me and has cheated many others.'

'He is dead' replied Fidus. He touched my arm gently, a most un-Fidus-like action.

'Lately I have seen you bowed down with worry. Leave it to me.'

Departure seemed imminent. My men waited a respectful distance from the Government carriage, loaded with its gruesome burden. I expected the suggestion of a bribe at any moment.

The casual insidious comment 'Oh one more thing Marcus Cassius…' and the nightmare would start up again.

Aquilinus Drusus marched out with barely a nod. He turned to me. He was smiling.

'Oh one thing Marcus Cassius…'

I looked up at him. My face felt as though it had turned to the consistency of stale bread. It would crack into rocklike crumbs if I dared show any reaction.

'I hope you don't mind, I had a walk around your farm. You seem to be doing a good job. Looks very productive, for a small island that is. Providing the the locals with work keeps them happy and out of mischief. The Empire needs men like you. Oh, and please say goodbye for me to your delightful daughter.'

My starchy face, stiffened in confusion, lifted to his ruddy complexion and wide laughing eyes as he turned back towards the cumbersome raeda.

'I know who she reminds me of...Postumia... my betrothed. They are as alike as two perfect golden walnuts in their shell.'

With a nod that almost seemed courteous, he sat down with a bump as the procession moved away.

Fannia had appeared beside me.

'Who is Postumia?'

Walnuts in a shell indeed!

Summer had turned into Winter. All had been silence. From the Government. From everyone. Except for Fannia rounding up the cats, not an easy task. Finally, she disappeared and returned with a bowl of some foul smelling offal.

'Come on' she called in the high squeaky tone she reserved for the animals. They hurtled after her, out of the villa, out of my life, I hoped wholeheartedly.

Actually our lives were very empty, Fannia's and mine. Lacking in stimulation and vitality. Tied to the villa because of bad weather, she had abandoned the visits to old ladies. I wasn't too dismayed at that. But Fannia had another problem. Her one friend, the young serving woman from Gaul who taught her to dance like a nymph. Claudia's only objective nowadays was to be in the company of Finnius. I interrupted the two of them on more than one occasion, whispering guiltily together in his cubiculum. Oh, his papers were spread out in a semblance of work but Finnius's mind was not on bookkeeping. I sent her flying back to Melania Lupurca's villa. And Finnius tidied my paperwork with his usual efficiency. But Fannia's friend had deserted her. Claudia was in love.

Fannia even asked when her brother would arrive. Any unusual event to relieve the monotony. I had to explain, as I had explained once before, that he might not have survived the journey. I privately decided that there was little doubt that he had perished and along with him, his nurse, my devoted concubine. I was convinced that they had been murdered, in Rome.

Fidus made a great noise as he entered.

'A message. From Londinium.'

The message was thirty days old. Melania Lupurca wrote:

"The situation very bad. The people giving up. Families even those with businesses are leaving. Talk of Saxon raiders. No-where is safe. I am staying with a Christian family. I am frightened every day…"

Fannia and Finnius, summoned so abruptly, stared at me, eyes wide in surprise.

'I am going to Londinium. Immediately. Finnius I leave you in charge of my daughter and my property. Make any decisions you feel right in order to safeguard everything. And that includes the villa of Melania Lupurca. Fannia, my darling *domina*. Take great care of yourself. Do not roam far from the villa. I will return as quickly as possible. But that may not be too quickly.'

'You must make an offering to the Lar' Fannia told me, all sweetness and practicality. 'To safeguard you on your journey.'

Goodbye to the safety of Vectis

I intended to travel as lightly as possible. It was not only for my convenience. I had to consider the horses and the long unknown journey that lay ahead. It was still dark. Fannia called after me as the *raeda* pulled away from our villa. 'Don't worry, I will make an offering on your behalf.' She knew without checking that I had not done so. Finnius stood near a flaring torch, contemplating my departure with that characteristically supercilious look of his. But I felt completely confident leaving him in command. He and Fidus working together should keep the place as secure as it was possible. I turned from the villa no longer visible, and looked forward, concentrating by the eerie flicker of our lamp, on the broad rough-shirted back of my driver. Stichus was one of the native slaves on the island. He worked hard. He possessed enormous strength. He was very loyal. He'd even accepted adoption of a Roman name. He seemed to find it amusing that none of us could get our tongues round his indigenous one. Fidus chose him as my body slave, and if Fidus approved of him, that was good enough for me.

The way down to the harbour was no more than a track. No such luxury as metalled roads on Vectis. Rome had not thought it necessary to engage in engineering programmes for the enhancement of such a remote place. My own affection for the island however had been kindled over the years until I loved the place fiercely. The charm of Vectis, lush undulating scenery contrasting with dark mysterious forestry, cliffs like teeth pointing from the watery jaws of the sea that surrounded us. Neglect and criticism of Vectis felt as hurtful as a personal attack.

Early light had started to filter through the leaden sky as the boat sailed. Needless to say, I did not enjoy the sea crossing. It was bitterly cold and the sea spat up sharp shards of spray like icy clouds of arrows and the waves sometimes leapt to terrifyingly heights around the boat. I don't pretend to be a good sailor. Furtive swigs of honeyed mulsum helped, but not much. Stichus spent the journey pacifying the horses. When we eventually stumbled, wet and shivering, onto dry land at Clausentum, we did not delay in the port. I dislike it anyway. And it looked neglected, dirty and deserted under the forbidding winter sky.

I knew exactly where I was heading. And I had to reach it tonight. My determination was twofold. We needed to rest, men and horses. I needed to obtain advice on the fastest route for my journey to Londonium.

A strategically sited milestone, but then aren't they all, Roman milestones are renowned worldwide, pointed the way. To Venta Belgarum.

What bliss to be on a good road. The horses trotted eagerly. The countryside, in fast fading light, looked very much like Vectis. It helped me feel I belonged to Britannia and it was not the unknown province I had all but forgotten.

But I was haunted by the vision of a sudden deadly attack in the darkness, the silence of the terrain only broken by the hoofs of our animals, and Stichus occasionally breaking into the unintelligible words of some strange song.

Hours later, traversing endless hills and valleys, we at last made out the flickering lamps that heralded our approach to the city. There was a long building just visible a little distance from the city walls.

And joy of joys, it was a hotel. The Romans knew how to accommodate travellers. The massive complex would contain, within high blank walls and a guarded gate, everything necessary for rest and sustenance.

The guard let me through the gates into the wide well illuminated courtyard. I had removed my rough but cosy cloak exposing a smart toga. I thought I'd be prepared; I had to appear respectable to gain entry to anywhere decent including the hotel.

'Where are you from?'

I'm fairly sure the guard was Italian in origin, possibly a freedman, a recent freedman, and insolent.

'Vectis.'

I would try the country bumpkin approach. It might amuse him, make him feel superior to give me the benefit of his knowledge. But I might get some useful advice.

'I'm travelling to Londinium. Do you know the best route?'

'Londinium?' He spat and used a disgusting Roman swearword I would never repeat.

'You don't know what's going on?' he sneered. 'No you wouldn't, being from Vectis. You'd do better to stay there. Any jobs going where you are? You must have a villa? I'm a hard worker. No encumbrances. I shan't stay around here when the troops pull out.'

I wouldn't have employed him if he'd been the last man in Britannia . But I needed to hear anything I could glean from him.

'It is necessary that I get to Londinium.' I thought fast. 'I have family there and as you rightly hint, it's not a safe place.'

He spat again head bent as he examined the result on the smooth wide stones between my strong leather winter shoes and his poorly clad feet. It seemed to concentrate his pathetic mind.

'You'd need an escort. You won't get far on your own.'

A shadow fell across the stones and he looked up in some amazement at Stichus who had lumbered over to my side. I felt very safe with Stichus at my side. The guard showed the first sign of respect.

'…he a Briton?'

'He is. My slave.'

The guard looked impressed.

'Fast with a deadly weapon too, I bet. He'll be handy. Speaking the lingo too. But I'd still say, travel with others. The Military if you can. But they are for the most part coming away from Londiniun not going there.'

'How do I find the officials, to ask the question?'

‘First get a good night’s sleep. Then go through into the *civitas*. The morning guard will direct you to the best Gate. Now, go through there. Someone should be on duty. Follow me’ he said to Stichus who looked down on the guard from his immense height as though he were an insect, but he returned for the horses and followed.

After refreshing myself in a small but adequate bathing area designed for quick visits by people in a hurry, I was then served hard bread and a bowl of vegetables stewed together unappetisingly. But the servant was a rather attractive, sinuey girl with alluring slanted eyes and abundant dark hair that hung over her shoulders and back like a silk shawl. I couldn’t tell her origin. And she didn’t speak. I seemed to be the only guest, which perhaps accounted for the uninspired food. But I lounged back enjoying the lavish surroundings furnished with comfortable chairs and benches, and colourful if not too well depicted frescos that covered the walls, purporting to represent scenes from hunts and Grecian myths. The servant brought me a cup of quite respectable wine. I must have unwittingly showed a little too much gratitude, because she sidled up to me as we approached the cubiculum to which I had been allocated, and indicated that she should join me. I patted her arm as I would a father. ‘I am an old, tired man’ I said. She slunk away after giving me a pitying if disbelieving glare. I was gratified by the disbelieving glare. And I was surprised at myself that common sense prevailed. But I was tired. As I climbed up the steps to the bed, my bones and muscles ached and I groaned, like an old man. Well it had been a long day.

Refreshed, horses harnessed, we left the hotel early, after I had settled the bill with a snarling porter who seemed to require a tip, but unfortunately for him, our language communication failed dismally. And good as his word, the guard had passed on my request to the relief shift, an equally surly fellow, but he pointed out the way to the

North Gate. We drove round the impenetrable walls that made one recognise the importance of Venta Belgarum in the Roman scheme of things. At the approach to the North Gatehouse, I noticed a cemetery lying adjacent to another road. Indicating to Stichus to stop, I perilously stood up on the carriage shielding my eyes to take in the unusual sight. The vast cemetery, punctuated by stone shrines, many of them ancient, stretched silently, turned white by an unexpected gleam of ghostly sunshine. I sat down sensing a rare feeling of piousness, as Stichus drove the horses forward, resisting an urge to glance back to be certain it was not a figment of my imagination, a portent of what lay ahead.

The gates opened for us, after I dutifully supplied my name, origin of birth and where I lived. The guard didn't seem too concerned. I don't think he had even heard of my beautiful island.

Venta Belgarum had woken up, bustling with folk, making their way to the market place, others shouting their wares, children running to school, dogs barking and leaping at carriages, mine included. Ordinary urban activities. Normality prevailed. It reminded me very much of Durovernum. I sighed reminiscently as the raeda clip-clopped along the narrow but well maintained street between shops and houses. I had been very happy in Durovernum. Until the Government put the squeeze on. And my wife succeeded in making every area of daily life except my work, unbearable with her vicious temper and constant moaning. And her unforgivable dislike of our baby daughter.

We passed a man carrying dead chickens hanging from a pole, off to the market place no doubt. Gods. How I hated chicken. Chicken reminded me of Durovernum too. And things suddenly got themselves into perspective. That was then…

I heard a strange sound from my driver.

'Stichus?'

He half-turned to me. His stone features had cracked into an expression that could only be interpreted as distress.

'My family were the Belgae tribe. I was born near here.'

I resisted asking why he was reduced to slavery. So far as I knew the Belgaes were a respected hard working people. Something must have gone horribly wrong. He must have committed a serious crime. Perhaps he had fled to Vectis, so willing to adopt a Roman name. I didn't dare ask. But I made a mental note to ask Fidus.

Beyond the Forum lay the imposing Government building that also possessed gates, and a guard. He was a Briton. He did not understand my increasingly irritable request to speak to someone about travelling to Londinium. Stichus came to my rescue after listening, po-faced and patient, to my inadequate linguistic efforts. Thank the gods for Stichus. Whatever uncomfortable secrets lay in his murky past. The guard let us through. Stichus pointed me towards a lofty doorway.

As I approached on foot, rehearsing my speech and hoping to find an official that would understand me, I encountered the biggest surprise in probably the last few hours, the world was so full of surprises nowadays. Mostly not good ones. This surprise was of a different kind. It presented itself in the form of Aquilinus Drusus, walking towards me, ruddy-faced from the cold wind, very smart in his red winter cloak. He also looked very surprised. Like me.

'By Jupiter! Marcus Cassius from Vectis. The last person I expected to see, today or any day. Have you got another dead body?'

'Aquilinus Drusus. What a very pleasant – surprise! No no, no more bodies. I am seeking some advice. I am travelling to Londinium.'

'Taken leave of your senses have you?'

He laughed too loudly, head thrown back. I gritted my teeth.

‘I know it’s not considered a particularly clever idea. But the fact is, I have to try and locate somebody who I believe may be in danger.’

‘If you’re in Londinium you are in danger. Believe me. Come inside and we can talk. Are you alone, or is your lovely daughter accompanying you?’

He craned his neck, unable to see the *raeda* and Stichus, beyond the magnificent archway.

‘No no, I would not take my daughter on such a mission. She is safe at home.’

‘At least you have that much sense.’

We walked towards another imposing façade.

‘How exactly do you intend to get to Londinium?’

He was not taking me seriously.

‘I have a good man, a slave and a strong one, and my two-horse *raeda.* I need to be shown the most direct route. And if possible’ remembering the advice of the hotel guard ‘to be safer, to travel with others, a military detachment?’

‘Londinium is practically a no-go area these days. Armed detachments are being gradually drafted away. They are urgently required in Europe. It does mean that Londinium could be wide open to attack. But there is no other way.’

‘I recall you telling me not so long ago that Britannia was a safe zone.’

‘Things change quickly these days. I still believe that Britannia is safer than say Gaul. But now tribesmen are starting to mob cities… and they are home grown troublemakers. The Empire frankly has had enough. What good is Britannia to us anyway? We pour money in, and there’s nothing in it for us. The sea makes journeys impossibly dangerous during the Winter Solstice…’

(Tell me about it.)

‘So I must go to Londinium alone?’

The man actually showed some compassion. He seemed genuinely worried that without any protection or experience of urban or indeed rural disorder, I intended to make the journey.

'Stay here.'

And he was gone. Through a massive oak door that slammed with a resounding crash. I wandered about, studied the floor, and its mosaic designs. One depicted a swirling sea creature surrounded by unusually repeated lines of black stone. I walked around it admiringly seeing it from different angles. Other mosaics including a clever twisted rope border that seemed to have been created from terracotta, brick and what was most likely a local stone. My critical eye derived a certain satisfaction, because the mosaics in my villa contained very similar designs. My villa. Would I ever see it again? I shuddered in the cold entrance hall. The stove had gone out. And Aquilinus Drusus had been gone a long time, too long.

I walked back through the archway, to see if my man and horses were coping in the now biting wind and drizzling rain. Sol had obviously reserved his beauty for the cemetery beyond the city walls. Stichus sat hunched sideways on the carriage steps, his face hidden in the hood of an old cloak I recognised as my own, that I'd left on the seat. I wondered briefly if he were scared of being recognised. But upon my approach, he flung it back and unfolded to the incredible height that always startled me.

'I think we are on our own, Stichus. It's going to be a tough journey.'

The erect man stared stiffly ahead, his profile as expressionless as a herm on a Greek pillar.

We both looked up as a horse and rider galloped swiftly through the archway.

Then a shout caught my attention. Aquilinus Drusus came quickly across the paved yard.

'You are in luck, Marcus Cassius.'

The only annoying factor being forced to retrace our journey and go to Noviomagus. It meant two days delay. But Aquilinus Drusus, obviously concerned for my safety, had sent ahead a horseman carrying daily messages. The horseman I had seen leave. Aquilinus Drusus who must have considerable sway with a certain centurion, had requested that we join a detachment of a half century of soldiers that he knew from his records was due to travel to Londinium.

Drusus threw a cursory glance at Stichus hunched hugely under my cloak on the driver's seat.

'See what you mean. But you should have brought four of him. Call here on your return. I would like to hear your story. Don't forget. You can stay in my house.'

Despite being overwhelmed at his generosity I craved an answer to the question over which I had pondered fairly often. I decided it was now or never as he turned away from the force of the rain.

'The man who died on Vectis. Tell me, if he was only a pen pusher, why did the authorities arrange for you come over?'

Aquilinus Drusus threw his head back in the way I was beginning to recognise.

'Marcellus Fronto a pen pusher? That's a good one. Did I really give you that impression? My little joke. He was a bit more than that. He was the Provincial Governor's private secretary. Very private secretary. ...got over Fronto's death pretty quickly though. He whisked Fronto's darling out of the secret police and made him his right hand man. What a laugh.'

I couldn't manage more than a watery smile that matched the weather as we parted. I didn't dare look back. Stichus, urging the horses into a swift trot seemed glad to leave too.

The fortified walls of Noviomagus, as we approached through chill mists and drizzling rain, seemed as formidable as the walls of the city we had left behind. Again we passed cemeteries near to the city but not so wide and awesome as the silent necropolis at Venta Belgarum that had so unsettled me.

Once through the formalities of the Gatehouse, we found ourselves almost immediately in the centre of the city and the forum lined with hefty pillars where Aquilinus Drusus had instructed me to wait. I despatched Stichus in search of a pie shop and I sat on a broad step near a drinking trough. There was a convenient post to secure the horses that seemed very tired, heads nodding stiffly revealing the strain, by the time we arrived here. I prayed, to whoever listened that they wouldn't go lame.

I watched people milling around. Smartly toga-clad lawyers and businessman deep in conversation. Local people, many attired in the Roman fashion, others poorly clothed, all involved with the daily events of their lives whilst I sat idly, contemplating the madness of my scheme to reach Londinium. But I had no option. Melania Lupurca was in serious danger. The damaged wax tablet bearing her stylus-scratched message, more than thirty days old, was hidden in the *raeda.*

I calculated another five or six days and nights to reach Londinium. And then I had to find Melania. There was an address but I couldn't bring myself to examine it until we had made some progress on the journey. Were the Christian family still sheltering her from danger? Sheltering her from what danger? Who would wish harm on a woman? Who were these marauding tribesmen anyway? Home-grown villains if Aquilinus Drusus was to be believed. Was the whole country at war? Gazing around the sombre forum of Noviomagus, watching people bustling, chatting, even hearing occasional laughter, I found it difficult to believe that it was so.

A shadow had fallen across the tiled ground in front of me. Stichus with pies. I stood up ready to congratulate him. It wasn't Stichus with pies. It was a soldier complete with short sword, red army cloak and a shiny, face hugging, plumed helmet. He muttered at me, but the helmet kept his face straight and distorted his words.

‘I am Marcus Cassius…’ I said hoping that was his question. ‘I have been sent here by Aquilinus Drusus of Venta Belgarum…’

What relief to see the soldier’s gruff features relax, as much as the metal moulding that bound his face would allow. It must have been horribly uncomfortable. Why wear it in the middle of a protected city? There seemed no problem here of any kind.

He beckoned me to follow. And where was Stichus with our food? I groaned as I untied the horses. Managing to lose Stichus in Noviomagus before we had even commenced the journey to Londinium would have been at best carelessness and at worst disaster. I dawdled as slowly as I dared pretending to have difficulty with the reins.

The soldier glanced back. I flinched in alarm as without warning, he lunged forward, causing various citizens to stop and stare. Jupiter, he was thrusting his vicious sword in my direction. A man shouted. A woman screamed. Was I really about to die? I flattened myself against the *raeda*. What was going on? And then I realised. Stichus was running heavily towards me, great hands full of pies. But his determined sprint made the soldier think I was under attack.

‘Stop!’ I yelled. He pulled up, seeing the soldier, as did the soldier hearing my urgent shout.

‘It’s all right!’ I gasped. ‘He is my slave.’

How easily a moment’s mistake could have led to a dreadful killing by the sword happy squaddie! True, the man was protecting me, almost too efficiently, seen from Stichus’s angle. But my slave, unruffled by his brush with death, calmly put the pies in the *raeda* and relieved my shaking hands of the reins. Noviomagus resumed its daily activities.

As Stichus steered our carriage towards the Gatehouse, to join the waiting men and horses, somewhat motley batch of the Empire’s gold and red attired military, I saw with horror that amongst the chariots and horsemen were men on foot. Jupiter! Speed was imperative. Foot soldiers would make the journey far longer. I called to Fabatus (the name of the impetuous soldier who had nearly run his sword through Stichus).

'Why have we foot soldiers?'

He laughed at my ignorance.

'To form a testudo in case of attack.'

Despite my earlier deprecating view of him, Fabatus was obviously the Centurian in command. We had proceeded no more than a few paces beyond the Gatehouse when Fabatus pointed with horror at my horses' feet.

'They can't travel to Londinium like that.'

'Like what?'

'These metalled road surfaces…'

'Metalled?'

'See for yourself. The carriage wheels run along the grooves, no problem, but the horses run on gravel and flint that will make them lame. Can't believe you don't know that. Where do you come from?'

Here we go again, more vitriolic comments about Vectis. At least on Vectis the horses seemed comfortable trotting along on sandy paths, delicately avoiding pitholes. Most of the time.

'…haven't travelled long distances for years…' I muttered.

But Fabatus obviously more concerned for the horses than me, and the fact that we had already covered many miles. After a bit of shouting, another soldier turned up with some strange leather strapped enclosed sandal-like items that they fastened around the hooves. The horses stamped about a bit as though getting used to new boots.

And then we left the fortified walled city of Noviomagus. I felt extreme irritation as our route looked as if it were approaching Venta Belgarum again. (I shut my eyes so as not to glimpse the distant vast menacing cemetery.) However the convoy moved along briskly despite the marching auxiliaries whose heavy sandals rang on the metalled surface. The journey to Londinium had commenced. And the weather thanks to the gods, turned suddenly dry. And the day got suddenly dark. Tents were efficiently erected including one for me. I slept, thankful for the wariness of the night patrol who were listening, so Fabatus told me, still amused by my ignorance, for warring tribesmen banging their shields, and even more alarming, the sound of prowling wolves.

A cry went up. I thought I dreamed it, dozing uncomfortably during a wet, windy day, as I did most wet and windy days while we were on the move. But then the cry woke me. Were we under attack from hostile tribes? Would I actually get to see the Squadron implement their tortoise formation. It was the last thing I wanted to see. That would mean danger. I am a coward.

'Calleva!' came the cry again.

I leaned forward and jerked on Stichus's cloak, actually mine, he seemed to have appropriated it, but I was glad of my previously hated heavy clothing.

'Civitas' said Stichus.

We were apparently to rest in Calleva. My irritation at more delay mounted, but I also knew that a break was necessary. And the good news was that we were about halfway to Londinium lying to the east. We were tired. The horses were near to exhaustion. Our food supplies were almost finished. Stichus's hastily purchased selection of delicious pies lasted us two days. They were good. If I ever go back to Noviomagus, I have to find that bakery.

Calleva boasted thick defence walls marking it as another important city and I glimpsed an arena before we passed the impressive gateway. Within the city walls, I was directed by Fabatus who seemed to be in charge of everything including the billeting of his men, to a small house where he said he had stayed on previous Londinium journeys. She greeted him pleasantly and agreed to put us both up. Stichus, cloak flapping, was hovering urgently beyond the door of the house like a hungry outsize bluebottle. I knew what he wanted.

'Is there a good pie shop hereabouts?' I called to my landlady.

Fabatus took me up to the Basilica that looked extremely rundown. The proud Roman standard blew about dismally, torn and dirty, some tiles from the roof had crashed to the courtyard, remaining there in dangerous fragments. My only remaining image was that of a magnificent bronze eagle his claws spread, balanced inelegantly on a plinth not designed for him; he would be more at home straddling a globe, except that his wings were badly damaged. He had obviously been through a war. I wondered what war. But Fabatus drew my attention away.

'We are pulling out of here soon. When all the troops leave Londinium, the Roman Empire will have no more use for Calleva.'

Chilling words to match the icy wind blowing through the important gateway that would soon cease to be important.

'How long before that happens?' I said, fearing the reply.

But the wind blew away my words.

A harassed looking centurion met us in a vast deserted *triclinium*, and after brief discussion of our uneventful journey, told us that Londinium was not yet under siege and still possible to enter, even conduct a reasonably normal life although businesses were closing down and long term prospects were grim. The citizens were not looking forward to the army pulling out.

I tried to get an answer my question again. The phrase 'not yet under siege' was disturbing.

'How long before Londinium is left completed undefended?'

'Could be years or months. We could get a message tomorrow. Do you intend staying there?'

‘I have to find someone, a relative. I think she is in danger.’

‘She isn’t alone? Why is she there anyway?’

Did I come clean about Melania Lupurca? I decided that honesty could only help.

‘She is a lady with a mission. She travelled to Londinium because she is very concerned about how the poorest people are coping. She does a lot of good works; helping to relieve the suffering of the poor…’

‘I think I might have heard about her. She is a Christian?’

Compared to the vast extent of the Empire, Londinium was a small place. I nodded.

‘Well, we haven’t found the Christians entirely helpful in our peace-keeping efforts. They have been smashing up what they call ‘pagan effigies’ and a lot of statuary erected to our gods. As you can imagine, it hasn’t gone down well in the Roman quarters. But surely she is not in Londinium alone?’

‘I only know that she is staying with a Christian family. I have an address. In a street off the Basilica Forum, running towards the river.’

The two men looked at each other.

‘Well you must be prepared for trouble anywhere in Londinium.’

‘He’s got a bodyguard, giant of a fellow.’

‘He’ll need him.’

The men wandered off discussing army supplies and left me alone. I found myself once again examining another wide expanse of Government floor. Exquisite Geometric mosaics, an intricate urn design. How appalling that it would all be abandoned. Would new leaders in the future appreciate the workmanship? Not that mosaics would be high on anyone’s list of importance during unsettled times. And my thoughts revolved to Melania. I remembered the two us of admiring my Medusa mosaic. It seemed a long time ago. I had to find her. It was as simple as that. And I had to carry her back to Vectis, to my daughter, and my villa.

As my tired eyes swam around the excellence of the floor patterns and my weary mind waded through the problems lying ahead, Fabatus returned with the officer, if he had told me his name I hadn't retained it.

'Is it possible to send a message to my daughter?'

'Where is she? Not in Londinium too?'

'At home, in Vectis.'

The officer frowned. I could see Fabatus thinking hard.

'Oh, the island of Vectis. Is that where you are from?'

I nodded. Here we go again.

'I went across the sea to Vectis once on a fact finding mission. But there wasn't a lot of facts to find. Except… have to admit… it's a beautiful island. Very quiet. What do you do there?'

I liked him better. He said good things about Vectis. I tried honesty again. I was bold now I knew I wasn't going to be investigated.

'I run a farm.'

'A farm! Good for you. I should think Vectis will be a safe area for some time. Go home and stay there.'

'I must find the lady first.'

The two men exchanged glances but politely said nothing. It wasn't difficult to guess what they were thinking.

'So is it possible for me to send a message to Vectis?'

I could be single-minded too.

'A message, yes of course. I think there is still a delivery at least once a week from Venta Belgarum, when the weather is safe for a sea crossing.'

Writing to Fannia made her feel nearer to me. It was a good feeling. I found that I was smiling as I concluded my message and laid down the stylus.

'I'm very grateful.'

'My pleasure. I will see that it goes at the first opportunity.'

I fervently hoped that his first opportunity was a good deal speedier than Melania's message to me.

Goodbye to the (dubious) safety of the Roman Army

I lay awake in the tiny house. I might have been tired as tired as a dog, but the snoring Fabatus too close to me for comfort, kept sleep well and truly at bay. His snuffles, screeches, groans would have be highly comical if they hadn't been so annoying. Occasionally he woke himself up with his own snores, but the next moment, off he went again. I heard something else. Noises in the dark, in the street beyond the house. I got up stifling a groan at my stiffness not only from the hard pallet but the past torturous hours in the carriage. Through the tiny, badly glazed window I could detect flaming torches. And in the glimmering light, I could see that the perpetrators of the commotion were a group of Fabatus's auxiliaries, the motley lot I mentioned earlier. They were not only scruffy, they must have been the dregs of the glorious Roman Army. The meaning of discipline had passed them by as their yells and swearing rent the night air. They had obviously been drinking heavily and I heard shrieks from a girl or maybe two girls. I couldn't really tell whether the cries were of happiness or fear. They could have been screams of fear. In fact I knew they were. I shook the snoring Fabatus and he woke as bad tempered as a bear. I gabbled my fears to him.

'I think those girls outside are being molested…'

'Nar…they love it…'

'I don't think so. I think perhaps you should intervene. The men are very drunk, they will give the Roman Army a bad name in Calleva too…'

'The Roman Army a bad name? There soon won't be a Roman Army in Calleva to have a bad name. Go back to sleep. I don't interfere when they've been drinking…'

He had warned me. He settled back to his snores. I shrugged on my endromida. I needed it. The air outside the fug of the cottage, embraced me with it frosty breath.

The soldiers had moved farther away, I could still hear the uncouth swearing. A movement by the wall of the house startled me. A massive dark shape veered towards me. I had been warned. I stifled a cry of fear.

'Master!'

'Jupiter you scared me.'

As my groggy eyes accustomed themselves to the ghostly night, I could make out Stichus. He was clutching his stomach, or thereabouts.

'Stichus, what's wrong?'

'The men… punched me. Five of them. Didn't see them coming. Little …..'

We moved to a low wall between the house and a shop. He slumped down groaning.

I was horrified to see the giant brought so low. But the miserable swine would have had to jump up and down to reach his chin for a knockout.

'Not only me' he said after a long pause.

'Who else?'

'They have taken two women.'

I made to dash off in the direction of the unpleasant uproar but Stichus grabbed my arm.

'No.'

The cold night was filled with an ominous silence. I could have cried for the fate of the girls. I thought of Fannia. They could be her age. In my rage I could have killed them. Except that fortunately Stichus knew my limitations. They had all but felled him.

'What can we do?'

Stichus was quiet. He was recovering slowly. I could also almost hear him thinking.

'We should go.'

'We leave tomorrow by first light. If those monstrous fiends are sober enough.'

'We should get out of Calleva. Now.'

I knew that I had gone mad; following my slave, doing as he told me, taking the surprised horses from the stable, coupling up the carriage and heading for the city walls. We seemed to be creating a tremendous racket but at the gatehouse, all was darkness and silence. Stichus unclasped the gate that wasn't properly secured and I drove swiftly through the great stone arch, as he closed the gate after us and ran to leap onto the carriage. He had obviously recovered from the cowardly assault, thank the gods. I didn't pause for a couple of miles until we were certain we hadn't been followed. Then we changed places. Stichus was a much better horseman than me. Travelling through the night was fearful to say the least. We had no choice. In his stuttering broken Roman, my slave explained his fears.

The soldiers were out for blood. He had listened to them while we camped on the journey to Calleva, being in closer proximity to them at night than I was alone in my little tent. They intended to make the first move whenever any potential pockets of resistance were met, or any potential pockets of any kind. Brutality seemed to be their sole aim. They were intent on robbing anything or anyone before they were disbanded, which was likely to be their early fate, unless they were forced to serve their full twenty five years in some more dangerous outback of the Empire, even more of a fate. They had also taken a strong dislike to Stichus. More than mere dislike. They had openly threatened his life. Stichus was no coward, but if I lost him to the hands of these desperate remnants of the Roman Army, I could see the likelihood of robbery and death being my fate also.

Stichus seemed confident that he could handle any possible confrontation with any Britons we might meet. From gossip he had overheard, he thought it unlikely that we would encounter any trouble from Saxon immigrants. They have come over to Britannia from Gaul, he insisted. To work on our farms. Despite rumours to the contrary he didn't see them as a threat. Yet.

One thing he asked. To revert to his real name. I could well understand that. But it was a mouthful. So

Kendreague he became once more. I said it over and over to myself, it might be fatal for him and for me, to make a public mistake if, the gods forbid, we were ever surrounded by Britons who hated Romans.

The gods must have been with me. Our journey was peaceful, except for Stichus's – what am I saying? Kendreague's tuneless singing, but I even got used to that. My back ached as my tired eyes constantly searched the road behind us. I didn't give much for our chances if the army caught up. Fabatus would be pretty annoyed too. I didn't think that subtle hints about escaping from his snores would hold much water. Talking of which, we had none. Again, the gods were with us. Over the rise of a hill, there were many in this part of the countryside, lay a tiny rough encampment, just a circle of thatched huts, smoke spiralling from their fires, a river running nearby. Kendreague took control whilst I hunched in the carriage, my head covered, pretending to be his ancient father, of all people. These were indeed desperate times. I could just about hear, though I didn't even dare peep, that he was being received in a kindly manner. He was gone a long time. The horses stamped and shifted. They must have been a lot thirstier than me.

Eventually, I heard friendly cries of farewell as Kendreague returned. He moved away from the encampment before stopping in the shelter of some trees. We left the horses free to roam about, and drink from the nearby river. Kendreague (it's getting easier to say all the time) filled a large leather bucket that he had brought from the friendly tribe.

'I have warned them of the approach of the soldiers. They are prepared. They take to the hills over there and the men pass by thinking the village is abandoned. They have done it before. We have to call on our return. They want the bucket back. They gave us bread too. No pies' he added regretfully.

Kendreague was becoming very talkative, in broken Roman, and simple phrases of his own language, for my benefit. I watched him reharnessing the horses, patting their heads affectionately. There was a gentleness about his massive frame in the way he handled the animals. There was intelligence in his manner as he thought through problems and took control without apologies when he knew it was necessary. I pondered again over possible reasons why he was a slave and how he had come to be in Vectis. But the time for those questions hadn't arrived yet.

Crossing the wide river Tamesis on the outskirts of Londinium was no joke. We were very fortunate that the tide was out. There was a ford, many people and carts crossing to and fro so we joined them. The horses were not amused. We would have to search for another, safer crossing on our return. On our return. I hardly dared think about our return, as we approached the massive walls of Londinium.

We left the horses at a shabby waterfront hostelry for a larger deposit of sesterces than I liked to hand over. But this was Londinium.

Outwardly there were no signs of the problems we had been warned about. A bustling urban culture. Identical in most ways to Noviomagus. Perhaps the buildings were closer together, there were certainly more official looking structures, more bazaars and bars. And pie shops; Kendreague's eyes lit up needless to say. But apart from these obvious big city differences, there loomed an intrinsic tension, difficult to identify, but a tension nevertheless. The passing public seemed hostile, defensive, glancing over their shoulders. They scurried to and fro, no time for lackadaisical pauses in conversation that I saw at other civiti.

Kendreague and I walked doggedly towards what was clearly, by its magnificently aligned masonry, the Basilica Forum. Here we paused. There were less ordinary folk; more smart togas, more learned looking men engaged in furtive conversation between the colonnades, traversing the pavements in twos or threes. Lawyers perhaps, or accountants? Finnius could have told me. But Finnius would not have been comfortable here. Finnius the scapegoat. Surveying the features of the men nearest to me, I read of intrigue and hypocrisy in the deep etched lines of their deceitful smiles. Above all, I held on to my belief that Finnius was truthful and honest. Positive disadvantages in a corrupt society, corrupt from the Government down.

I could not become embroiled in such matters now when my target had to remain on course. I turned impatiently away from the Basilica Forum harbouring its secretive plotting denizens.

To my right and back towards the waterfront, lay a temple. The importance of its structural contours could not be refuted.

'Stay here' I told Kendreague.

Although the day was coloured a wintry grey, within the temple, composed mystical light flooded the two narrow aisles of the Basilica. The apse, built slightly higher than the floor of the nave reflected a luminescent purity. I noticed a couple of soldiers quietly meditating, not even aware of my entry. Mithras was important to them. I fervently hoped that their prayers would result in improving the army's seriously relaxed morals. And I needed help too. I sank to my knees. In all piety I asked Mithras. My beloved lady might be a Christian. But she was in danger and I loved her.

I gazed at the ghostly myriad of particles dancing in the rays of light that filtered through the carved stones of the nave. I stayed there on my knees, until they ached. Staggering to my feet, I left the Mithraeum.

The strangest phenomenon occurred. Rain like spikes of ice clattered to the stones of the street. A nerve-shattering clap of thunder rent the air. People were running for shelter. I saw Kendreague further down the street, his stone face impervious to the onslaught of the gods. He was beckoning to me. There was urgency in his gesture.

Goodbye to Londinium

Kendreague, my circumspect slave, had located the site.

A building grand enough, from its intricate pilasters and statues of unrecognisable officials, to be a palace although it seemed unoccupied, lined almost the entire length on the right as far as the waterfront. The left side of the street was crowded with wooden dwellings and the odd shop squeezed in between. The surface of the carriageway itself had not been repaired for some time, full of dangerous cracks, wheel ruts filled with undrained rainwater. But the strange storm had passed over. I stood, transfixed with the realisation that we were here, after all the long days and nights and near disasters. I thanked Mithras humbly, there in the street in Londinium.

'The house opposite palace entrance.' So the stylus message was scrawled. Frantically I splashed down the street searching the gatehouse to the deserted residence. An oak door locked to the world was the nearest equivalent. I gazed desperately to the other side.

Two dwellings joined as one, but separate in the design of the windows, and the shape of the doors, caught my attention.

'You knock on one door, I will try the other' I instructed my slave.

Simultaneously we struck the doors, urgently. Perhaps too urgently. We waited in vain.

Kendreague shrugged his great shoulders. He looked as though he thought our mission was hopeless. He also looked hungry.

'Go on' I said wearily. 'I'll stay here, just in case…you go and find some pies.'

Exhaustion had again assailed me. I felt terrible. I crossed the silent street to the abandoned palace, and lowered myself onto the chill marble step, head in hands. I must have dozed, I seemed to have developed the knack of sleeping anywhere at any time. It was raining again when

I regained consciousness and shook myself, like a wet dog. I fixed my wavering gaze on the two dwellings.

Dim lamplight could be discerned behind one of the windows. Almost with a single bound I crossed the street and knocked with more restraint on the door. It opened. I could not define the figure in the entrance except to know it was that of a man.

'My apologies for the intrusion' I said using the Brittonic tongue as best I could, my lips quivering with cold. 'Is this the house where Melania Lupurca stays?'

There was no reaction. I began to repeat my question in Roman. Before collapsing there on the threshold.

My first sensation was to be violently sick. This was in part due an overpowering dizziness. Followed by a vision of Kendreague demolishing a faceful of pastry. Perhaps I was really ill. But as everything stopped spinning, I endeavoured to take in my surroundings. I was in a fine room, elegantly furnished, the walls painted in the newest Empire style, utilising a scheme of red lines and whorls and interspersed with delicate urn designs. The man whose vague outline I had seen at the door, sat opposite me, watching me compassionately. Kendreague was regarding me with something like relief. I hadn't died then, and he recommenced the devouring of his pie. The man's appetite was insatiable, no matter how desperate the situation.

I gingerly swung my legs to the floor and raised myself to an upright position.

'Sorry about that' I attempted, to the young man, unsure of the language.

'Don't be sorry' he replied. He was Roman thank the gods. But there was a hint of an accent I couldn't recognise.

'Your slave has explained your terrible ordeal in journeying to Londinium. Take your time. Would you like a little mulsum?'

He couldn't have offered anything more welcoming. I nodded gratefully.

Then I heard a cry. A thin little sound. A baby's cry.

The man smiled warmly.

'Our child' he said.

Through a doorway appeared a young woman no more than a girl, holding a small mewling bundle.

We sat companionably, his wife nursing the infant beside her husband on a modern couch, I occupying another equally contemporary item, Kendreague cross-legged on the tiled floor. He'd finished eating I was relieved to see. A stove gave warming heat. I had removed my damp *endromida*, and was starting to feel pretty good again

When everyone seemed comfortable and my mulsum had been generously topped up, we started to talk. The pleasant young man was Paulus and his wife the serious young mother, Statilia. They had been born here in Britannia. Both their fathers had served in local Government a long way over to the west of Britannia in Venta Silarum. But ambitions for a different future for himself and his new wife, Paulus had journeyed across to Londinium where they had been living for four years, the baby was two months old. Paulus ran a fast food shop near to the Baths above the Forum. It was doing so well that another man now lived on the premises and ran the business for him. People always wanted fast food. His pies were famous for their high quality. I could tell that Kendreague had no fault to find! Paulus preferred, he said, to stay in the house with his wife who was of an anxious disposition since the birth of their son, but as luck would have it, they had been down to the shop for a walk and to check all was well, when I first knocked at the door of their house.

Would they be staying on in Londinium? Did they know that the Army would be leaving sometime? I half wished I had not spoken out for fear of upsetting the young mother.

But this was Londinium.

'Yes we have of course heard the rumours. But my business is growing and I am on the point of expanding it. There are pottery works over to the west of Londinium, and I'm negotiating with the owner, to supply food in that area. City folk are always hungry and most have no means of cooking. He's even willing to give me use of a kiln to adapt for bread making. I feel safe here, at least for the present. Leaving Londinium now would be more potentially dangerous than staying.'

'And being a Roman - if the Roman Army should leave?'

'Our problem is not being Roman, there are plenty of us and a lot more Britons who have happily adopted the Roman way of life and like it. Look at what we have given Britannia . The Baths are not least of the huge advantages. If the Roman Army leave? They are not much good now anyway, mostly rabble, the best soldiers have been drafted out of the country to serve in Gaul and places like that. If we eventually have to toe the line and obey the law of any future Government, then we shall. If the city was raided by greedy foreign tribes, they will still want food!'

A bit of an idealistic view, I mused. Would the greedy foreign tribes be charming enough to hand over currency in return for their pies?

'Our biggest concern at the present time is our religion. You see, we are Christians.'

His confession came as no surprise to me. I was certain that they were the family mentioned in Melania's wax tablet.

'Do you know the whereabouts of Melania Lupurca?'

I was right. My supplication to Mithros, combined with Kendreague's dogged instincts, I had found the house near to the Basilica Forum that sheltered my beloved Melania. Paulus told me, his smile displaying genuine fondness, that she was visiting some poor people down on the riverfront.

She would return before dark. I glanced through the small window not yet shuttered. It was already very dark.

Paulus talked on. He seemed glad of my company, cloistered indoors for the most part with his nervous little wife. He told me about the stupidity of a few Christians who so carried away with their religion that they had destroyed Roman idols to the rage of others. A house had been torched in revenge and it was rumoured that a young lad found mutilating statues of gods had been killed.

'…many saintly men in the past have gladly been tortured and executed for their belief. But I prefer to be quiet and not endanger my family.'

He smiled fondly at Statilia who gazed trustingly up at him.

'It's hard now, but one day the whole world will be of a like mind.'

'You mean we will all become Christians?'

'Of course. There is no other Way.'

I had no answer. I recalled my feelings of piety and the amazing revelation of light, when I stood humbly in the temple. And surely Mithros had shown us the way here. The way to Melania. My thoughts moved on quickly. We would have to leave as fast as we had arrived. I remembered the dodgy ford across the Tamesis. I related that small adventure.

The couple laughed as they imagined the picture of our swerving *raeda* and the unwilling horses splashing through the muddy current.

'Just around the next bend in the river there is a Legionary Bridge, a fine strong bridge. The ford is impassable when the tide is full or even partially risen. You were lucky today.'

A Legionary Bridge. That meant soldiers. That meant trouble if the wrong soldiers spotted us.

My premise scared me.

'Can one cross the Bridge at night?'

Yes, Paulus told me, day and night. But I was still worried. And where was Melania?

'Should I go and search for Melania Lupurca?'

Paulus looked up surprised at the blackness of the window.

'I will go with you.'

Little Statilia gasped.

'Don't worry darling. We will be careful.'

'Look after her' I instructed Kendreague sharply. He jerked up, he had been dozing from the combined effects of the warmth of the room and an over-full stomach.

'We will look around the forum first' Paulus decided. 'She may have gone to fetch something from the market place. It stays open late' he added.

We left the streets composed of old timber-framed houses and entered the more imposing area with newer stone properties, and on to the Forum lit brightly by strategically placed torches.

'Over there…' Paulus indicated an imposing building set at the end of the forum.

'The Provincial Governor's Palace. He's out of town needless to say…and that's the City garrison. Not fully occupied any more …The Bath Houses are to our left just around that corner. And there is the Temple…'

'Yes' I said eagerly, too eagerly. 'I went there today – during a cloudburst' I added wondering why I had to justify my visit to the Mithraeum.

'You are not a Christian then?'

'No.'

And I wondered whether I could ever be persuaded. My deeply rooted loyalties to the Roman gods would be hard to abandon. Except for the Household Lar, who frankly got on my nerves with his eternal posturing. Constantly reminded me of unfinished jobs attached to the villa. My piety didn't extend to him. But Fannia seemed attached to him.

The market was noisy, smelly and bustling like markets everywhere. But there was no sign of Melania. We retraced our steps down towards to the River. It was much quieter here, the silence made me nervous. Old buildings cast strange shadows in the swelling surging water that, as Paulus had predicted, was now at full tide and looked dangerously deep.

'I think we had better go no further along the waterfront' said Paulus, wisely I thought as we uneasily returned, both now silent. Our mission remained disconcertingly unaccomplished.

The window shutters had been fastened against the unwelcome darkness. As Paulus unlocked the door of his home, we could hear women's voices, chattering.

I had never been so relieved or happy to see Melania Lupurca. She sat with Statilia, dandling the baby, both women laughing at the scawny infant. Melania looked up. She calmly passed the baby to its mother and rose to meet me.

'Marcus Cassius. It is you.'

I held her in my arms. What a good feeling it was to hold Melania Lupurca tightly again, in my arms.

The little family retired early. Kendreague was given cushions and a cover in the back of the house. They knew that Melania and I would find our own level. We held on to each other.

'We must leave Londinium' I said.

'I am ready to leave.'

'Where were you outside in the dark? We searched the forum and market and down by the waterfront.'

'A poor woman was giving birth. I stayed until the child was born. And tended to them and gave her food. The plight of some of these people is terrible. But there is little I can do. I thought to return to Vectis, and come back to Londinium again with more chattels to sell, freeing money to help. But almost every night, we hear of trouble, and rumours of the army leaving, and invasions following…it's hard to know what is true…My journey here was very frightening. I and my servant were fortunate to join some business people returning to

Londonium but one night we were attacked and they were robbed although I hid and they did not find me – or my goods…I know I am weak but I have done everything I can. I just want to go home.'

'We are leaving as soon as the morning light comes. If the tide is out, we shall cross by the ford.'

'There is a good bridge…'

'I have already had a nasty brush with the Roman military.'

If I could have been certain of meeting Fabatus, I think I might have chanced explaining to the reasonable side of his nature. But he had no control over his troops especially at night.

'I'm not inclined to risk meeting them again. Kendreague will be our protector.'

'Who?…'

I covered her mouth with kisses. And we slept.

Before it was properly light, having not slept, I woke Kendreague. As we prepared to leave, Paulus appeared.

'You are going' he said, sadly and a little obviously.

'Take care of your family' I said, also a little obviously. 'Be prepared to leave Londinium and return to your parents if things look bad.'

'It is always in the back of my mind, but with God's will it need not come to that.'

I hoped that his faith would see him through. But I haven't reached my considerable age without learning that the gods can let you down, often when you need their help the most. If you put all your faith in the gods, then why don't they just take over? I have a problem with that. But Paulus was young and impressionable. However my own father became a Christian when he was very old. I have a problem with that too.

Melania thanked Paulus, but she seemed strangely distracted.

As we walked carefully down the street slippery with rain, Melania tapped my arm.

'We need to make a stop. Here.'

Surely she was not going calling in to see the poor nursing mother again. We had halted, I very unwillingly, near to the River where a tumbledown wooden shack formed the last dwelling. The rough opaque glass of its windows were broken and stuffed with rags. The door was roughly repaired with a plank of driftwood. The building looked as if it would tip into the River mud at the slightest push.

Melania approached and called softly, as simultaneously the door creaked open.

Dangerously overloaded Raeda

Crossing the ford seemed simple in comparison to the turmoil going on in my head. I hardly noticed the deceivingly benign waters, only just recognising that Neptune had turned the tide, as I tried to untangle the greater confusion that now confronted me.

My passengers screamed and clung to each other as the river mud churned over the wheels and the horses tossed their head in fear. The water that now and again sprayed up into the *raeda* felt icy cold. Once again Kendreague was our hero. He had, as on our inward crossing, sensibly removed the horses' bootees. This time he waded alongside the horses through the threatening tidal stream, holding the reins steady and encouraging them with comforting noises. When after an interminable time, we reached the safe green swards of the south bank, Kendreague was shivering uncontrollably as he tipped his boots and the river water gushed out. But he knew as I did, that we had to keep moving. We replaced the horses' footwear. I silently thanked Fabatus. Fabatus wasn't that bad a person, he just had no control over his men. Not that I would relish running into him again, not after running out on him. I had also earlier, grudgingly thanked the people in the waterfront hostelry who had sheltered, fed and watered the horses although they had the nerve to charge me an exorbitant sum for the privilege. But I wouldn't be seeing them again either if I could help it.

Looking back at Londinium as we gathered speed, on the hard surface of the good road, I glimpsed the formidable structure of the Legionary Bridge. I had a curious feeling that I had been right to avoid it.

We kept going, mile after miserable mile. Cold and hungry and tired. Nobody spoke. But I knew where Kendreague intended to stop.

The small settlement lay peacefully in the dull evening light. The sharp welcoming odour of woodsmoke threaded towards us through the velvet dark sky. Kendreague went on ahead and announced our arrival. We were exhausted but the welcome we received was overwhelming. And naturally, they were anxious to hear all the news of the civitas. After we had joined a group of people and children in the largest of the simple dwellings, and given quantities of delicious food, Kendreague spoke at some length with the elders. I was surprised at the ease with which he discussed matters of Londinium. I was also amazed at the reverence with which the villagers treated me until I remembered that I was supposed to be Kendreague's ancient, silent father. I forgot to be annoyed and was relieved instead when he reported to me that the soldiers from whose dubiously safe clutches we escaped, had galloped past the settlement without pause, a few hours after we had departed.

We were given use of a hut with pallets to sleep upon, even a place to wash. The villagers rushed around with cloaks and bedding. They wanted to make sure we were comfortable.

In particular the women and the boy.

Late into the night, long after the feeble child was asleep, Melania and I talked. And with us, a paler, thinner Quinctia than I could have ever easily pictured.

Melania told me how she had discovered the woman and child on one of her daily searches for such women in distress along the banks of the Tamesis. Together they hammered the piece of driftwood in place to strengthen the broken door. It had been kicked in during the night by a bunch of drunks but Quinctia had hidden herself and the child in the roof space. I wondered if the drunks were other disreputable soldiers.

Quinctia had endured a treacherous sea crossing and being turned out of the boat with a sick child, onto the muddy banks of Londinium by sailors whose only concern was to dump the army supplies they had ferried from Italy and get on their way home. It was obvious that whoever had placed the two innocents in the hands of the seamen, had no intention of ensuring their arrival at the right harbour in Britannia.

Quinctia could not say how long she had been living rough in Londinium, only that it felt little safer than in Rome. The gods only knew what terrible ordeals she had experienced there. In Londinium she managed to find a job in a bar, leaving Philippus (how strange it sounded to hear his name) locked in the roof space of the tumbledown house.

Melania and Quinctia had known each other perhaps two months. And on Melania's frequent visits Quinctia told her more and more about the orphaned boy in her care and the rough treatment they had both received from the familia in Rome. Melania slowly realised that she could be face to face with my son.

Apart from the fact that Quinctia had been forced to return to Rome, she did not seem to have confided to Melania the closeness of the relationship between us. In fact the two women seemed careful to avoid any personal secrets. When we were all too exhausted to talk any more, they went together to the larger of the pallets behind a screen of animal hide. I lay carefully next to the little boy and listened to his soft breathing. This was my son. But I could still hardly believe I had found him and Quinctia, both so thin and vulnerable. And strangest of all, they had been rescued by my lover, Melania Lupurca the woman I had risked everything to find.

And there was a long way to go. Not only miles either.

During the following day, when we were very refreshed and wrapped in warm woven cloaks and given provisions by the generous villagers (Kendreague had remembered to return their leather bucket), the journey was almost enjoyable for a while. The rain had blown away. The air felt warmer. The road was deserted. We watched the hills and the trees. And I watched somewhat nervously, not only the two women, but for signs of ambushes on the horizon.

Philippus became curious about me. I started to talk to him. It helped to take away my fears of ambush.

I asked him how old he was.

'Ten but I will soon be eleven.'

'You are a tall lad, for ten nearly eleven. When we get home to Vectis, I will measure you.'

He frowned solemnly. He was fair haired, with large brown eyes. He was also very pale and very skinny. He put his head on one side.

'I don't understand.'

'We will choose a wall and you will stand against it and I will make a mark on the wall where the top of your head comes. Then in another while, we will do the same thing and see if you have grown taller.'

He liked that idea.

'When will we get to Vectis?'

'You have to be very patient. This is a very long road. Vectis is by the sea.'

'I don't like the sea.'

'You will. Because now you are home and nothing bad will happen to you.'

My son leaned sleepily against Quinctia and she put her arm round his small shoulders and kissed his dark hair. I wished that had had chosen me to cuddle up to. But he did not know me. I had to be as patient as I had instructed him to be.

Sitting with my back to Kendreague and the horses, facing the women and my son between them, I could look at the two women, as they stared sideways at the passing scenery. The women were both very beautiful in their different ways, even wrapped up against the cold air in old shabby garments. They could almost have been strangers to me. But they weren't strangers. I had loved them both for their separate attributes. I had loved them both as they had loved me, with unconditional, generous affection. They were both so proud. Nothing in their unguarded gestures or the looks in their eyes betrayed how they felt. I wondered uneasily for how long on this endless journey, they could remain silent and undemonstrative towards the man they both loved. And how did I feel? I confess I had adored the silent Quinctia all those years ago. She had helped me escape from the irksome ties of an increasingly unfulfilled marriage. The sadness I felt when she was forced to leave Rome by my acerbic wife, had been a painful process. And Melania? Her companionship, her patience with my daughter, and our mutual affection had blossomed as naturally as the Summer Solstice follows winter. In my desperation to rescue her from the dangers of Londinium, I had willingly left my daughter.

Along the endless miles the horses pulled the raeda and Kendreague sang his tuneless songs. We both knew that stopping at Calleva was definitely not an option. The nights were the worst. We had no tents, little bedding. The ground was iron hard. It was difficult to find a protected hollow for shelter. The women huddled close with Philippus in between them, often sobbing because he was cold. I slept as best I could whilst Kendreague seemed to exist with hardly any sleep. Five more days and nights, food and water disappearing fast, fearful of attack. Well I was. And I caught Kendreague nodding off as he drove, one unusual afternoon when Sol touched everything with unexpected warmth.

False Alarm

At last we approached the menacing endless cemetery and the intimidating walls surrounding the city of Venta Belgarum; the last place I wanted to visit again apart from Calleva. But I had no option. Despite a danger of possible penalty, if news of our untimely departure from Calleva had filtered back. I did not dwell on what form such a penalty might take; it could be anything an intolerant officer of the army fast losing its credibility, decided to administer. Nevertheless, I needed to accept Aquilinus Drusus's generous offer of accommodation. These people, and animals, in my care were at the end of their endurance.

I left Kendreague with the raeda and everyone in it, once we were through the city gates. I nervously retraced my steps of many days ago, through the same street, past the same noisy, bustling throng. It seemed like yesterday.

At the imposing entrance to the Government building I paused remembering when Aquilinus Drusus, his head turned against the driving rain, and I had coincidentally met. I prayed that it would happen again. Today though, the Sun God gave us the benefit of his good humour. The air was clear, and the evening light seemed unwilling to fade. And there was a man walking briskly in my direction. I felt a smile lighten my weary jowls. The man walked straight by me. He was not the man I hoped I would encounter. But in an emergency he would do.

'Can you help me!'

He turned, staring in disgust at the filthy stranger who dared ask him for assistance. He obviously thought I was a beggar. I probably would have thought the same if I had been him.

'Can you tell me where to find Aquilinus Drusus?'

'He's away. On leave.'

The man walked intently on.

Desperation overrode my fear of annoying him. Too late. I had annoyed him.

'When will he return?'

'He has only just left. I don't know when he's due back. I don't even know where he's gone. Now if you will excuse me…'

I sat on a wall. I could have wept. Instead I set about finding accommodation. Nearer to the city wall, I succeeded. A homely old woman sitting on a stool outside her timber clad cottage, watching everyone that passed by regardless of the freezing air, beamed at me as I asked her if she knew of anywhere I could stay, in my broken Briton accent.

'I have travelled many miles. I am heading home to Vectis. My family need to rest for the night.'

'Never heard of Vectis. How many in your family?'

'Two ladies, and a child and myself. And my slave.'

'Got two wives have you?' She grinned wickedly. 'Oh I am not interested. If you have the money I can sleep the ladies and the babe. Her over there…' She jerked her thumb towards another house, smaller and shabbier than hers, tucked beneath the walls.

'She can put you and your slave up. Aine!' she yelled nearly deafening me.

A matching smaller and shabbier woman appeared wiping rattails of hair from her face. She gave me a wide toothless grin.

After my serious misgivings, our enforced night in Venta Belgarum turned out to be a very sociable and interesting one.

Kendreague went off in successful pursuit of pies, and I watered and secured the horses by Birkita's cottage. Some precious hay was also supplied by her. To go on the bill she said firmly. I gratefully concurred. Birkita was a businesswoman and good for her. All of us, including toothless Aine, gathered around Birkita's roaring fire and devoured our pies. They were nearly up to the appetising standard of the ones Kendreague had purchased in

Noviomagus. I regretted not sampling Paulus's cookery. I would have to ask Kendreague the pie expert for his analysis. Birkita, keeping a mental tab I am sure, supplied milk for Philippus and the women. And beer for me and Kendreague, herself and Aine to imbibe. It looked rather too cloudy for my liking. Kendreague remarked that his father used to make beer from barley and Birkita agreed that she too used barley, from an old family recipe. I stared warily into the heavy emulsified substance. It wasn't a drink that I enjoyed, even in the old days, although I knew that my servants and farm hands grew barley especially for the purpose of producing beer and brewed it for their own consumption.

Surely it was us Romans who had brought the art of beer-making over here. But I kept quiet. Kendreague was staring into the dancing flames, his stony expression reflecting that he was lost in some deep secret thought. Perhaps it was the talk of beer making and his family. I remembered that there were questions to be answered. I hoped the answers were not of a type I would rather not hear, but I needed to know. The air surrounding that particular mystery needed to be cleared away.

The cottage air heavy with wood smoke could have benefited from clearing away too. I bravely if gingerly sipped the beer. By Jupiter, it got better with every gulp. It was very drinkable. Soon Kendreague brightened up, and he and I were accepting another refill from Birkita's huge jug. It was a surprise to everyone when Quinctia nervously asked if she might have a drop. Birkita was only too happy. She had of course guessed that we were Roman. She wasn't fazed. Birkita knew that everything in Britannia was best. Including the beer. And Quinctia, after her first sip, smiled and nodded at the surrounding company. I was delighted to see her pale face become lively, and her cheeks begin to glow. Quinctia was beautiful. Memories of her silent beauty caught up with me and I nervously glanced at Melania. She was observing me, from her bench seat in shadows away from the fireplace,

Philippus next to her, his little hands cupped around his milk bowl. I smiled across the dim room lit only by the fire.

I raised my cup of beer and my eyebrows questioningly. But Melania shook her head. I knew she would have relished a cup of wine tonight, this night of relaxation and comparative plenty. But I doubted that the ladies living simply in the shelter of the city walls could be bothered with wine. I resolved to keep firmly away from the direction of the beguiling Quinctia and quaffed more beer instead. The flavour increased in appeal, the strength seemed to be increasing too.

'Where is it you're from?' Birkita demanded.

'The island of Vectis…'

'I know it!'

Aine's shout took us all by surprise.

'My brother went there to find work on a farm. I think he is still there…' she added uncertainly.

I was very interested, as Birkita refilled my cup yet again.

'What is his name?'

'Eh? Speak up!'

'Your brother's name!'

'Tegan. His wife and children were there too. He's only bin back once to see us here. But he seemed 'appy enough. That's the important thing. Me? I like noise and gossip. Not much of that thereabouts I guess.'

Vectis might be quieter, but I wouldn't encourage her to bet on the gossip issue. I turned to my silently imbibing slave.

'Kendreague. Do you know a Tegan?'

I thought the name sounded familiar but I wanted back up before committing myself.

'Tegan works on the farm in the summer. He mends fishing boats during the winter solstice.'

Aine crowed loudly with delight.

'Well, 'ow about that! Your farm! Make sure you give him a message from his ol' sister. I'd like to see him and the little ones some day. ‘e needn’t bother to bring his wife though…’

Aine’s joy resulted in another helping from the jug as she chuckled away about her brother and his children of whom she was obviously fond. Not his wife though. I wondered what she had said or done to fall out of favour with Aine. Married Tegan perhaps. Families!

But Birkita wasn’t appeased.

‘No. Where do you COME From?’

Now I had got her message. It was my roots that interested her.

‘I come from Rome. I came here along time ago. I have been here many years. My daughter was born here.’

‘And where is your wife?’

I had an uncomfortable feeling that Birkita had been closely examining my female companions, and arrived at her own decision that neither woman was my wife. I was also concerned that Philippus might be listening. I glanced over to where he lay, his head on Melania’s lap. Asleep.

‘My wife returned to Rome where she died.’

Birkita seemed satisfied with my answers, as she heaved another log onto the glowering embers. She turned her enquiring attention to Kendreague nursing his beer.

‘You’re not Roman!’

‘My family were of the Belgae tribe. I was born near here.’

His words struck a familiar note that clamped around my heart and made me shudder in the fierce heat of the cottage. The pride in his voice, the way he drew himself up from slumping over his beer. Of course, we were at the very heart of his ancestors.

Birkita was clearly impressed but she hadn’t finished with Kendreague.

‘Have you got a wife?’

A rather drunken Aine, nursing her damaged arm, decided that she was ready for bed and that meant everyone else should be. Birkita doused her fire, causing more choking smoke to fill the rafters. She beckoned to the women, scooping up my sleeping son, as Aine indicated that we should follow her outside into the freezing night.

Aine's cottage was almost as cold, but it was a relief to be able to breathe. Aine staggered away moaning about her broken arm that she had nevertheless managed to wave about, leaving Kendreague and I to decide where best to lay our heads. I was instantly wide awake. The sharp air of the cottage cleared away all the drowsy effects of the beer. Kendreague crouched on the cold flagstones by the fireplace and poked amongst the dead logs until a lick of pale flame leaped round the wood followed by another. I moved nearer and sat on a rough box with a rougher blanket covering it. I would be so glad to get home to the clean comfortable orderliness of my villa.

Kendreague looked up at me. It was a shock to observe how the tiring journey had taken its toll. His eyes were sunken into sockets of stone. Deep grooves of tiredness lined his face. But he would recover. He was a young man. Compared to me that is.

'We have to talk.'

'You want to know the truth about me.'

'I do. I have to know about you since you are serving me. You should not be a slave if your tribe are such respected people. As respected people they should also have wealth of their own. What happened to you Kendreague? What made you run away to Vectis and willingly become a slave and take a Roman name? Did you have a wife? A family? I am surprised that Venta Belgarum's chief Gossip let you off so lightly. It's lucky for you that we are leaving early tomorrow.'

He had resisted answering Birkita's question. Instead he had stood up and left the cottage, to the old womens' amusement. They knew where he'd gone. After all that beer. By the time he returned, Aine had caused a commotion by falling off her stool and hurting her arm.

Broken it she complained. And it was then that she decided it was time for everyone to sleep.

'You are right. My tribe has its own wealth. My father farmed. He was a highly respected man. But I let him down. I disgraced him.'

'What crime did you commit?'

'My only crime was to fall in love with the daughter of our elder.'

As he poked at the logs, one crashed over. Sparks flew upwards lighting his tormented face, throwing a grotesque shadow against the cottage wall.

'Why was it a crime?'

'Isolde was betrothed to someone else. But she and I loved each other. We met in secret, until we were discovered.'

I knew all about being discovered.

'And then?'

'Oh I was forced to leave my village. I would have been killed. My brother helped me to escape. If that old woman over the street knew anyone from my tribe, she would have heard the scandal. I just kept travelling south until I got to the sea. And then I got on a boat to Vectis.'

'Were you pursued? What about the leader's daughter. Was she punished?'

'Isolde would not have been punished. She was a cherished only child. She must be married now. She might have babies now.'

I watched his faraway eyes; seeing his beloved with another man, bearing his children. And thinking of Kendreague.

'Did they give chase?'

'If they did, I never knew. I have heard nothing from the village in five years. My father was a sick man. I think by now he must be dead.'

'Who would inherit his farm?'

'It will be mine. No matter what I have done. My brother told me that they would look after it for me. He knows that one day I will return. Perhaps I will get a message. Perhaps when the elder is dead. I don't know. One day.'

'You will continue working as a slave?'

'I like to work hard. It stops me thinking too much. Only on nights like this, drinking too much beer. The memories are rekindled.'

'You must be manumitted. I will arrange for you to be a freedman. One day you will need your freedom. And we have to be prepared, when that day comes.'

'You are very kind. Fidus always talks well of you. And he is right. But I should like to be allowed to continue working for you.'

I wondered how long it would be before the Romans living in Britannia had to take their places among the indigenous population and ceased to be the masters. How long before all the slaves were freed? Instinctively I knew that slaves would be slaves long after Romans ceased to be in power.

I thought of Fidus. How strange that Kendreague should mention him now. Fidus, a freedman who preferred to work for me, accepting without any sign of indignation occasionally being mistaken for a slave. I remembered clearly how my father oversaw the manumission of Fidus on condition that upon my father's death, Fidus should serve his heir for five more years. Then Fidus would have unconditional Roman Citzenship. After the five years following my father's death, by which time we were in Britannia, Fidus approached me and said he and his wife wished for nothing more than to continue serving me. It was humbling to experience such overwhelming loyalty. I pay him well, but I know that my reliance on Fidus is priceless.

Kendreague curled up on the hard flags, his head cushioned by my old cloak. I dozed on, almost falling off my box. I was too restless to sleep. Somnus had deserted me. I thought about the women I loved, lying together in the cottage over the street. Would Melania pray to her

Christian God before she slept? Would she invite Quinctia to join in her prayers, or did Quinctia still adhere to our old Roman deities. How little I knew of Quinctia now. And Melania too, seemed distant, pointedly avoiding close proximity with me. I wondered gloomily how Melania would react, if she had not reacted already, on learning that Quinctia had been my concubine all those years ago. Would Melania, a highly principled woman, decide to coldly sever the close bond that had been lovingly forged between us? If Quinctia were to reveal her affection for me, I would be in dangerous waters. Quinctia had raised my son. She might regard herself as having been a sort of long-distance wife, mothering my son in my absence, regardless of the many dangers in Rome. Were the two of them whispering confessions to each other? Were they dissecting me, bit by bit, clinically discussing my attributes but far more likely, in my experience of women, my weaknesses? I cringed there on my box, almost too frightened to imagine their secret conversation. But if their confidences were being revealed, perhaps at this very hour, I would have to bear the consequence. And the outcome would be that I would lose them both.

Sleep was impossible in the dark smoky confines of Aine's cottage, with anxious thoughts assailing me. To add to my discomfort, Aine was groaning from somewhere in the depths of her cottage.

How uncanny that my fear upon our entry to Venta Belgarum had turned out to be nothing but a trivial false alarm. The new dread that assailed me and sent the god of sleep scampering fearfully away, was almost worse that anything Aquilinus Drusus not to mention the whole Roman army of disagreeable thugs could have hurled at me. Even in the murkiest depths of the Styx there was nothing more intimidating than the wrath of women.

And the deceitful jug sitting invitingly on Aine's rough hewn table was found to be dry and dusty.

Home again – but not quite

The first chilly light crept past the murky cottage windows and varied sounds of a city awakening rent the peaceful air. Our hag of a landlady appeared looking more unsavoury than the night before and despatched Kendreague to buy bread. I was about to protest at her taking over my slave but Kendreague nodded. He was happy to go. He was hungry.

Not long after he had departed, Quinctia appeared at the door followed by Philippus lagging behind. Quinctia looked very pale again. She regarded me with nothing more than a gaze of undisguised concern. Not for me though. Philippus was crying.

'Philippus has a pain' she explained.

'Where, Philippus, where is the pain? Come here so that I can examine you.'

He approached me sideways like a small reluctant crab, putting his hand on his stomach.

'Here, in here.'

'Lie down on the box' I told him.

I carefully pressed around the little flat tummy but there was no reaction.

'Does that hurt?'

He shook his head. He seemed bored lying there and stood up very quickly, too quickly for a child in pain.

'I'm hungry' he whined.

What a relief.

'Kendreague has gone to find bread. Go outside and look for him, but take care not to stand near the carriages passing by the cottage.'

He fairly skipped outside.

'I was so worried' confessed Quinctia quietly.

'Children can do that. But he is in fine form. You have done a good job looking after him here and in Rome.'

She looked down, her dark lashes protecting the expression in her enormous eyes. I remembered gazing into those eyes, a long time ago, in very different circumstances. I wondered what they would have told me today. As she stood, very close to me, I examined my inner thoughts, watching this lovely woman, black hair flowing around her narrow shoulders. She seemed very small and too thin. It was all I saw. No warmth for Quinctia invaded my confused feelings. I didn't even want to touch her arm to console her. She moved away anyhow.

'I had no choice' she whispered.

Aine appeared again, muttering angrily, more like a bad spirit than ever.

'How is your arm today?'

'What? Speak up!'

'Your arm, how does it feel?'

'Hurts. Agony. Couldn't lie on it. Couldn't sleep.'

She wasn't the only one.

'May I examine it?'

'What? You a doctor or summut?'

'Yes as it happens, I am.'

Aine obligingly moved nearer, her arm had obviously prevented her washing herself too. She watched curiously as holding my breath, I grasped her elbow, then her upper arm. And then her shoulder.

She gave an ear-piercing yell followed by a stream of Good Old Brittonic swear words. Then she stopped. Quinctia nervously took her hands away from her ears.

'You done it! It don't hurt no more! 'Ow did you do that?'

She stretched and flexed her arm in obvious delight.

'Your arm had become dislocated from the shoulder socket. I apologise for hurting you.'

'That don't matter. You done it!'

And she grasped the dusty jug and disappeared, presumably to fetch water.

I grinned at Quinctia.

'Hope she uses some of the water for her person' I said.

Quinctia smiled, such a pretty smile. It broadened into a giggling sound, just as Kendreague stomped in, bending his back and lowering his head to negotiate the doorway.

Kendreague only paused briefly to look first at Quinctia and then at me.

'Bread. And pies!' he said triumphantly.

The old women watched us depart. They looked quite sorry to see us go. But they were pleased with the coins. Rightly so. I had been pretty generous. But we had all appreciated the night's hospitality. And Kendreague had revealed his secret to me. It was out in the open, so much easier to deal with, out in the open. The problem was now shared. What I didn't know was whether Melania and Quinctia, like me unable to sleep, had used the night in the cottage to reveal secrets of their own. I shuddered and put the thought out of my mind.

We left the gatehouse without incident. Melania remarked upon the vast cemetery. It was the first time I had heard her speak today.

'Over there' she pointed but I couldn't really see exactly where. 'There is a Christian burial ground. See the chapel?'

We all went 'Mmmm' but there were so many structures scattered among the miles of statuary, graves and steli I doubted anyone was sure. I resisted stopping, although I knew that Melania was hinting that we should. My urgency mounted as the miles passed and every hill and valley seemed interminable and again we were short of food. I have never known such a small person as my new-found son to have such a gargantuan appetite. I saw Kendreague's stone face exhibit dismay as the last pie was devoured, by Philippus.

The weather deteriorated as we approached Clausentum. Driving rain soaked us. Angry winds battered the raeda making the journey even more uncomfortable. Philippus was crying again and I found myself getting short tempered with him. Son or no son.

'It is as bad for everyone!' I snapped as the mounting gale threw away my words with its fierce howling. But it also drowned Philippus's crying, so it wasn't all bad.

We were a sorry sight as we drove into the port as blackness started descending. There was more blackness than light these days. We left the exhausted horses with a kindly couple, Britons, whose business was running a stable for travellers' animals. And I quickly found shelter in the form of an unusually open-fronted house with a bar and a bakery run by a Roman needless to say, who wanted to enjoy little bit of home about his establishment, he said. Not much to enjoy here, rain driving in, wind howling round the deserted tables. However, in the back room there was a glowing stove. So that eased the pain.

I left my little group warming themselves and eating some good smelling pies, and made my way nearly blown from my feet, down the slippery cobbled path to the puddle-filled waterfront. I asked a group of seamen hanging about in the sheltered archway to a bar about the next sailing for Vectis. Even as I enquired, the stupidity of my words were blown back at me. The waters frothed angrily, white edged waves trying to wash me away as they swept over the crumbling stone walls.

The men nudged each other and chortled at the possibility of a boat to Vectis.

'Won't be one tomorrow, nor the day after. This storm's set for a while yet.'

'When did the last boat leave?'

'Two days ago.'

We had missed the boat by two days. Of all the bad luck. I silently cursed Neptune and then regretted it. A curse, even a silent curse would not be well received at a time like this. I should have taken Fannia's advice and made an offering to the dratted Lar. Then I wished I hadn't murmured that impious thought as a particularly enormous wave nearly drowned me much to the amusement of the sheltering seamen.

‘Come back in two days’ one of them hissed through broken teeth but he was smiling quite sympathetically through the gaps. ‘Live over there on Vectis, do you?’

I felt that the moment had come to push for a bit of respect.

‘I am Marcus Cassius and I have a farm on Vectis.’

‘Oh yes? We took a friend of yours over. On the last boat for Vectis that got back.’

‘A friend? What name?’

The men shrugged their huge cloaked shoulders.

‘He just said he was a friend. And he wasn’t a Vectian. He was visiting you. Don’t know how long he planned on staying but he’ll be over there a while yet. And there’s not even a bar on Vectis.’

There was uproarious laughter at the idea of being stranded on Vectis without the convenience of a bar.

There didn’t seem to be much advantage in lingering, doused by icy salt water, ridiculed by bored sailors.

‘I will come here every day to see when a boat can sail.’

They sniggered amongst themselves at such an unlikely event. And I left with as much dignity as I could muster, my legs almost blown from under me at every step.

Grateful to be within the warmth of the mock-Roman establishment, I explained that we could not get home. The owner, one Modestinus, boasted that his sleeping accommodation was better than anywhere else in Clausentum. I wouldn’t have thought that said very much. Clausentum is a place I have always disliked and it looked much more rundown, even making allowances for the rain, than when I had moved to Vectis. The approach road was full of holes. The sea defences were unrepaired, hence my sodden cloak and boots. I had noticed the line of *borrea* that were empty and closed. This port used to be quite important, and ten years ago these storage sheds and warehouses were open and busy. The place was a depressing symbol of the changing face of Britannia.

Modestinus, delighted to have paying guests, took us proudly, carrying a cheap smoky taper to light our way, to look at his rooms. The first was not promising. A leather bucket caught rainwater as it dripped relentlessly through the roof. The rooms were very cold, though Modestinus said no problem, he would have stoves in place by bedtime. He realised by our faces reflected in his smelly flickering tapers, that we were actually near to exhaustion and that bedtime had arrived for us. He craned his neck to look up at Kendreague hopefully and my reliable man followed him to deal with the chore.

Too weary to complain, except for whining Philippus, we managed to sort ourselves out in two separate rooms. For a change Kendreague and I had a bed each. They were very hard and the bedding inadequate. Rain pounded relentlessly on the leaky tiles as the wind whistled around the building and in through the rotting window frames. But tiredness overcame us.

When gloomy daylight searched us out of the uncomfortable beds, I also searched my head for a clue to the identity of the person who had travelled from here to Vectis, announcing himself as my friend. I did not need that sort of problem. I probably did not need that sort of friend. How far would the army go to punish me for abandoning their help on a journey to Londinium and why should they care whether I lived or died in the attempt? And if it were not the army, who was it? Had the Government decided to pursue me? I was puzzled. I was frankly scared. I couldn't bear to think about it. Except that I did.

My son Philippus did not endear himself to me, during the next anguished two days waiting for a boat, that turned into a third day. I caught him taking some coins from the three-legged table by my bed. He jumped guiltily as I entered the room to retrieve my boots to go down and face the grinning sailors.

'What are you doing?'

‘I want a pie.’

‘You only have to ask. You do not take anything without asking, son.’

‘Am I your son? How do I know I am your son?’ he demanded defiantly.

‘You most certainly are. But that does not give you the right to take coins without asking me. And if you ask Modestinus, he will give you a pie and add the sum to my bill.’

Philippus fell into a sulk. He was a sulky boy. He was starting to prompt my memory about someone I would rather have not been reminded of. Yes, the journey had been long, tiring, painful. But his sulks continued long after his tummy had been regularly filled, and we had sorted out better bedding with our genial if surprised host. No-body else had ever complained about his lodgings he said. He had a good name hereabouts. His food and services were impeccable.

The food was only just acceptable. Kendreague had not located another cookshop or bakery. The beds in the draughty damp rooms were falling apart. I heard rats scrabbling in the roof space during my restless nights. People unfortunate enough to be travelling through Clausentum were either too tired to notice where they slept, or had no palate. Or perhaps they simply did not dare to voice complaints in the short spaces between flows of self-adulation that streamed non-stop from Modestinus. I dared. I had dealt with worse people than Modestinus.

Darkness started to fall and with it the wind. Encouraged, I dragged my unwilling, sulky son at the close of our third enforced stay at Clausentum, to talk to the sailors. The men had grown used to my twice daily trips. I almost imagined they looked forward to my appearance. They greeted me quite warmly, particularly if I bought them beers in their little stone haven of a bar where they seemed to do nothing but drink and laugh at nothing.

‘This your boy? Hello lad’ they said grinning at Philippus who stared rudely back.

‘The weather is changing’ they said to me.

I was right about the wind.

‘Tomorrow?’ I hardly dared to ask them.

‘Tomorrow’ they agreed.

Vectis

I must have done something right. Sol rose early, kissing the ugly port with his golden smile. Neptune obviously hadn't taken offence at my silent curses because he had calmed the waters until they echoed the rippling qualities of a lake. I could have almost swum home.

The eloquent Modestinus accepted my minimal payment without a murmur of discontent. 'We will see you again when you are passing through Clausentum' he said ingratiatingly and waved a last goodbye as he turned and made his lonely way up the broken path back to his Roman monstrosity of a dwelling.

It was then I realised how tough it was getting for him. Less trade meant less traffic passing through. He was probably the only hostelry surviving, but only just, in the port. He had been here twenty years he told proudly me one night, when out of boredom I shared a beer with him, or was it two. He had surrounded himself with reminders of the good old Roman days. There were wall paintings, now rather faded, long ago executed by an artist on his way to Londinium, I particularly admired the cavorting Bacchus, and another, fighting gladiators with net and trident; he even boasted a small larlarium. When he was alone, and nowadays that would be most of the time, he must fear for his future. But I couldn't waste my compassion on Modestinus. I probably needed it for myself.

The island looked beautiful. From this distance, the Winter Solstice had not spoiled its lush appearance. The day was so clear that the dark forests were visible stretching inland. I even imagined I could see the deer that roamed there.

The horses seemed eager and lively as they delicately avoided the holes in the terrible road. They knew they were home too. Melania was smiling. My son merely looked his usual sulky self. Quinctia? She was out of my direct range of vision. It was probably better that way.

And there lay my villa. Just as I had left it. Nobody waited to greet us. But nobody knew we had arrived. No matter. Kendreague helped the ladies down and then unloaded our baggage. Where was Fidus? I called loudly. Had he given himself a day off? That seemed very unlikely. My shout however had attracted attention.

Finnius solemnly escorted us inside the villa where he revealed his devastating news.

Finnius reported the death of Fidus with a brutal lack of emotion. He could have been recounting the conclusion of a balance sheet.

'Four days ago. One minute, directing the men sorting the ancient stones that I intend to sell for you. The next, collapsed on the ground. His wife handled all the necessary formalities. The funeral has taken place.'

Very efficient. But Finnius's efficiency rendered me emotionally incompetent as I slumped down on the nearest stone bench, speechless with the shock. And I should have been here to examine the body of Fidus myself. I spoke slowly to give myself time for composure.

'Do you know the cause of his death? Had he showed signs of illness? Were there been any problems here?'

'Everything has run normally in your absence. He was an old man. It was his heart.'

Finnius paused showing uncertainty for the first time.

There was just the matter of the visitor.'

'Visitor.'

Oh yes, the unnamed, uninvited guest. I felt a sudden onslaught of fear replace my grief. It must have showed because Melania moved quietly beside me. Her first instinctive movement since we left Londinium. Her understanding presence helped me gain self control.

'You remember the person from the Government? Aquilinus Drusus.'

As we gathered together, except Melania who went back to her villa saying she would return tomorrow, Finnius confessed that the sudden appearance of Aquilinus Drusus had obviously caused Fidus concern.

'He did not like the unannounced visit. 'Why has he come here now? he kept asking me. When the master is away.'

Philippus was swinging his legs, higher and higher, until he kicked my favourite low wooden table with the carved feet and edges inset with brass studs. It was an expensive table, from Rome. My irritability rose to an unmanageable level.

Jupiter! I am as devoted to Roman memorabilia as poor old Modestinus.

'Don't do that' I bellowed. He stopped and sulked. I addressed Finnius again, with an open question.

'How did you feel about the arrival of Aquilinus Drusus?'

'I was surprised to see him. But he seems very genuine. He is taking Winter Solstice leave apparently.'

I recalled with a shudder someone else who used an official holiday for the sinister purpose of visiting Vectis.

'One thing, though. He showed no surprise that you were not here. He volunteered the information to me that you and he had met in Venta Belgarum and he had hoped that he would see you on your return journey.'

'He didn't wait very long in Venta Belgarum' I said gloomily.

Why had Aquilinus Drusus had made his visit to my villa, particularly if he knew I would not be here.

I asked Finnius for his opinion. Another open question which he chose not to answer. I sensed that Finnius might also have been nervous about the official's return. Finnius had a dark past of his own.

We were silent, each with our secret thoughts.

But someone important was missing.

"Where is my daughter?'

Approaching the bath house I knew that Finnius had got it wrong. When I heard the high giggles and low male laughter I knew that Finnius had got it right.

They were in the caldarium splashing each other like happy children, causing steam to erupt and swirl and they plunged and wallowed, chasing each other, she squealing as she attacked him with a giant sponge, he grunting as he lunged this way and that, together creating a crazed whirling dance in the foaming water. It looked like innocent fun. Until I realised that my daughter was naked.

I bellowed; the same enraged noise I had used to check Philippus for kicking my table and they reacted with startled gasps. I could have been a Shade from the Underworld looming through the vaporous mist.

Fannia, quickly recovering her composure, all pink and pretty, mounted the shallow steps from the pool, keeping her pert back to me, and grabbing a stolla from the long stone bench, wrapped it around her lithe form. She ran the length of the room, her feet pattering wetly on the mosaics, to where I stood very angry and red-faced. She flung her arms around me.

'Oh I am so happy. You are safe.'

That smile, I recognised it from another of the wall paintings in the loser Modestinus's house.

She was the Personification of Flora. Fresh, young, beautiful, the rebirth of Spring. I kissed her flushed cheeks and smoothed her dark hair away from her sparkling eyes. And then I remembered the other person in the water.

But under cover of our embraces, Aquilinus Drusus had skipped out and donned his robe. He approached me respectfully.

'Marcus Cassius. I too am happy that you are safely returned.'

I sat down on the bench. It was hot in here. Fannia landed airily beside me, fluttering all over me, like a springtime butterfly, in her delight. I wondered grimly who was giving her more delight.

'I expected to find you in Venta Belgarum on my arrival after an extremely stressful journey from Londinium. As you invited me to do.'

'My apologies for that. I was ordered to take some leave and being unsure whether – when you would return – safely – I decided to come here and await news.'

'How long exactly have you been staying in my villa?'

'Six days.'

Timing sounded right. Even if everything else felt wrong.

'You are alone?'

'I am. And may I express my condolences over the death of your slave…'

'Fidus was a freedman.'

I had barked at him. I relented. There was no point in putting the man's (soaking wet) back up.

'Thank you. I too am very sad that I was not here. Shall we change our attire?'

I gave him the benefit of my disapproving glare.

I was feeling in need of a cooling bath. Alone.

'And how long are you staying with us? I don't mean that…'

It was precisely what I did mean. I wanted him out! I could not allow the chance of a repeat performance in my bathhouse between my daughter and Aquilinus Drusus. Besides which I had just recalled his comment about Fannia as he drove away from my villa the last time. With the corpse, destined, with a little help from my men, for the sea. No wonder poor Fidus was taken fatally ill when Aquilinus Drusus turned up again.

Another few days – if it is suitable.'

What could I say? No it is not suitable?

Instead I dismissed them curtly, ignoring Fannia's imploring smile, whatever it meant. After all it was my house, and my bathhouse. I locked myself in and indulged in a long relaxing soak. I needed to carefully work out my questions. So many questions these days. But at least I could conduct enquiries within the safety of my own home again. An advantage, of a kind.

The stammering slave had been well trained. I was astounded by his expertise; in washing our hands, in serving our meal, in pouring our wine, in faultless politeness, in silence. He listened for instructions and acted upon them quickly and efficiently, in silence. My dear servant Fidus had left a legacy I could not fault, almost reducing me to tears as the man backed silently out, leaving us in silence and a long pause.

'What is his name?' I eventually asked Finnius.

'Duane.'

I would remember his name from now on. Meanwhile, refreshed and reclining contentedly across my couch, grateful to be home, sipping my mulsum, I looked round at my guests. Melania Lupurca smiling as graciously as ever. (As I left the bathouse, I saw Kendreague outside in conversation with a small girl slave from the kitchen. A budding Romance? I dismissed that idea along with the girl. Kendreague would soon be manumitted. Jupiter, another task to be organised. I had told him to run to Melania Lupurca's villa and invite her to join us.) And happily she had appeared, exquisite in a white and silver stolla, hair coiled gracefully and held by silver combs. Fannia, my delicious Flora, her golden stolla flowing to her dainty gold sandals, her bright eyes afire. Her usual sweet nature had dictated without prompting from me, that she reclined near Quinctia, who gave an impression of awkwardness in her new status as dinner guest, wearing a long midnight blue tunic and a sad countenance. Finnius to my left, handsome, enigmatic, sipping his mulsum, looking completely relaxed in the elevated position he found himself occupying. I had created Finnius my unofficial advisor and official senior clerk; that he was my only clerk was irrelevant. And our guest of honour. Aquilinus Drusus rested on the couch to my right. He too, was smiling over the rim of his cup of wine. He was smiling at my daughter.

The meal proceeded companionably. Aquilinus Drusus was anxious to hear my experience of the present political climate in Londinium. I guessed that he also wanted to know why I had cunningly slipped the clutches of Fabatus. I could tell from his quizzical expression that he had already heard about my disappearance. I ignored his obvious curiosity.

'Londinium is full of more rumours than anything. But people are very nervous. People are leaving. But others want very much to stay put. People I met… a particularly hard working family…'

I thought with affection of Paulus and Statilia who had so kindly sheltered Melania, and desired nothing more than to be allowed to live and work there. I caught Melania's eyes. They were telling me firmly not to name names. How wise she was. I revised my script accordingly.

'I met families who do not want to leave. But without the army in control there seems to be a very real threat of invasion by insurgents…'

'Yes they are right to be afraid. Londinium citizens are in a vulnerable position. Rebels are always attracted by a wealthy place like Londinium.'

'Londinium won't be wealthy if everyone runs away. It will fall into ruin.'

He waved my remark into the lamp flame.

'You have to appreciate that the Roman army is badly needed in the Northern Empire, to protect transport services and important cities. The whole Northern Empire is in trouble. And Rome too is under serious threat from Goths. They are potentially the worst of the insurgents. Britannia is least likely to suffer.'

He hadn't changed his views. Or was he quoting from those whose job it was to make sure he heard what they wanted him to hear.

‘ Britannia has to learn to cope on her own. The Roman armies’ priorities do not allow them to stay and coddle her for ever.’

What a very helpful comment! I was beginning to feel cynical about the Roman armies’ priorities.

‘And you Aquilinus Drusus. What does Britannia hold for your future?’

He paused. I could sense his uncertainty. But I looked him in the eyes. I wanted to know. Would he return to war-torn Gaul or to Italy? Or to Rome? Surely not Rome.

‘I have a few options. But for the present, my position in the Government at Venta Belgarum is secure. Very secure.’

I saw his eyes flicker slyly to meet Fannia’s.

The meal progressed amiably if quietly. I was careful not to indulge in too much wine. I could not have described what I ate. Everything laid out on the tables seemed to be laced with richly provocative smiles that wreathed across the room between Fannia and Aquilinus Drusus.

Melania announced that she was weary and would retire to her villa and Finnius offered to escort her. I was disappointed to see her depart. But in all the circumstances, it was probably as well. I had need for a private discussion with at least one of the remaining people in the *triclinium*. I was impressed at the concern of Finnius until I caught my daughter’s eyes that held a meaningful twinkle. Of course, Claudia. Finnius would have concern for Claudia too. So Finnius possessed an ability for emotional calculations too, tucked somewhere not too deep beneath his methodical mathematical intellect.

Quinctia, looking nervous, looking even more out of place, did not delay either. She heard Philippus crying she said. I thought to myself that it would not do Philippus any harm to get over his crocodile tears by himself but I quickly abandoned such cruel reflections and thanked her. She was obviously glad to have some task requiring her absence from our company. Quinctia was going to be a problem too. I could not imagine where she fitted in, now that we were back. Only as nurse to Philippus, a thankless task, I imagined. Perhaps she accepted her role in return for her freedom from the terrors of Londinium. It didn't seem much of a future but maybe she did not envisage much of a future anyway. I felt guilty. It was my fault as usual. One hopeful sign was that Melania and she betrayed nothing to suggest that they had discussed their innermost secrets together. But I had had not a moment alone with Melania Lupurca. How I missed our intimate moments, listening to her wise observations, loving her warm nearness.

I was being eyed suspiciously by my daughter and my uninvited guest.

I cleared my throat, which made time to consider how to handle the situation. I dismissed my daughter who was not amused.

'I would love to stay with you a little longer' she pleaded prettily. If Fannia had possessed a cat's tail she would be swishing it ticklingly all over me, and purring in my ear. But I managed to turn a deaf ear, both of them.

I was alone with Aquilinus Drusus. He was a big man lounging there, no denying it, but well proportioned. I noticed for the first time the excellent quality of his evening toga, a rich purple that set off his bronzed features. How had he managed to keep his Roman radiance in this sunless place? Fidus and I had long lost ours. Aquilinus also sported a finely shaved chin. A despairing thought descended as I stroked my unbecoming and unfashionable beard. Who would shave me now? I had almost forgotten that Fidus was no longer a part of my world. It was a very depressing remembrance and not only because he shaved me so expertly.

'May I pour you more wine?'

I held my cup out. Actually shouldn't I have asked him? I sipped from my cup, unable to speak.

'Please let me say at once, now that we are alone, that I quite understand your displeasure at seeing us together in your bathhouse today. Particularly as you have only just returned.'

I kept quiet and let him talk. My wine tasted good after an evening's abstinence. More like many days' abstinence, when I thought about it. I leaned back, savouring the warmth as the crimson liquid slipped easily down my throat, while I let Aquilinus grovel.

'Fannia has been the perfect hostess. She has not been able to do enough for me.'

He obviously realised this was not a strictly acceptable premise to make to a father.

'Fannia made sure that my roo was to my liking and provided every comfort...plenty of cushions...enough lamps. A wax tablet...'

I jerked out of the amusement I had derived from his discomfort. It was my turn to experience apprehension. What wax tablet?

'Are you aware that Fannia kept a record every day while you were away. The pages tidily bound with leather thongs that I believe your – servant – assembled for her. She records the weather...personal comments...how much she missed you... and Melania Lupurca. She is a devoted daughter. You must be very proud of her.'

'Of course. I also have her best interests very much in my heart.'

'Of course' he agreed, almost soothingly. 'More wine?'

He was getting cheekier, and I was getting sillier as I held out my cup to be refilled.

'Please understand I have the utmost respect for your daughter.'

'I am glad to hear it. I was beginning to have my doubts especially as...'

What doubts?' He interrupted me, looking surprisingly agitated, for a self-assured man from the Roman Government.

I swung my legs to the floor and leaned towards him. He looked even more anxious.

'I do not consider that it shows respect towards a young woman, if a male guest enters the bathhouse knowing that they will be alone. More particularly when the male guest is betrothed to another.'

He made to interrupt me but I waved him into silence.

'No, not respectful at all. I would like to feel that you are welcome in my home. But now I feel that the welcome has been abused.'

Aquilinus Drusus had turned red in the face.

He stammered the words.

'But … I am not betrothed to anyone.'

'You told me yourself. To my face. I even recall her name. Postumia… your betrothed. I even recall your words. They are as alike as golden walnuts in a shell, you told me.'

Too much wine late at night, and too many confused thoughts contributed to another sleepless night. I certainly wasn't appeasing Somnus at the moment but I was careful not to grumble about him even in my fermenting mind.

By morning, I was tired and fractious. In the bathhouse that felt almost disapprovingly deserted, I cut my face trying to shave, and I yelled for Duane who appeared silently and almost at once.

'How competent are you to shave my face? Did Fidus instruct you?'

Duane nodded silently, respectfully.

'I hope you do a good job as he did' I told him sternly and with not a little regret.

'Your g-guest is p-pleased.'

'You shave him?'

Duane nodded solemnly. Not a glimmer of expression.

I was speechless, again. Not only was the man attempting to woo my daughter but he was commandeering my slave.

However when Duane had finished, I felt a little better. But the difficult day still lay ahead.

My two children and Quinctia were in the triclinium that appeared clean and freshened after the evening's activities. The floor positively shone. Fidus knew that I appreciated such attention to detail. His staff had been well trained. Oh Fidus, I still miss you. Chasing around on your gammy legs, never letting any matter go unattended; making time to create a note book for Fannia. Watching over everything. In the villa and at the farm. There would have to be some reorganising. I doubted the rough farm hands would take too kindly to Duane and his stammer. But Duane had been trained as a body slave that was now obvious. Ha! Kendreague! The farm would have to fall into Kendreague's strong hands. He had proved himself a capable and reliable man. I would talk to him later. I felt cheered. Things were not so bad. Or were they?

Philippus was playing with a kitten, a creamy-mottled little thing whose colours caused it to blend into the mosaics so that it was almost invisible like a chameleon, when he put it down to run and greet me. I almost felt he had been told to.

'Good morning. Please may I go outside? It is not cold today.'

Perhaps my son's demeanour was improving with the fine fresh air of Vectis. I smiled at him realising that I hadn't been in the habit of smiling at him. Perhaps he needed to feel my approval.

He ran into the garden, letting out loud whooping noises like a swan.

Fannia laughed.

'It will take time to get used to a little boy around the place.'

And bigger boys too, I thought.

'How are you today Quinctia?'

The sweeping eyelashes dropped again.

‘Fannia I need a quick word with Quinctia about Philippus. Could you perhaps keep an eye on your brother? And take that animal with you!’

I could not allow myself to be entranced by a kitten no matter how appealing. Fannia scooped it up, as it meowed pitifully, and was gone. My children were suddenly extremely obedient which had to be a cause for suspicion.

I somewhat nervously approached Quinctia. Quinctia, of whom I had once been so fond. She had been through tough times. She would need careful handling. I rested my hand upon the long sleeve of her morning stolla. I recognised it as belonging to Fannia. The wretched woman probably had no suitable garments of her own. The one she wore last night had looked very familiar.

Her eyes remained downcast, her mouth also turned down at the corners. She had possessed a beautiful mouth and a wide sensuous smile, rarely seen even by me in the old days.

‘I want to help you. I am deeply indebted to you’ I said.

‘I’m sorry.’

She moved her arm away with a tiny flinch. I was right. Quinctia was still in love with me. What a terrible situation. If I gave her clothes, they would be seen as loving gifts. But my fondness for Quinctia had been swept away by passing time. There had been too many disturbances for too many years to restore something as fragile and transient as our brief clutch at happiness, and that so long ago.

She moved over to a window and stared through the green glass lit by morning sunshine that transformed her hair to fiery emerald.

‘I am happy to look after Philippus if you want me to. He is not an easy child. He has not had an easy life. But…’

She turned towards me and at last lifted her long eyelashes revealing dark sad eyes that looked straight at me. There was pain in their intensity, making it difficult for me to return her gaze.

‘I have to say something, Marcus. I am grateful to you and to Melania Lupurca for rescuing me. To be your servant again will make me very happy. A return to the old days. Except, what happened between you and me. That is in the past. I have no regrets. I have the greatest respect for you. That is all.’

We both heard Philippus yelling again. Whether in fright or temper I could not tell. Fannia never screamed like that when she was little. The boy did not seem able to amuse himself without a tantrum for long. I sighed. My sigh released an undeniable gratitude that Quinctia had shown herself to be the quietly understanding woman that I remembered. She had not clung to a slender hope that we could rekindle passions long extinguished. She was also willing to continue the responsibilities that I saw as so onerous. I certainly did not yet love my son. I took her small hand for a brief moment.

‘You will be well looked after and well rewarded for your task’ I said.

Quinctia hurried away. I had not discovered whether she and Melania Lupurca had discussed me together. I really needed to know. It would help me regain a necessary sense of proportion over my household. There were too many secrets abounding either real or imagined.

Fannia was next.

And there she was wandering through the entrance, reincarnated like a muse from a tragedy.

‘What’s wrong? Why is there mud on your face?’

What a sight, not much like a muse, they were always white and perfect. As she got nearer I could see that she was pink from crying. Not forced tragedy-inspired tears either. And she was limping too. She raised the hem of her gown to examine a graze on her knee leaking bright spots of blood.

‘That child. I don’t like him. He is vicious.’

‘He is nine or ten years. What happened? Duane!!’

‘He threw a stone at me.’

‘What did you do to him?’

‘Nothing. What could I have done to him. I do not throw things.’

That was true enough. Now her mother I recalled, had perfected a very good aim when throwing things at me. My dinner. My shoes. Insults. The green umbrella… Oh yes she had excellent aim, Flaccilla.

‘He just threw the stone at you. For nothing.’

‘I was walking in the garden. Thinking, while I kept an eye on him as you told me to. He ran up to me and said that he hated me. He said that he is the number one member of the *familia*, because he is your son. He said I was nothing. I did not answer and kept walking. And then he ran ahead of me and threw the stone. Little monster! Look at me!’

I was concerned at the blood. Duane appeared and I sent him for water and a clean cloth.

‘He will not get away with talking to you like that’ I said. ‘Sit here Fannia. I will clean your knee when Duane returns.' When...

It was teeth-gritting time.

‘Fannia, last night I spoke with Aquilinus Drusus.’

Her colour heightened even more, but attractively. A pretty blush. But she did not speak.

And Duane came with bowl and amazingly, a clean cloth. When he had gone, we bathed her poor knee amidst wincing, mine, and little shrieks, hers. It was a nasty wound. I was very angry. Holding her gown clear of her knee she sat primly, remembering my last words.

‘Where were we?’

I couldn’t recall my last words.

‘Your conversation with Aquilinus…’

‘Ah yes. I was, as you know displeased with the manner in which I found you both yesterday. On my return from a long tiring journey. Moreover, that was the time usually allotted to servants to use the bathhouse wasn’t it?’

She nodded.

'I asked them to come back later. Aquilinus had been around the farm…'

Snooping again? I was even angrier.

'… and he was in need of washing.'

'So you helped?'

'No, I, we, oh it was just a game!'

Just a game was it? And the result was that everyone's time schedules were put out. No wonder Kendreague had been lurking outside. The servants had a set routine. It was all very annoying.

'Can I go now?'

'No.'

I was not going to be sidetracked again.

'Aquilinus Drusus confessed to me that you and he are very fond of each other?'

She nodded enthusiastically.

'In so short a time too.'

'It only took one glance' she said romantically. 'We are very fond of each other. In fact…we love each other. And when you give your consent, we will become betrothed.'

Children can be Difficult

We we sat in her beautifully furnished hall. I realised that it was only the second time that I had been inside the villa of Melania Lupurca. The first was on the solemn occasion of her husband's funeral. And where I recalled the solemnity broken by a mysterious peel of tinkling laughter. Now we were both solemn for very different reasons. And laughter was not appropriate, any more than it had been then. But this was now. We faced each other across a fine low table. It would have matched my favourite table almost perfectly, the feet overlaid with elaborate brass fittings, and upon the top, a handsome pottery one-handled urn and a bowl containing apples that blushed like my daughter's cheeks.

'And how do you feel about Fannia becoming betrothed to Aquilinus Drusus?'

I hesitated unable to answer immediately. After all, he had diffused a very sensitive situation last summer, more sensitive than he knew or would ever know, Jupiter willing.

'He seems to possess a good heart' she added.

'You see no disadvantage with such a match?'

'Not unless you reveal a disadvantage to me.'

'The problem I see is…' And I instantly recalled another one.

'When I first explained about her brother, Fannia immediately replied that she would leave me when she found her husband. Almost as if she desired to depart, once her brother arrived. If this is just an excuse, her betrothal to Aquilinus Drusus thereby extracting herself from a situation she did not like is not a good enough reason. And she and Philippus had a fight this morning.'

'A fight?'

'He has already started pulling rank on Fannia. Boasting about his superior position as the only son etc etc. I don't know where he gets his nasty comments or temper from. Unless they are hereditary. Jupiter forbid!'

Melania winced.

I'd have to watch my tongue.

'Inherited?'

'My deceased wife, I'm afraid. He certainly has her capacity for ill humour. Quinctia has known him since his birth, perhaps I should talk to her.'

'Yes' Melania Lupurca said slowly. 'It might be a good idea.'

I gulped. I had unwittingly created the moment to address the dreaded subject of Quinctia. As if there was not enough confusion.

'By the way she is staying on at the villa, as nurse to Philippus. Although I fear that it is Fannia who needs a nurse. The little wretch threw a stone at her too.'

I hoped I might have deflected the issue. I had always been fired by the idea of a diplomatic career.

'Quinctia was in love with you once.'

My visions of a diplomatic occupation fizzled out forever.

'Although she took extraordinary care to emphasize to me that it was many years ago…You knew of course, of her infatuation?…Marcus?…Where are you…because you are certainly not here in my villa.'

'Mmm, what? Oh I am so sorry. I caught sight of your magnificent water clock. Clocks hold a magic for me, never having owned one myself.'

Melania Lupurca was not deterred.

'You knew of Quinctia's love for you of course?'

'Quinctia was of great solace to me when my marriage was breaking down. I started the tedious process of her manumission in my gratitude. But she was nervous at the thought of having to make her own way. She was not fond of my wife and I was surprised therefore, when she returned with her to Rome.'

'Quinctia told me that your wife found out about your affair - with your concubine.'

So did that also mean that Quinctia knew about my liaison with Melania. Did it matter now?

'It was a short-lived affair.'

'But an affair nevertheless. No wonder your wife was displeased. I would have felt the same.'

Melania Lupurca knew everything.

She stood up, in as dismissive a way only she could accomplish without displaying bad manners. She was not smiling.

'As for Fannia and Aquilinus Drusus. Personally I think she could do a great deal worse than become betrothed. Goodbye.'

And Women too…

I retained an image as I left. Upon the pavement in the hallway I saw an intricately devised mosaic, a bearded man before a globe. He looked like a philosopher. I badly needed such a man's wisdom for I had none of my own. But the tiny tesserae forming the philosopher's expression portrayed an unhelpfully vacant stare. He was not prepared to advise me, even in spirit.

I had walked to Melania Lupurca's villa and now I walked away. I could hear the angry sea crashing and rolling. As I neared my own villa, not daring to allow myself to think for fear of frightening myself, a figure seemed to be approaching. Or was he retreating? From that distance it was difficult to observe whether he was coming or going. I felt like that myself. And I had only just realised that it was raining. At first he was unrecognisable through the cloudy air.

Duane reached me, lifting the hood from his worn cloak.

'M-Master I must speak.'

Duane spoke, lucidly for Duane, and his words depressed me further. The wife of Fidus had lost her senses. The kitchen women had been agitated for some days because of her erratic behaviour. She no longer seemed to understand anything that was said to her, she made no attempt to mix and bake the bread for which she was famous, she lifted bowls and cups and dropped them seeming not to know how to carry them. My beautiful red Samian ware was becoming sadly depleted. And there was no bread. I'm not sure what upset me most.

'I will come and look at her' I pacified Duane. At least it took my mind off terrible qualms that explained to me that I had lost Melania Lupurca forever because of an unwise infidelity so many years ago.

It was the first time that I could recall visiting entering the kitchen of my villa. Not a proud admission but I was always put off by the tremendous heat and noise that three women seemed to be able to create. The kitchen was built separately from the villa for the obvious reason that it occasionally caught fire. Nothing too serious but not the sort of excitement I would have welcomed. Mostly I never knew about the conflagrations until Fidus told me later.

Near the kitchen entrance stood an iron trivet over a place for an open fire, built after a series of potentially dangerous accidents on the original old stone fire range in the corner of the kitchen that had been the only means of cooking and retained as the bread oven. The outside hearth had been Fidus's construction, from a design of the one installed many years ago in the grounds of my Roman villa.

The kitchen interior consisted of the usual shelves for holding cookware and tables for food preparation, and baskets for waste to be taken to the pigs. High on one wall near to a barred window, a hare and two pheasants hung. They smelled pleasingly fresh and would be prepared for my table while still in that condition.

Below them on a stool sat Fidus's widow. She smelled stale and unwashed. Her scrawny hands continually wrung each other in the lap of her long black tunic that was stained and torn. Sunken in a wrinkled ashen face, her eyes were shut against the world. Her hair was as matted as the hags' lank locks in the house by the sea. But those old girls had each other. She was alone.

'Donata' I said softly. There was no reaction. I repeated her name louder as the two cooks shuffled nearer to watch.

'She don't speak no more sir.'

'She don't hear neither.'

'Does she stay like this all day? Does she eat anything? What happens to her at night?'

I hoped they understood my faulty use of their language and that I could interpret their replies.

One of them contributed a comment. I looked up at Duane for help, from where I crouched next to Fidus's widow.

'She – she stays here all the t-time, she does not return to her cottage. She eats only when food is put in her hands.'

'She cannot stay here.'

What could be done with the poor woman. There was a slim hope of the malady passing as her grieving for Fidus lessened. But at that moment, Donata opened her eyes and stared vaguely at me. No glimmer of recognition reflected my worried gaze. She looked around as if in a dream, got up unsteadily and wandered to the table.

'Are you goin' to bake some of your loverly bread then?' asked the more outspoken of the two cooks.

The empty eyes reflected nothing as Donata slowly returned to her stool and lowered herself with a grunt. I stood up from my uncomfortable crouching position, also grunting, and left the kitchen with Duane.

'She is a risk to herself and the others in there. Can anyone look after her in her cottage?'

Duane shook his head. It was a bad situation to see the wife of my lifelong servant, sick in her mind, with nobody to care for her.

When Duane spoke again, I noticed an interesting phenomenon. The more he talked the less pronounced was his stammer.

'My mother and Donata are friends. My mother has knowledge of medicine. She would help, but Donata would have to move to us. I can arrange that.'

My gratitude showed as I unthinkingly clasped my slave's huge hand. It was sad that Donata would be unable to register her own appreciation. I gave him the rest of the day to organise the safe removal of the pathetic widow to his cottage. And I made myself a mental note to visit and talk to the mother of Duane. This medical ability that he mentioned could prove interesting. I was learning, probably too late, that no knowledge should be ruled out, no matter how unlikely the source.

One problem had almost been resolved. I returned to the villa. There were many more problems waiting. The first was Fannia, curled up like one of her kittens, on a couch.

'How are you feeling?'

Nobody ever asked me that question.

She looked up at me with red eyes.

'While you were out, my beloved Aquilinus has departed.'

'Gone?'

'Gone. He knows that you do not like him. He could stay no longer where he says he is not welcome.'

'Oh Fannia my dear child. I had no time to digest your news. So much had happened, even since my return from Londinium.'

And my darling Melania has closed the door to her villa.

'When did Aquilinus leave?'

She shrugged.

'Not very long.'

'Come' I said. 'We will catch him before he sails. Kendreague!'

The smaller of my two raedas pulled by only one horse, in Kendreague's capable hands fairly flew along the stony path to the harbour. The sea looked very rough and threatening.

'No boat will sail' I told Fannia, being the expert on marine conditions since my homeward-bound experience. Fannia's eyes brightened. She hugged my arm.

'I do love him father.'

'Love! Ugh!' squeaked the small voice of my son. I had no option but to bring him along. His piercing screams at the threat of being excluded were more than either of us could tolerate and I did not feel like facing Quinctia. Not yet.

'Ignore him' I whispered to Fannia. I patted her arm.

‘Fannia you must understand something. When Aquilinus left the villa last summer, following the er… tragic accident with that man from the Government, Aquilinus said you were the exact image of his betrothed. He even told me her name…’

‘Postumia. I know all about her.’

‘Now he says that he is not betrothed. I find it very confusing.’

‘He wanted to explain that she is not now his betrothed. Her family moved overseas, to Africa. And she didn’t want to stay here without them. Not even to marry Aquilinus!’

The emphasis on Fannia’s last phrase easily showed her amazement that the young woman could so readily leave him.

‘I would follow him to the ends of the world’ she added simply. ‘Aquilinus confessed to me that at first he doubted he would recover from losing Postumia. But now he has found me, she has gone from his thoughts completely.’

‘Fannia’s in love… Fannia’s in love’ chortled the irritating small boy beside me.

‘Yes I am and you shut up’ she said angrily.

Fortunately we had reached the harbour and the tumultuous roaring of the sea drowned our voices. Aquilinus’s horse, tethered roughly to a log, tossed his mane at the deafening sounds. I was right. There was no boat. Aquilinus stood alone on a flat rock, his back to us. Fannia leapt down and ran towards him, my shout to her to be careful was swept away on the screaming wind.

I watched, as he turned instinctively at her approach and I saw his arms clasp her slender frame, her hair streaming away as her pretty upturned face met his mouth.

Bringing the couple together gave me immense satisfaction, although probably Aquilinus would have returned to the villa anyway rather than spend a damp cold night on the harbour wall.

He and I drank, reclining alone before dinner. I refilled his cup from the bottle of my best wine residing on the lagoena.

'You want to take my daughter as your betrothed?'

'I crave your permission more than anything in the world sir.'

'Then I cannot refuse. You must promise to look after her in these uncertain times.'

'She will be my first consideration. We will be very safe in Venta Belgarum for some time to come.'

Venta Belgarum. It was slowly dawning on me that I was losing my daughter. It was as she had predicted. Philippus had arrived and she would leave. But I had no doubts that she and Aquilinus were in love. As Melania Lupurca had said, she could do a great deal worse than become betrothed to Aquilinus Drusus.

We drank another cup of wine. I tried not to think of Melania. Instead I concentrated my thoughts upon my daughter and I watched Aquilinus and liked him more. I was to have a son in law. It didn't sound too onerous. We smiled over the rims of our drinking cups.

'By the way' said Aquilinus. 'Why did you rush off alone from Calleva? Fabatus couldn't understand it…'

'I don't care for the auxiliary company he keeps' I replied, and he laughed loudly.

Marriage Plans

The second half of June was decided upon; in deference to Juno, the Goddess of women. But also in deference to Fannia who had the last word. Aquilinus Drusus would have liked to organise the marriage for the very next day. But he had to return to Venta Belgarum which was fortunate in view of the organisation to be thought through and discussed with my determined daughter who knew just what her she wanted. But the day Aquilinus left Vectis, saw Fannia in tears and Aquilinus in clear distress. They were indeed very much in love.

Because it was all the rage nowadays, I agreed that the marriage would be conducted *coemptio*, the old fashioned sale of a daughter to her husband, luckily for Aquilinus Drusus, now in symbolic form only. But it did mean that my legal power over Fannia was conveyed to her husband. The final irrevocable deed that caused me sadness to contemplate. But I needed to reflect that Fannia could have legally married and left my home at an even younger age. Marriage was her right. I had to console myself over my good fortune to have kept her with me this long.

The days grew longer and lighter. The farm work load got heavier. I left Kendreague in full charge and he was doing a good job. The men respected him. He also liaised closely with Finnius on matters relating to farm management, selling of stock, replacement of farm machinery. They made a good team.

In my villa I have a wall panel of which I am very proud. It is a constant reminder of the crops that my villa farm produces in heavy abundance. Ceres, goddess of corn is depicted handing an ear of corn to Triptolemus the inventor of the plough. I grew to love the farm more and more, especially now it was almost the summer solstice, when lambs arrived, mothered by the lofty long haired sheep with their great horns. The workers seemed to welcome me as I tramped about in the mud and animal dung and not caring about it. I often wandered to the far end of the land. From there, I could see the villa of Melania Lupurca among the new green leaved trees. Of the lady herself there was never a glimpse. Claudia came regularly to the villa, ostensibly to visit Fannia, but she was usually to be found with Finnius at some time of the day. They, like Fannia and Aquilinus, seemed very much in love.

Philippus grew well, but I found it hard to warm to him. A terrible thing to say of one's own son. I could see nothing of myself in his nature, good or bad, nor had he any feature resembling my own appearance. He had developed a snarling countenance that I tried very hard not to liken to his dead mother. As much as I showered gifts upon him, the last a bow and arrows (he proceeded to shoot a kitten (good aim I'll admit), he demanded more, saying it was his right. He boasted so much about his position that eventually, having kept out of Quinctia's way, and she mine I might add, I called her one day when I saw her alone in the garden.

'How are you Quinctia? It is a long time since we spoke.'

She ate her meals with Philippus, in the little *cubiculum* where spare cupboards and furniture were stored. For some reason he liked the gloomy room.

She lowered her eyes and murmured that she was in good health thank you.

'How do you find young Philippus these days? He is sometimes uncommonly rude both to his sister and to me. I confess to not knowing how to handle his moods. Have you any suggestions?'

She seemed relieved that the topic was about someone else and not her.

'He is improving. He does not keep awake so much at night nor wet his bed so often.'

'Oh.'

I did not know of this habit nor whether he should be beaten for it. And I am a surgeon. Or was.

'How do you handle the bed wetting?'

'I praise him when the bed is dry.'

What a perfect person Quinctia was. What a good wife and mother she would have made some lucky man. But the woman was in her thirties now. Such chances had sadly passed her by. And her youthful prettiness had faded and she was still unbecomingly thin.

'Are you comfortable? Have you enough clothing, bedding, er…'

The ineffable guilt still haunted me. But she nodded, her eyes on the grass as though concentrating on her sandaled feet.

A brooding impatience cut through my guilt.

'Why did you tell Melania Lupurca?'

She didn't speak for a moment. But she knew what I meant. She sighed deeply.

'It was not in my mind to tell her anything. Perhaps it was the beer that the old women gave us that night. I just told her, when we lay in the cottage trying to sleep.'

'Why?'

'She mentioned that you and she dined together often.'

'So you decided to set about destroying our friendship? I took you for a discreet woman.'

But I fear there is no such thing in love or war as discretion, just as there are no rules. The first enormous striped ginger bee bumbled past, searching for budding foliage. The woman I once thought to be prettier than almost any other stood before me, her eyelids lowered. I suddenly disliked the coy habit. It took the form of slyness. Avoiding eye contact.

'That is all. You may go to your tasks.'

I tended to forget that Quinctia was a freedwoman (or almost, the formalities never having been finalised). But Quinctia seemed to forget too. She had not broached the subject. As she left me, walking hastily towards the villa, I recalled another matter of manumission that lurked unfulfilled. I had made a promise to Kendreague.

Yet another problem caused me not a small amount of anxiety. Fannia raised the subject, during one of our comfortable evenings, alone together for a change. Finnius had excused himself and Fannia whispered to me that he was with Claudia. Her earlier annoyance at losing her friend's undivided attention had of course completely faded now her delight in Claudia's love affair blossomed alongside her own. She occasionally enquired as to the absence of Melania Lupurca, queries that I dismissed airily suggesting that she was a busy lady with a life of her own. Fannia was too engrossed in her future plans to think about my throw away line.

'Who do we invite to be *pronuba* at my marriage ceremony?'

It was a baffling dilemma, the pronuba being a very important lady not only because she attends the bride in her preparations. She also conducts the important rituals of the marriage ceremony itself. The other significant attribute of the pronuba is that she must be a univira and taking into consideration the escalating divorce rate it might be difficult to locate a woman who had been married only once. There were married couples we used to know in Durovenum. For example Curius the dentist had a wife, a vivacious, energetic networker. I recall that Flaccilla hated her. But I didn't relish another tiresome journey any more than rekindling old cronies. Besides the wife of Curius might have divorced the vapid man by now and remarried and who would have blamed her? Fannia of course thought she had the answer.

'Melania Lupurca. We have to ask her!'

'Melania Lupurca is of the Christian faith, you will recall, and would therefore not be willing to attend a marriage ceremony held in the Roman tradition.'

Fannia's sweet face fell.

'We could ask her.'

'No Fannia, we will not ask her. Even her husband's funeral did not adhere to Roman formalities.'

Not strictly true, but in essence correct. And I could not bear the thought of my child being snubbed, however politely, by Melania Lupurca. I leaned down from my couch to where Fannia sat on her little stool below me, and patted her hand gently.

'I will think of somebody, darling child.'

Easier said than accomplished; but after Fannia left me I had a thought.

Further around the coast of Vectis, lived another villa owner; a retired civil servant. We had met only once or twice after I had settled to Vectis and he seemed pleasant enough. He was the one who couldn't understand my dislike of peacock meat. But this matter was of far greater importance.

At the sixth hour next day, because the sun felt warm and because Fannia was an impatient girl, I drove the raeda for a change, through the dry and dusty terrain to the villa of Laetorius. Fortunately, or not, the villa lay in the opposite direction to that of Melania Lupurca, a precious glimpse of whom who I alternately dreaded and yearned for.

Laetorius was pottering around his garden accompanied by a slave. He was more stooped than I remembered him, and wore a strange white hat to protect his head from the dubious heat of the sun. He had obviously been in Britannia many more years than me. I still did not find the warmest day that Britannia could accomplish comparable to Rome's ferocious heat.

I called out to him as Fannia and I approached. The slave looked up. Laetorius did not. As the slave attracted his attention away from the all absorbing plants, the elderly man straightened with some effort and squinted at us. As we drew closer I saw a cataract clouding his right eye. Oh no. Not again. But I didn't recall telling him on our previous encounter of my former profession, nor did I intend to.

I attempted to explain the reason for my visit while he beckoned me to follow him to a shaded terrace where ancient large Greek pithoi were placed randomly like fat centurions.

I realised that Laetorius had not understood anything I had carefully said. And when the slave haltingly explained that his master could not hear, my resolve softened. He could not lose both his sight and his hearing. But the invitation of a consultation could wait.

'Is your mistress at home?'

The slave nodded and spoke into the ear of Laetorius. Then the slave ran into the house.

'Nice weather for the time of the Solstice' croaked Laetorius.

I agreed that it was, by dint of nods and smiles. Fannia walked about impatiently peering into the Greek urns.

The wife of Laetorius was a tiny lady only slightly less infirm than her husband. She hobbled painfully using a stick like a little lopsided bird. But she was friendly and mercifully she could hear, as I explained again, why Fannia and I were calling on them. By this time the slave had brought some refreshing watered wine and we all sat and sipped and thought about the problem facing my daughter and me. Laetorius's wife jerked her head on one side, her bright eyes blinking.

'As you can see, I am not the best person to enlist for your daughter's marriage ceremony, much as I would have enjoyed the honour.'

We all agreed including Laetorius, who hadn't got a clue what was going on. His body slave obviously did not speak or understand enough Roman to communicate anything of use to his master, or had simply lost interest.

'However...'

We looked at her hopefully.

'My daughter, I am sure, would be delighted to partake. She was *pronuba* for her friend's marriage ceremony very recently, last June I think...or was it July? No no, it was June.'

Her daughter. It sounded good. But where was her daughter? Probably away at the far ends of the Roman earth.

'Wait one moment.'

The gracious lady rose and leaned on her ivory topped stick.

To our surprise, she called out loudly.

'MarCIA!'

After a pregnant pause, during which Fannia looked at me nervously, a figure, short and matronly, approached us rather suspiciously.

'May I introduce my daughter Marcia.'

Marcia relented and smiled at us as formal introductions were completed.

'Sit down my dear. These people are our neighbours, though we seldom see them! They would be very grateful for your attendance at the young lady's marriage in your capacity as *pronuba.*'

She looked at me for assertion to which I nodded not too enthusiastically. Marcia flopped near her mother. She would not beautify any ceremony. But it was Fannia's day after all.

Marcia asked when the wedding was to be and where. I told them.

'Venta Belgarum!'

Mother and daughter spoke in unison, looking shocked. It was after all a long way for Vectians to consider travelling. I assured them of the safety and speed of the journey. I had only recently completed such a trip without encountering problems.

Something confused me.

'Will your husband accompany you?'

I wondered where he was. The lady could not be divorced. They knew the rules as well as I did.

'Marcia is widowed' her mother explained gently as Marcia's plump face creased unattractively. Oh dear. Fat women should not make a habit of crying in company.

‘Her husband was killed in a nasty skirmish north of Londinium, three years ago or is it two, no. Three. Marcia is still grieving.’

So nasty skirmishes were indeed occurring. An unsettling revelation. And Marcia had obviously returned to the comfort of her parents in safer Vectis.

‘I am so sorry’ I said humbly.

We hastily made our excuses to depart as Marcia seemed overcome by my thoughtless question. Her mother fluttered around as best she could in view of her lameness. She would have been a bright butterfly in her youth. Now, she shepherded her stout sniffing daughter towards their villa. Marcia was at least twice the size of her mother.

‘Come and see Marcia when you wish to make your marriage plans’ she called.

‘Will it not upset her too much?’ responded Fannia as though Marcia was not present. It was certainly upsetting Fannia.

‘No no. She will recover.’ Her mother replied firmly. ‘It is very good for Marcia to have a project. Takes her mind off her misery. Come over and see us whenever you are ready my dear.’

They disappeared through the villa entrance, Marcia seeming unconcerned at being talked about as though she had not been present. And it was obvious that Marcia’s mother was reaching the end of her patience after two or was it three years of interminable displays of grief. It seemed unlikely that poor Marcia would ever abandon her hallowed state as *univira,* for where could she find a new husband? But it probably suited her to have nothing to do but accept the kindly fussing of her parents. I distinctly heard her mother saying

‘Let’s see what the cook has made for you. A little honeyed treat?’

‘Yes come over whenever you are ready my dear’ echoed Laetorius vaguely.

‘What do you think?’ I asked Fannia as I drove us slowly back, the first swallows swooping in front of the horse.

‘She will probably be all right if she can stop crying. Anyway’ Fannia added petulantly. ‘There is nobody else. And how will I ever have a wedding dress and my flammeum and pretty shoes, with no emporiums to supply the material?’

By the time we reached home, I was feeling very inadequate and there was not much I could do about it. And the one person in the whole world with whom I yearned to discuss everything had turned her back on me.

Thoughts on Seneca

The following week, Fannia, growing impatient to have her marriage plans in order, asked me to take her again to the villa of Laetorius for the purpose of meeting with his plump lamenting daughter. Fannia's growing impatience at the lack of arrangements, had revealed itself in another way, as I found her giving her favourite girlhood doll to the simpering Lar, a formality that even I knew should not have happened until the night before the marriage ceremony.

'Just a tiny bit premature, isn't it darling?' I whispered as she finished her devotion and turned away, tears in her eyes.

'He won't mind. I need all his help and so I want to give him plenty of time to solve my problems.'

'Everything will work out' I soothed her

'Anyway it is all a big problem because I won't be here at home on the night before my marriage. You said yourself that we should allow two days at least to travel to Venta Belgarum. And please make sure that we take some charred hawthorn branches with us too.'

'Charred hawthorn branches' I muttered not able to recall for the life of me the purpose of that strange request.

I drove Fanna to the villa. She gave me a sweet kiss on my smooth cheek, thanks to Duane, and ran to the entrance. I waited a few moments to be sure she could stay and drove home remembering her request to meet her no longer than two hours time. Two hours, I muttered again. Well it was a sunny day so perhaps I could squint at the sundial and work out an approximate deal with it for my return to the villa of Laetorius. My daughter's visit worried me, amongst all the other worries. Supposing she could not strike up a friendship with fat Marcia. Where would we go from there? Durovernum? This was how to make me really fed up. I handed over the reins to a slave, wishing I could hand all the other reins over to somebody else and walked to the sundial. I looked at it this way and that and made a sort of decision on the moment when I would return to meet Fannia. I remembered my glimpse of the fascinating clepsydra with its clever displays showing the passing of time. I recalled a bell, and tiny doors and windows that I knew would open to reveal little figures. There was also a complicated dial and a pressure regulator that I would have liked to understand. The clepsydra was in the villa of Melania Lupurca. I wondered if I would ever see or understand either again.

Not daring to be late, Fannia was strangely impatient over matters of time, not something that was ever a cause for concern to Romans, I returned to the villa where I was delighted to see the young matron and my daughter sitting in the garden together. Fannia waved as she saw me and she and Marcia kissed before she ran to me.

'Well done. Right on time.'

How would Fannia know? Unless Laetorius also possessed a clock. Now that would make me really envious.

I hardly dared ask her, but not about the clock, as I turned the horse away from the villa.

'How did it go?'

'Wonderful. She is such a nice person.'

'Marcia's mother?'

'No! Marcia. Oh. Sassia is lovely too. They are a lovely family.'

'Sassia?'

'Marcia's mater.'

'Oh.'

'We are invited to dinner tonight.'

'No tears today?' I asked while I digested the news of dinner at Laetorius's villa.

'We had a lovely time.'

Of course. At the lovely villa with the lovely family. Sarcasm is very frustrating when you have to keep it to yourself.

'And it gets better! Marcia has a flammeum, such a gorgeous orange. I would not find such a veil even in Durovernum. And she has a wedding dress, a simple white tunic beautifully made. Her friend borrowed it for her marriage and Marcia says I can have it too.'

Now I may not be an expert on female clothing. But Marcia must have been three times the size of Fannia.

'Surely the lady is larger than you? Have you tried on the garment?'

'Oh of course I have tried it on and it fits perfectly. Six years ago when Marcia married her husband, she was as small as me. Now she says all she wants to do is eat. It is such a shame. She will never find another husband if she gets any bigger.'

Or the size she is now, I thought. But I was very relieved about the dress. And Fannia was euphoric. Until later in the day, that is.

Finnius and I were going through the books; or he was. I watched in awe at his efficiency. Columns of figures defy my understanding.

'On the matter of the pay for Kendreague. You requested a substantial increase in his pay upon your return to the villa. I would like to clarify that it is correct.'

'Perfectly in order. But I appreciate your thoroughness in querying the matter of Kendreague's pay. He is now my ordinarii. My most valuable man. He saved my life on at least two occasions during the journeys to and from Londinium. In fact, I am thinking of arranging manumission for Kendreague. There is another reason for that particular decision and I must request your discretion if I explain. A few years ago Kendreague was forced to leave his tribe. His father is a respected farmer, who since Kendreague left the farm, may have died and the property will be Kendreague's. One day he will be able to return and claim his rights.'

'Why did he have to leave his tribe? Is that the reason he chose slavery?'

I explained about Kendreague and the chief's daughter, and Finnius smiled. An accountant's calculating smile, weighing up the financial possibilities, considering the outcome.

Then Finnius relaxed his professional deliberations.

'He is fortunate that he came to Vectis and you employed him. Fortunate for him. Fortunate for me also.'

'Why do you say that?'

'I think that you bring out the best in people' he said.

Not always, I thought ruefully. But the compliment raised my flagging spirits. Sometimes Finnius surprised me.

'What is the best way of bringing about the manumission of Kendreague? I am completely out of touch with the laws these days and I am sure they must have changed.'

'Praetorian law requires only that you give an open sign of your willingness to free your slave. By *manumissio censu*, the master must enter the slave on the Censor's List as a Roman Citizen.'

That would mean another tiresome and possibly dangerous journey, who knows where nowadays. To my knowledge there was no Censor's List here on Vectis. The most likely place would be the Government offices at Clausentum, if they were still operating, which I doubted, having seen that rundown tip.

'But' continued the knowledgeable Finnius, who had seen my face fall.

'...By *manumissio per mensam*, the master invites his slave to lie down at a meal with him, thereby expressing his obvious intention to free the slave.'

'As simple as that?'

'As simple as that.'

I shook Finnius by the hand.

A weight off my mind. One by one the problems seemed to be solving themselves. Except the most important one. My heart ached as my mind composed a picture of Melania Lupurca. Her gracious smile, her composed dignity. And the madness of the moments when we had melded so exquisitely together. Now it seemed that it was all in the past. Our mutual rapport as defiled as the ruins of Rome. The evening air beckoned me outside, my peacocks strutted around and as if he recognised me, the male bird spread his magnificent tail displaying the turquoise fanned perfection.

'Come on, and show father…come on. 'Σύ έχθρός παίς'

Fannia was half dragging Philippus who was screaming.

'What did you call him?'

'Oh it's Greek! Come on Philippus, show father!'

I didn't know that Fannia was able to express anything in Greek. I wondered uneasily what she had said, although he had probably deserved it whatever it was.

'No' he squealed. They are mine!'

I wrenched Philippus from Fannia's grip.

'What is going on?' I shouted.

'Look in his cubiculum'was all she would say as she flounced off.

'We had better take a look' I said to the writhing child.

The room was as untidy as any small boy's room. As an unpleasant extra, I detected a sour whiff of dried urine. So the problem had not gone away.

'Did you have an accident in your bed?' I enquired trying not to display any emotion.

'Quinctia didn't come in and wake me in time.'

'Does Quinctia normally come and wake you?'

He nodded sulkily and added

'It's her fault.'

He had mastered the art of laying blame elsewhere.

'Now what have you got to show me?'

'Nothing.'

He sat defiantly upon a wooden chest that I recognised as an item of furniture from the store room where he and Quinctia ate their meals.

Impatient now, I hoisted him up and released the rusted clasp of the lid.

A leather bag that I instantly recognised lay inside. Protruding from it were my silver embossed drinking cups. The precious silver cups that I had reluctantly handed to the ill-fated Marcellus Fronto on that portentous morning.

'Where did you find these?'

'No-where. They are mine.'

'Philippus, these silver cups belong to our family. They were…stolen.'

'I didn't steal them.'

'I know that you did not. They disappeared before you came to Vectis. So where were they?'

Wriggling with childish temper and glaring at me with an expression, interpreted best by the Latin word *contumelia*, he grudgingly described a winter walk along the path to the harbour. Inquisitive, like all children, he had clambered into a deep ditch and discovered the leather bag and its expensively shiny contents.

I marvelled that I could have forgotten it. But the morbid scenario to that fatal accident encouraged me only to get away, with my gold, quite forgetting my silver. Until today when Fannia, finding him in his room, asking him some question, probably related to her marriage day, had peeped innocently into the chest and seen the bounty.

'Did you show them to Quinctia?'

He nodded.

'And had she told you to give them to me?'

'They are mine. I found them. And one day everything here will be all mine.'

How I disliked the boy's childish arguments that combined a coarse element of mature reasoning. It seemed wholly unnatural in so young a child.

Philippus bawled as I left his disgraceful room, meeting Quinctia outside. She displayed alarm on seeing me holding the leather bag and hung her head to hide her eyes, long dark unbraided hair falling in unattractive rattails either side of her pale face.

'Oh! I thought he had taken the bag straight to you.'

'Why did you not check your assumption?'

But she had slid into his bedroom, closing the door.

For no reason I can think of, I stayed where I was, and listened in surprise.

'You were supposed to give them to your father. Now you are in trouble again. Will you never learn? Our future relies on your good behaviour, remember what I have told you so often.'

As I handed the silver cups to Duane for cleaning, the peculiar phrase spoken to Philippus by Quinctia hung around me. Eventually I persuaded myself that I had misheard. Listening through a door never did anyone any good. Back in the old days, Roman folk played that whispering game in the echoey atriums of their palatial homes. By the time the murmurs had circulated and become distorted, they had lost their original intention. It seemed hilarious then. But under treacherous circumstances people had been slayed for acting on misinterpreted information.

The more I dwelled on the character of the little boy who through the mysterious whims of the gods had become an inseparable part of my life, the more confused I was. True, he had never known his mother. Flaccilla would have tolerated a son, and basked in the pomp and pleasure that accompanied the birth of a boy. But the gods had decreed otherwise. As Fannia had told Melania and me, in her mimicked epode all those months ago. When I felt strong enough to face simpering words and shifty eyes, as I now saw them, I would have to speak again with Quinctia, who after all, had taken Flaccilla's place from the start of the boy's life. Did she see herself as his mother? What had she whispered to him, during their journey to Britannia and when they were stranded in Londinium, and here in Vectis? I did not understand why she instilled elevated ideals into such a young child or for what purpose. That he would inherit was undeniable. Why press the point so hard into his blond head, and in the process turn him into an unnaturally aggressive little person. I needed to find a tutor. Perhaps properly organised education would bring everything into perspective for him. And I needed to try harder with him. And that is when I started to remember the philosophy of Seneca. Of all the famed personages at whose feet I would have gladly sat given the opportunity, and that included the gods with whom I have to admit I was starting to become disenchanted, Seneca would be at the top of my imagined list.

It was Seneca, whose work 'On Anger' I read idly, as a young student when I could have never imagined such matters would concern me. It was Seneca who dictated that a child must not be allowed to indulge in tantrums, nor be given everything he asks for, or always comforted when he cries or allowed to do everything he wants to do. When I described Philippus as indulging in a show of *contumelia*, I remembered Seneca's explanation, that a badly behaved child can not be described as insolent because he is not in a position to hold anyone in contempt, the Latin *contemptus*, and the word from which *contumelia* is derived. His elders are by their mature position in the familia beyond contempt. It did not help too much, except that I saw my almost uncontrollable son as benefiting from some of the aspects of the Stoic philosophy. Control to overcome rebelliousness was the correct way forward. Not in an avenging manner, but purely to improve the child for his own benefit. A tutor was the way forward, preferably a mature mentor conforming to the Stoic tradition of education. Be very afraid, Philippus. The problem was that at the present time it was I Marcus Cassius that felt afraid. *Contemptus* or no *contemptus*.

'Finnius!'

Scuttling sounds like terrified mice issued from the cubiculum of Finnius. Through the doorway, a pert little girl I recognised as Claudia appeared. She was followed by Fannia looking embarrassed. What in Jupiter's name was going on?

'Where's Finnius?'

'We don't know.'

'Why are you in his room then?'

My patience was running out.

'You will see soon enough' said Fannia and the two girls ran off towards the garden giggling as only mischievous girls can.

I wanted to see Finnius on two counts. To instruct him to find a tutor for Philippus. And to ensure that he attended our evening meal the following evening and that he bring my *ordinarii*, suitable attired, for his inaugural dinner.

I found Finnius in the garden. The girls had discovered him first. There was a great deal of showing off, and prancing around and of course giggling, while Finnius sat on the stone bench, smiling at the two delectable creatures, who seemed to be practising a dance together. They broke off when I advanced and ran away light as muses vanishing into the evening sunset.

'Tomorrow – dinner – bring Kendreague along and make sure he wears something respectable.'

'Tomorrow night is the night then' said Finnius.

'Might as well get it done' I said grimly, making it sound like unpleasant medical surgery.

'And do you know of a tutor for Philippus, preferably well-versed in the Stoic form of teaching and discipline for the young?'

I made that sound rather unpleasant too.

'I think I know the person' replied Finnius.

Finnius must have been proud at the efficiency with which he produced the tutor but the introduction was at a highly inopportune moment, as Fannia and I prepared to depart for our dinner with Laetorius and his women folk. Fannia immediately ran back to her room. The tutor was no stranger. He was none other than the arrogant young Greek.

'We meet again' I said.

Too many Dinners

My stomach was churning before we even got to the villa of Laetorius. Fannia moaned so much I was glad that Kendreague was driving us there. It would have been difficult to concentrate on controlling the horse in the darkening gloom of the roadway under the constant barrage of her anger.

'Why have you recalled that insolent tutor to the household? The place is suddenly full of detestable people.'

'You don't need to worry. You will not be here much longer' I reminded her.

She was quiet for a moment, silenced by the indubitable fact.

'Well, you are left with all the detestable people. I hate Philippus. I know I should not. But just because he is my long lost brother, I do not have to love him.'

'You don't have to love him but perhaps you could try to like him. I am trying and that is why Marius has been sent for. The boy needs a firm hand.'

'Ha! He did not manage to handle my education very well.'

'You my little minx, were older and had your thoughts on more artistic forms of education. You are now I believe an accomplished dancer. Philippus is still at an impressionable age. Marius has experience in disciplined philosophical training aimed at children like Philippus.'

'Marius thinks he is so clever! We shall see.'

'I shall see' I corrected her again. 'You will be a married matron in your own home with matters of your own to take up your thoughts.'

'And a wonderful husband.'

'Indeed. So let's have no more talk of all the people you do not like in my villa.'

'Quinctia gets on my nerves too!'

The horse swerved and the carriage felt as though it would overturn as Kendreague pulled it up fast. Fannia was screaming.

'It's all right darling. Kendreague, by the gods, what happened?'

But Kendreague was busy clicking at the horse and doing something complicated with the reins as we moved off again.

'Fannia. Enough of this silly talk. I would like to be calm before we reach our destination. By the way…'

I had to pacify my distraught daughter somehow.

'The silver embossed drinking cups. It is the time that they should pass from my ownership. I am thinking of presenting them to Aquilinus as a wedding present.'

Fannia squealed with joy.

'Oh he will love them. Thank you thank you.'

I was not meant to keep those cups. But at least they were going to a good home. And not ended up with a rascal or at the bottom of the sea. Or hidden by an arrogant child.

Sassia proved a wonderful hostess. Her organising skills revealed that she would have made a very suitable *pronuba* except for her obvious mobility limitations. Laetorius reclined, leaving everything to his wife, including the placing of his dinner on a handy repositorium by his couch and for the very good reason that he could hear nothing of any conversation.

We dined on chicken. Always a difficult bird for me to swallow, some unpleasant culinary memories never go away. But it was well seasoned and accompanied by delicately prepared vegetables; followed by the honeyed sweets of the type that we had overheard Sassia describing as a consolation prize for Marcia. I was very comfortable, sipping a good wine that I did not recognise, regularly topped up by Sassia, watching Marcia and my daughter chatting wedding talk as they ate. Marcia talked with her mouth inelegantly full, devouring a great deal more than

Fannia delicately toyed with. The overweight young matron, soothed with quantities of food, became quite animated and not, as I feared, in any way morose about comparing the happy bride-to-be with her own widowed state.

Sassia asked me the dreaded question about my wife. Fortunately, the girls were totally involved in their own talk of the arrangements, including mention of hawthorn again, I had to find out the hidden implications of that particular perennial, but not now. Reluctantly, but because she was a good listener, I related to Sassia the gloomy tale of my marriage and the amazing rescue of my son, in as succinct form as possible. I left out mention of Quinctia.

'The things that happen these days defy understanding. I am a little old fashioned in my views on marriage. I see marriage as for life, not to be cast away on the slightest whim. Having children is a women's duty. Alas children in our marriage did not happen for many years. Marcia was born when I was almost past my childbearing time, and Laetorius is very much older than me.'

She glanced at Laetorius who seemed to be dozing off. I leaned across and gently detached his wine cup from his slackening grip. He didn't notice. She nodded her appreciation.

'He is a good man. How could I ever leave him? Especially now with his sight deteriorating.'

'I may be able to help there. It is not too advanced.'

How could I do otherwise? And its early stage meant that surgery would not be too uncomfortable especially if he accepted a compound of opium. Like the physicians in the past, I do not advocate anything other than a very small dose. Anaesthesia is a dangerous area of medicine where careless administration of the drugs can lead to destruction of the nervous system and death. Speed in surgery is the best way both for comfort and safety. I explained my method, and she neither flinched or cringed at my (toned down) description. However, she swiftly changed the subject to discussion of the forthcoming marriage.

'Do you know of a house where we can stay?'

I had completely overlooked guests and their accommodation. The gods only knew where all these good people could lay their heads in Venta Belgarum. Staying at the dishevelled hovels of Aine and Birkita was hopefully not an option, particularly not for these fastidious ladies and certainly not the bride. I was not sure that I wanted to recommend the hotel either; if it was still in business, remembering that I had been the only guest. I would have to send a message, furtively so that Fannia didn't know I had forgotten about so important a detail, to my future son-in-law asking his advice.

Sassia shifted awkwardly on her couch. The dining room here was narrow and therefore the seating cramped. The girls had left us to chat alone. How agreeable it was that women loved to share secrets. How regrettable it was that some secrets caused so much harm. Melania Lupurca was never far from my thoughts, even in the dining room of my new friends. Laetorius snored contentedly. Sassia poured me another cupful of their excellent wine.

'I cannot tell you the joy your company is giving me. The days of conversation with my dear husband are a thing of the past. And Vectis is very quiet. Do you know of the lady who has the villa beyond your own? I have often thought of calling there. When neighbours are so few, new friends can bring a fresh point of view. And perhaps gossip?' she added with a giggle.

'I believe she travels a lot' I said, changing the subject brutally, but I had no choice. To discuss Melania Lupurca with my new acquaintance so eager for gossip, would have caused me agony I could do without. Especially after chicken.

'As a physician I am concerned to see that you use a stick to aid your walking.'

'My husband was Provincial Governor at the Headquarters in Clausentum. When he retired, he had our villa built here. He wanted a quiet life.'

Her expressive hands fluttered along with her explanation.

'I fell and broke my ankle on the day we left Clausentum. We were down on the harbour. The roadway was in a very bad state of disrepair.'

It's a lot worse now, I remembered ruefully.

'Laetorius would not hear of a delay to our journey. My ankle was never properly treated.'

Any benign feelings I felt towards Laetorius quickly diminished. Pretty selfish of him. But perhaps, if Modestinus's insanitary hotel were the only available choice an unscheduled stay in Clausentum would have been as repugnant then as it is today.

'Marcia was only a baby. There was so much to do. And I was in considerable pain for a long time. And so now, my movements are much impeded. If we were in a large *civitas*, I would seek help. Now, it is probably too late and I will never walk normally.'

She drew up her birdlike shoulders like unformed wings.

I nodded gently. She was probably right. But…

'When we are visiting Venta Belgarum, we could try and find a doctor specialising in bones and joints. I am sure in such a large place there would be such a professional man. Better still…'

I was getting a bit carried away with my offers of help so soon after meeting my new neighbour, especially as she responded with such obvious attentiveness.

'…I will send a message to my prospective son-in-law, asking that he make enquiries.'

And make enquiries about beds too. The message was getting more complicated by the hour.

'How fortunate we are to have made your acquaintance, My Dear Marcus Cassius.'

I flinched at such intimacy, reminded of the last occasion when my name had resonated from the heavenly lips of Melania Lupurca.

Moreover, Sassia was regarding me in an almost flirtatious manner.

She rose from her couch a little unsteadily and I quickly left the comfort of my own cushions and took her arm as any correct Roman gentleman should do. Her birdlike hand became painfully clawlike as she clung to me, leaning her tiny frame against my heavy one, heavier after forcing down all that cursed chicken.

'I think that you are a wonderful man, Marcus Cassius. Do call again soon. Two or three hours after the sixth hour, my husband and my daughter sleep. We would be undisturbed. I would love to hear more about your fascinating life.'

The unwelcome advances of my neighbour's wife after dinner and the prospect of another dinner of a very different nature lay on my stomach unpalatably. I spent the day without resorting to food, a whole day inscribing, then smoothing out my text to replace with better definitions, my requests on a wax tablet to Aquilinus Drusus and despatching Kendreague to the postal office, only just in time to avoid Fannia discovering it.

Fannia was being particularly difficult.

'Can Claudia come to dinner tonight?'

'No child, it is a formal occasion, besides, is Claudia not a slave?'

'No she is not. Melania Lupurca hired her as her servant to help Claudia's family after their terrifying flight across the sea from Gaul. Melania Lupurca does not agree with slavery.'

I remembered. Melania Lupurca. A tolerant, compassionate woman, except where I was concerned.

'Even so, tonight is an official dinner, certainly not for servants, at which you and I, Finnius and Kendreague only will take part.'

'I am glad it doesn't include Quinctia' she muttered.

'What do you hold against Quinctia?'

Did this personal hatred reveal that my daughter was privy to my wretched secret? Would the nightmare never leave me alone?

'She is crafty. She listens at doors. She spoils Philippus. I don't trust her.'

Such harsh disapproval. But it did not appear that she knew of her father's long extinct indiscretion. Time to move on without dabbling in dangerous waters.

'At least Marius is keeping Philippus out of your way.'

'Oh yes…' she falteringly agreed as if she had only just noticed.

Marius was in fact making progress. Only two days in, peace reined throughout the villa. And I had seen Philippus fairly galloping in to the room allocated for his lessons. Catching up with the supercilious Marius as he approached with long-legged strides, I asked how he thought that Philippus's education would proceed.

'As you rightly request, I am following the doctrines laid out clearly by Lucius Annaeus Seneca, by whose works I abide without reserve. And of course it is much more satisfying to teach boys.'

I knew he couldn't resist a dig at Fannia's lack of concentration.

'His natural high spirits have to be encouraged in order that he gains self-confidence. But on occasions that energy must be restrained, as on others, encouraged. The boy lacks confidence and that is the cause of his aggression. He is very good at his maths work, therefore we are exploiting his talent in this section before advancing to other equally important but perhaps for him daunting subjects.'

I was impressed.

Finnius was not impressed; upon discovering my diminutive list of diners. Me, my daughter; him, Kendreague.

‘The whole objective of a dinner to which your slave is invited to lie down, is that it is seen by others and therefore you are displaying publicly your intentions to free him.’

‘What can I possibly do about it? Vectis is such a small place.’

‘Invite the lady Melania Lupurca for one?’

‘I believe she is very busy at the present time.’

Finnius raised doubting, neatly plucked eyebrows. (Was Duane also grooming Finnius?) But fortunately for Finnius he did not challenge my unfounded comment.

‘The family you visited last night for dinner?’

Bitter bile rose in my throat. But I remembered that Melania Lupurca, when revealing her fondness and her concern for my health, had given me a phial for just such a purpose.

‘Send Kendreague with an invitation’ I said tight-lipped, knowing that fluttering Sassia would take it as positive personal encouragement following so shortly on their invitation.

‘Better still, accompany Kendreague. Explain the reason for this dinner. But be sure to talk to the lady of the villa. Her husband will not hear you.’

Locating the precious phial was simple, hidden behind a secret compartment in a table within my cubiculum. I pulled out the tiny stopper. Breathing deeply I held it to my nose as if to inhale some aromatic memory of Melania Lupurca, then threw my head back gulping the contents, a few drops with a very strange flavour, remembering too late the ill-fated obnoxious Fronto who had not felt too clever after knocking back Melania’s remedy. But that was in the days when Melania and I loved each other.

Within an exceedingly short time I felt very much better and strong enough to cope with my public declaration of the manumission of Kendreague and almost strong enough to cope with any repeated onslaught by the lascivious wife of Laetorius.

The family of Laetorius arrived. They looked eager and they were early. Laetorius looked bemused. Marcia seemed excited; her second social occasion in a long time. Sassia, bedecked in expensive jewels, appeared more like a frivolous butterfly than ever; an exotic wounded butterfly on three legs.

We sat in the garden and everyone, except Laetorius, admired the *nymphaeum* that had been cleaned and restocked with little golden fishes. I must remember to enquire of Duane by whom and bestow praise accordingly. I was feeling horribly nervous. But I had to trust that Finnius had taken some part in setting a dress standard for Kendreague. He had. When Kendreague appeared accompanied by Finnius, the two men looked impeccable, shaved, hair trimmed, and clothed in smart evening togas. I even heard Sassia betray a tiny gasp of admiration upon her first sight of my handsome slave. His height, and his breadth of chest dwarfed almost all of us, if I am honest even me, as he approached and politely bade everyone good evening.

The dinner was a resounding success. All my favourite dishes were served. And no chicken.

It was gratifying to see that Kendreague lying next to me, seemed completely relaxed, drinking wine but not too fast, leaning forward to assist others, including the virtually swooning Sassia, with food and wine. Finnius must have given him close instruction on protocol.

It seemed to me deplorably sad that three men, myself included, relaxing late into the night, were without the benefit of feminine company. I yearned once more for the matchless companionship of Melania Lupurca. Marcia precociously eyed Finnius who returned the eye contact politely but not encouragingly. Kendreague, who lay, impassive as a Greek god, his thoughts on the evening impossible to fathom, magnificently weathered Sassia's fulsome gaze. Whereas the aged, expensively attired Laetorius, the man with the wife, sat gazing mesmerised at the flickering light from a lamp, the bronze base designed in the form of smiling comely muses posed as if dancing.

My daughter seemed far away in her own thoughts, an unsmiling comely muse tonight, too late for dancing, but there would be no guesses required as to where her thoughts were.

I sat alone after my guests departed, and Laetorius had thanked me profusely and enquired where we had met before. It seemed he might have another problem to contend with as well as eyes and ears. As I relaxed into a sense of contentment that many of the hurdles I had set myself had been overcome, a light step and then an even lighter kiss planted on my head announced my daughter's presence.

'I thought you would be tucked up in your bed.'

'It has been a lovely evening. And thank you for inviting our friends.'

I had no choice there.

'You and Marcia seem the best of friends.'

'Did you notice that Marcia was flirting with Finnius? Claudia would tear out her eyes.'

'Such a barbaric action would not be necessary. Finnius is true to Claudia.'

'Just as my beloved Aquilinus is true to me. Oh, my mind is constantly set upon my wedding plans. Is the accommodation settled in Venta Belgarum for everyone?'

'Would I not arrange such an important duty?'

A day spent frowning over a wax tablet, biting the stylus until it broke, rubbing at the wax until my fingers shone, had resulted in being able to speak to my daughter with assurance. She covered my forehead with kisses. I cherished those daughterly kisses. Soon enough there would be none.

'There is something else. It is on my mind and I have to speak.'

'Tell me.'

'I do not wish Philippus or Quinctia to be at my marriage ceremony.'

Too Many Dilemmas

Fannia's decision should not have been much of a surprise. I had seen it coming without wanting to. Sometimes surprises are like that. But only nice surprises are real surprises. The nasty ones leave you thunderstruck. I allowed the turbulence surrounding Fannia's unmitigated declaration to settle. It took three further days, before I could force myself to consider the correct strategy for a pater familias to adopt. My son could not be excluded from his sister's marriage rites. And another quandary arose that was connected, in a way.

Interrupting my tangled conscience, Fannia found me poking disconsolately amongst the bright algae that once again obstinately formed in the nymphaeum threatening the health of the golden fishes.

'I have thought of a problem attached to the marriage ceremony.'

Well thank Jupiter it was only one.

'Have you remembered that I am accompanied by three young boys on the procession to my husband's house?'

If I had ever known of the tradition, I had not remembered. All those years ago when I married Flaccilla I had waited dutifully as decreed, in my house until she arrived. By then I was in such a state of nerves a small detail like three children amongst the wedding guests would not have made a lasting impresson on me.

'Two boys hold my hands, and the other carries the spina alba.'

My powers of recollection had let me down badly. And what in Jupiter's name was the implication behind a boy carrying spina alba? But I seized the moment.

'Philippus can be one of your boy attendants.'

'No he cannot, because if you remember, both the boys' parents must be living. If not it is very bad luck.'

The way my world was spiralling downwards at the present, how bad could the bad luck be? Pleasure at assisting with my daughter's forthcoming marriage arrangements was fast diminishing.

'Then you will have to ask your husband to locate the three lads from Venta Bulgarum, for I recall no children but Philippus residing here on Vectis.'

I had heard that brides are nervous and prone to tears, but Fannia seemed only prone to exasperation with me.

'I will send a message to Aquilinus immediately. Kendreague can take it.'

'Duane will instruct a servant to take your message to the postal station. You must remember, Kendreague does not take orders now that I have freed him.'

'What is his status here in the villa now that he is freed?'

'Kendreague manages the farm. But one day he will leave here and return to his tribe.'

'All the nice people go away. Why do we not see Melania Lupurca any more?'

Oh to know that answer. If the lady loves me, how can she completely spurn me?

'Melania Lupurca is very busy.'

My old lame excuse trotted out again

'It is not what Claudia says.'

'I am not interested in gossip. Go and compose your message to Aquilinus Drusus.'

I alloocated a little of my sympathy, most of it was for me, to Aquilinus Drusus. The endless demands that constantly assaulted men! However, wedding preparations never run smoothly and he wanted to marry my daughter and soon I would lose her.

As I resumed my gaze into the pool, there was again an interruption of a different type, a much louder interruption for one thing. Marius bore down on me, sandals flapping, fury in his face.

'My most valuable slate, my copy of Seneca's works! All destroyed!'

The young tutor's poise had collapsed. He shook with rage.

'Sit down sit down, tell me slowly.'

He had, he explained to me in a distressed voice, decided (mistakenly as it transpired) that the time had come to instil a reasonable amount of discipline on his pupil whose attention span had not widened appreciably despite gentle encouragement. During a lecture explaining why it was necessary to put aside mathematics for a while to concentrate on new subjects, Philippus had calmly picked up a slate, one his master treasured having particularly succinct guidance on the treatment of difficult children and smashed it on the mosaic tiles at Marius's feet with such force that not only were Marius's toes bleeding abundantly but apparently a piece of the tesserae was also damaged. Not content with that act of violence, and stimulated by Marius's angry yelp, the disgraceful child had snatched Seneca from the desk and torn the fragile papyrus pages until they fluttered like autumn leaves at his bloodied toes.

'The child is beyond help. Yesterday he kicked my shin. I have never encountered such wilful destruction in one so young. I can no longer teach him! He is unteachable.'

'Oh come on Marius. Children misbehave and have trantrums all the time. You are an experienced tutor. You can handle him.'

Marius shook his head.

'No, no more. I have had only one successful day here followed by ten days of misery.'

When you left me on the first occasion…' Poor Marius. I purposely tried to make his exit sound as defeatist as I could. '…how did you find another post. Did you travel to Durovernum to the family I recommended you to?' (I had done my bit, Marius.)

He dabbed ineffectually at his toes with what looked suspiciously like a shred of Seneca.

'I travelled to Clausentum and thence to Noviomagus. I stopped there. I found travelling tiring and I was worried about being attacked by robbers. But in Noviomagus I found a position, instructing twin boys for a wealthy Roman family.'

'Ah that was extremely fortunate. Why are you not there? What made you return to Vectis?'

Even swift-footed Finnius could not have travelled so far so quickly to search for a tutor. Marius looked shamefaced.

'I have to admit that I was – almost - indiscreet with the wife of my employer. I was turned out of the house. I returned to Vectis to…'

Lick his wounds? Oh poor Marius; and poor Roman matron. I wondered if she had been turned out of the house too for her almost-indiscretion. Indiscretions, whether anticipated or real, seemed to be almost a daily occurrance. No one was immune these days, not even me. I couldn't even shake off a long past indiscretion, whilst the wife of Laetorius couldn't wait to become involved in one of her own.

'…perhaps study for a while and…'

'And Finnius saw you?'

'That is exactly how it happened. I was climbing off the boat when he brought the message about the hiring of a tutor, I believe he was despatching it to Venta Belgarum or Clausentum when we met, and I accompanied him here and the rest you know.'

'Go and clean your feet. You really cannot afford to give up this position so easily. And Marius…'

As he limped slowly away, my call arrested him and he turned a woeful face.

'I have a nicely rolled copy of Seneca. I shall give it to you.'

Marius had lost his arrogance. Fannia would be jubilant. But I was devastated.

Punishing Philippus was distasteful but necessary. For the first time in my life, I smacked a small boy. The surprising effect was the lack of reaction except on his red bum. He neither screamed nor struggled. Quinctia appeared, eyes downcast, but no doubt mystified by my presence in Philippus's cubiculum. I informed her coldly of the reason for the chastisement and left them. I went down to the bathhouse.

The villa settled to something like normality after that. Perhaps smiling Sol helped it along, with a spell of warm sunny weather that enabled smooth running of the farm, and Philippus to receive his lessons in the garden. He behaved much better out there. I wouldn't say that the tutor and the pupil gained any noticeable rappour, but they regarded each other with more tolerance, which was a start. And fortunately Fannia had heard nothing of the humiliation of Marius because she was at the villa of Laetorius as she often was these days.

And it was on such a fine sunny day, when I walked beyond the garden, smiling approvingly at tutor and pupil as I passed from the gateway into the stony lane. A woman stared out towards the sea, the shawl over her head defying recognition but as I neared the figure materialised as Quinctia, who turned, startled. Why did I always startle her? She was like a bony little goat these days, ready to leap away if she was threatened.

'Ah Quinctia.'

Time to unburden myself of some of the irksome details of the forthcoming marriage. They concerned Quinctia anyway. Because I had decided that she would not be attending the ceremony.

We walked slowly along the path as I explained my predicament.

'We have to cut down on guests because of the great distance we have to travel. You Quinctia, being not strictly a member of the familia, will therefore remain here at the villa, with Duane and the rest of the servants. My son and his tutor will accompany me to Venta Belgarum.'

Her question surprised me.

'Are you taking Kendreague to Venta Belgarum?'

'Kendreague and Finnius.'

She sighed a great sigh.

'When I spoke to Philippus about Fannia's wedding he told me that he does not wish to go.'

'Then Philippus will have to get accustomed to the idea. It would be very…'

(I thought of Fannia and her obsession with bad luck.)

'…bad manners if a family member were not present. It is particularly important that my son attend's his sister's wedding.'

Quinctia was silent.

'Is that understood?'

'Yes. No. I have something I must say to you, Marcus Cassius.'

Without warning, the Sun God slipped discreetly behind sudden formations of heavy black cloud, and a dreadful foreboding settled over Vectis. The lowing noise of cattle in the meadows ceased. The birds stopped singing. No breeze whispered. Even the sea was unnaturally quiet.

I lowered myself onto the gnarled trunk of a felled tree that formed a natural bench. Quinctia stood huddled into her shawl, staring hollow eyed. I waited.

She twisted round. Her utterance struck my chest with the violence of a centurian's knife.

'You do not have a son.'

'What are you saying?' I choked on the words.

'It is true. Philippus is not your son. He is the illegitimate child of Egnatius.'

'Egnatius?'

But he had gone to the considerable trouble of paying for a messenger to travel across the Northern Empire to Britannia with the news of my son? I forced myself to laugh, spread my hands, palms uppermost, to reject the madness of her declaration.

'What sort of spiteful game are you attempting to play? Are you trying to persuade me to believe that my wife and my brother in law were lovers?'

A strange whisper of fear flowed transparently through the silence of Quinctia. It slithered around me with clammy intensity, like a chill sea mist. The frowning clouds were gathering momentum. I heard the sea's tumultuous roar. A storm was brewing and not only in Vectis. Neptune had overheard the catastrophic words that I refused to believe.

'What malicious amusement do you derive from making a fool of me? Tell me some more of your jokes. If I am not his real father, who is Philippus's real mother?'

'Philippus is my son and Egnatius is his father.'

A spasm of exquisite agony tore through my body. I slumped forward, my heavy head cradled in damp hands that reaked of salt and sweat, chaotic episodes leading to the discovery of the woman and the child in Londinium whirling past me as though caught on a spinning top.

'I am sorry' she said.

'You are sorry? That is all?'

'Egnatius took me to his bed. Only once…'

I gave vent to a furious groan. This simple slave had certainly spread her favours. I wondered who was the most demeaned. I was about to find that out.

'Yes. It happened just before you moved us to Britannia. I was glad to return to Rome, although I feared the punishment that Flaccilla threatened, because of our indiscretion.'

'You risked ill-treatment at the hand of my wife, to be reunited with Egnatius.'

'But I was spared. Egnatius and I were reunited. And one year later Philippus was born.'

'Flaccilla didn't punish you? For dallying with her husband and her sister's husband and giving birth to a son? And did her sister never find out the truth?'

'Everyone except Egnatius thought the baby to be yours.'

I remembered Flaccilla's intentional mockery of me on the eve of her departure. However, being Flaccilla, she wouldn't want anyone else to have me either. Further, she would not have tolerated a male baby crawling messily around her beloved father's tastelessly ostentatious villa.

'But what of Flaccilla? If, as you say, you were spared any punishment and Flaccilla obviously did not die as I was informed by the messenger, then where is Flaccilla?'

'She disappeared.'

'Oh yes? Just disappeared?' Quinctia's tale got more fantastic. For a droll moment I wondered if she had turned her hand to writing tragedies and had derived her shocking narrative from an ancient Greek play. There is nothing new in the world. But this gruesome plot was a new one in my world. Distant thunder growled menacingly for effect.

'Please believe me. I am telling you only what happened as I witnessed it. I have held all these cruel secrets in my heart too long and I can hold back no longer. When the boat reached Portus Roma, Flaccilla vanished the same night.'

'How could Flaccilla just vanish? What unbelievable debris from the drains of Rome are you raking up?'

But Quinctia was calm despite my increasing fury. Her candid stare revealed a woman who had decided to no longer prevaricate.

'There was someone else on that boat. He was Roman. He was always very well dressed, woollen tunicae with an expensive looking belt, and a heavy cloak. But that is all I can tell you. I thought he might be a physician because of his attentiveness to Flaccilla. The rough sea journey from Massilia made her very sick. But when we reached Portus Roma, he too, vanished.'

Vanished. With my wife. Who was he? If Quinctia had guessed his profession correctly, it was very likely that I knew him. The probability subdued me. I wondered why they crossed by sea from Massilia to Portus Roma instead of by road to Rome. More importantly, I wondered where in the world they were they now. I did not understand why should I want to know. Perhaps only to discover if her scornful tongue was less cruel towards her mysterious unknown lover. It was the strangest feeling for me, being told that Flaccilla was alive. After years of not knowing her fate but imagining I knew; then believing a message that was revealed to be a lie. And now, yet another twist in this formidable tale. How much many more onerous revelations could I take?

'So after leaving my arms you returned to the waiting arms of Egnatius.'

'If he knew I was telling you all this, Egnatius would have me killed.'

I ignored her reflection, save to think I could at that moment have easily killed her too.

'And did Egnatius know about you and me?'

She shook her head, slowly, reflectively.

'Flaccilla threatened to tell Egnatius everything, and Galatia too, when we reached Rome.'

'All things considered, it was lucky for you that Flaccilla didn't make it to Rome.'

In Rome of course, the pater familias is at liberty to take a concubine. But in sharing her favours Quinctia clearly flouted acceptable conventions, added to which concubines were usually discreet enough to avoid producing offspring. Silly little Quinctia, her heart overruling her head. And I had played my part in it all. That cold Durovernum evening when Flaccilla was out, Quinctia smiling her sad, silent smile as she refilled my drinking cup. It had been too easy. She was lonely. Her lover far away, I unaware of her liaison in Rome with the slimy Egnatius. I was lonely. My wife was probably with girlfriends, perhaps with a lover, although I had no reason to believe it. Not then.

And now I learned that my wife had been unfaithful too. I stood up and paced around, kicking stupidly at stones like some lout. How inept I had been, and ignorant too, oblivious to my wife's moodiness that could have betrayed more than mere irritability at being forced to live in Britannia. But I was a busy man. I did not see into the eyes of the real Flaccilla. An incongruous omission, because I am constantly fascinated by eyes, appreciating not only the wondrous variations of the iris but observing expressions, humour, happiness, pain, misery, and very occasionally, glimpses of distant unimaginable reverie, perhaps composed of desire to be somewhere else with someone else.

Frustrated at my own incompetence, I ground my heel into a dusty hollow disturbing scavenging ants and beetles. Thunder crackled, almost over my bursting head. And what of the other lady? An unpleasing sour wife I had been told, but a wronged wife nevertheless.

'Did Galatia find out the truth?'

'She accepted my explanation that I had slept with a slave in Britannia. The pater familias and Galatia also accepted my description of the man on the boat and how they had gone away together. They were very angry but they were always mystified as to where Flaccilla had gone and with whom.'

Weren't we all.

'I think that the family tried to have Flaccilla traced. But there was never any news. When Philippus was born, we were kept together in the house against Galatia's wishes. But he was a strong child, and they said he would make a good slave when he grew. Despite my insistence that I was to be manumitted, they treated us like slaves. And then the *familia* threw us out.'

'When hard times came to Rome.'

'Rome has become a frightening place. You were concerned about the rough behaviour of the army here in Britannia. I have seen groups of soldiers fighting each other in Rome. It is not safe anywhere. The pater familias was left for dead one night outside the villa, and soon after that the family treasures and I think gold and silver coins too, were confiscated. Egnatius took me aside at great risk to himself. He told me that he would be taking his family out of Rome. He could do nothing for us.'

'Poor old Egnatius. That must have been a seriously hazardous meeting for him. One could almost feel sorry for him! Abandoning you and his child!'

'Except that he promised that he would send a messenger to you declaring the child to be yours by Flaccilla who had died. He said that his message would be the only chance that Philippus and I would have to survive.'

'A caring father, Egnatius! But of course he knew that I would raise Philippus and everyone would live happily. In ignorance, but happily.'

'Flaccilla might be dead…'

She saw my tempestuous face and quickly dropped the subject of Flaccilla's possible fate. However, knowing my wife I am convinced that she is alive. She is a survivor. I would very much like to know who in the Pantheon of the Gods looks after Flaccilla. I suspect that it is Minerva; leaping from Jupiter's brain all grown up and armed into the bargain without assistance of a mother, and becoming a powerful councillor to her father. Flaccilla's lack of maternal instinct coupled with her adoration of herfather would have warmed her to that deity. Flaccilla is alive and well and if she is running true to form, probably the ruination of her latest suitor.

I clenched my fists until the nails bit deep into the skin, but I did not inflict as much pain as was caused through recognition of the deceits that I attempting to recognise.

'I have told you the truth. I will leave here and take Philippus with me. It was hard enough for me, to live here acting a lie. Now it is impossible. And I have some gold hidden away to help us. A last gift from Egnatius…'

'That was big of him.'

'While you are away in Venta Bulgarum for your daughter's marriage, Philippus and I will leave Vectis.'

'Ridiculous. Where could you go?'

‘I will find some work somewhere on the mainland.’

‘The mainland is even less safe since we returned from Londinium and doubly dangerous for a woman and a child. Give me time to think. It’s quite a lot to take in. By the way, if you do not know the whereabouts of my wife, where are Egnatius and his incomplete family?’

I spat the words. Uttering the name was like eschewing foul matter. Quinctia seemed unaffected.

‘Their intention was to go to Africa.’

Far enough away as to be almost impossible to track the man down.

For the duration of Quinctia’s confession, I had managed for the most part, to remain controlled. But I might not hold onto my demeanor much longer.

‘I forbid you to say anything to anyone until I have spoken to you again.’

Her thin face looked less pinched as she stared unflinchingly with those enormous limpid eyes. I saw relief clearly written there. She was freed from those terrible restraints.

She had passed them to me.

Enormous rain drops splashed on us, darkening our clothes, as lightning tore the clouds apart.

Quinctia saw him before I did. Kendreague stood a little way off, looking very wet.

‘Kendreague. Do you need to speak to me?’

I hoped not. My mind and my heart were too full of Quinctia’s abysmal revelations. I tried to sound normal, but I had forgotton what normality was.

‘I was taking a stroll.’

All these people going for walks. The entire population of Vectis would descend on me at any moment. I needed to get away from here.

I nodded at Kendreague. Ignoring Quinctia, I turned through the stone archway into the rain-drenched garden, back to the villa. In the porticus I flung my wet garments and shoes all over the red and white chequers. Within his own mosaic panel Orpheus played his lyre, unoffended by the puddles, watched by the exquisitely designed animals and birds. For once I did not pause to admire them. I needed the privacy of my cubiculum. I need to lie down.

My hope to remain awake and alert was thwarted. My body felt as though it were pressed down with a provocator's shield and my mind remained firmly closed against my hope of constructive thought. I awoke in darkness, overbalancing on the bed steps, cursing and fumbling, when a knock on the door admitted Duane who mooched around in silence lighting lamps.

Thunder still rumbled distantly.

'Who is around for dinner?'

My voice was cracked, my throat dry.

'Your daughter is dining at the villa of Laetorius, Master Finnius is out; your son and Quinctia have already eaten in their room...'

How can she eat? Easily. Because her problems are now my problems. But I was grateful to which ever of the gods had recognised my need for peace and quiet.

'Please leave me, Duane. I shall not require dinner.'

The silence of the villa frowned at my thoughts that tumbled like a succession of bungling acrobats as I reflected first on one revelation closely followed by the next. I hated the recognition of my stupidity at having been made to look a complete fool by three people all of whom at one time I trusted. My wife, my brother-in-law and my ex-mistress. All scheming to deceive me to their own advantage. The greatest deception had been hatched in Rome, where cunning Egnatius had plotted to foist his unwanted son onto me under false pretences using the silent but not so innocent Quinctia. There had to be a lawsuit somewhere in this mess. There were no lawyers on Vectis. But during my stay in Venta Belgarum it should be a simple matter to trace an orator who would advise me in the preparation of a meditatio. Once the case was professionally drawn up I would gladly spend my precious gold and shake down the whole of the Roman Empire to find Egnatius.

Then there was the child to consider. The innocent victim with fair hair, unusual for a Roman, unknown in my familia for the very good reason that the boy was not of my familia. I wondered if the evil old man I detested so intently was aware of his son-in- law's embarrassment. It seemed strange that the child was not thrown out as a newborn infant; not until the familia fell on hard times; only when their wealth was depleted. Yes, he must have known. He always had a soft spot for Egnatius and never for me. But what could I expect considering our active mutual dislike of each other?

Reluctantly, because I deem myself to be, for the most part, unprejudiced in my judgment of others, I conceded that it was impossible to blame a mother's fierce protection of her child. Despite which she had confessed everything to me and in doing so faced losing their home and a proper education for her son.

And a falsely acquired inheritance. My fury flared again. Egnatius might even now be dreaming up some dastardly plot, one day claiming his son and worse, bogus recompence from me. Or from my estate.

As my imagination grew wilder, my mood became impatient. I could not forgive Quinctia. And I knew that forgiveness was made more impossible because of my own feelings of guilt; my thoughtlessness contributing to Flaccilla's displeasure, my impatience with a small boy. Myriads of despairing torments invaded me like spears from a merciless army as I cowered on my cathedra heaped with comfortable cushions, but affording no relief.

Aware that my forehead was furrowed by anxiety, my lips rigid lines of anguish, I glanced, abhorred at the unnatural set of my limbs; left elbow crooked, hand moulded against my face; right arm languidly resting on my thigh, right leg supported on a footstool while my left leg was stretched forward, heel resting on the tiles, upturned bare toes ridiculously splayed in the air, twitching with unrelieved tension. I presented a figure of abject failure.

Too many Disturbances

Only a few days remained before we made the journey to Venta Bulgarum for the marriage of my daughter to Aquilinus Drusus. The only decision directly concerning me had been made by Fannia, deciding what toga I would wear at the ceremony. It was actually a *vestis cenatoria*, not worn since Durovernum days, for a wedding, I seemed to recall. The well cut material and elaborate embroidery distinguished it as a garment for an important occasion.

'Whatever will Philippus wear? He has nothing suitable at all and we won't have time in Venta Bulgarum to look for anything.'

Fannia shrugged at my typical lack of response.

'I will ask Sassia for her advice. I have found a beautiful silk dalmatica for Quinctia to wear.'

Daily and nightly too, juggling all my dilemmas to no avail, it was hardly surprising that the significance of Fannia's remarks escaped me. When I eventually realised that Fannia had had a change of heart (she was a sweet girl) I summoned Quinctia.

'It is too late to involve Fannia in the unpleasant details of your confession and to upset her by acquainting her of the fact that she does not after all have a brother. You and Philippus will attend the marriage ceremony as though nothing has happened.'

Quinctia's response was something of a surprise.

'Thank you' she cried. 'We are very grateful and Philippus has promised to be good.'

The implications of Philippus's premature and uncharacteristic promise also passed me by. As I said, there was too much to think about.

The day before the journey to Venta Bulgarum, Duane interrupted me as I attempted unsuccessfully to soak away my problems in the bathhouse. I expected a scrape down with a strigil. Nothing was further from Duane's mind. He looked more worried than apologetic.

‘P-Pirates have been sighted out at sea.’

‘What does that mean exactly?’

‘Th-the men are keeping a watch. Th-they will raise the alarm if there is an attempt to come ashore.’

‘Where are these pirates from?’

‘G-Gaul most likely. If they land here, our men will fight them off.’

I couldn’t imagine my private army of steel-fisted, agricultural implement-wielding farmers having much trouble dealing with a boatload of exhausted sea-sick Gauls. But it was disturbing news.

‘Keep me informed. Oh Duane!’

He stopped mid-sprint skidding on the damp *tesserae*.

‘Make sure the other villa owners know of the sighting.’

Dinner in my villa tonight would see Laetorius and the dreaded enticing three-legged *Cerce* better known as Sassia, her dowdy daughter Marcia; why could she not have inherited her mother’s butterfly delicacy? Finnius and Kendreague were summoned to appear in their best togas, having been a resounding success on the first occasion. My darling daughter, bride to be Fannia; and Claudia, at Fannia’s insistence. I was not certain of the protocol here, but it was Fannia’s evening and this was Vectis and not Rome. Quinctia and Philippus had also been instructed to attend and this created something else to worry about, because I knew that Fannia, who had become sweetness itself now that her marriage was imminent, would introduce Philippus as her brother and probably make a fuss of him. I emphatically hoped that while in a different environment I would be able work out a plan for the future of both Quinctia and Philippus. The inevitable eruption of familia surprises could be dealt with later when the wedding was over and life had settled down again. If life were to ever settle down again. Pirates sighted in the bay did not feel much like a settling down period. There was something else.

At first the devastating idea, from only the gods knew where, arising like a phoenix from the fiery confusion, appalled me. Everything I valued was firmly established on Vectis. The ever-changing wondrous sea view, my exquisite strutting peacocks, the natural conformation from forest, fields to the shore, the seasonal activities of the farm. And my incomparable mosaics fastened forever in the soul of my villa. My villa on Vectis.

Slowly, against my will, I realised that the only solution to obtaining my peace of mind, took the form of a momentous decision to leave Vectis. From now onwards, my life could never be the same. How could I envisage a future in the home of which I was so fond, dogged by constant cruel reminders; a past infidelity; the presence of an illegitimate child who was nothing to do with me. And desperate memories of someone I could never forget.

The nearness but separateness of our villas was becoming more and more impossible to contemplate. It would be easier to leave them behind. Forgetting the child who I thought to be my son, would be far less agony than to chase the constant visions of Melania Lupurca from my tortured heart.

Putting a brave face on with my evening toga was difficult, more difficult than donning the toga. The wretched garment pulled and twisted and defied my attempts to arrange the pleats in the accepted manner.

'Duane!'

Kendreague appeared looking godlike and immaculate. An amazing achievement on both counts considering he is a Briton.

'Help me with this disastrous dress.'

Our guests assembled and we drank a toast to Fannia. I had never seen her look more radiant, a shining golden muse, insisting we withdraw to the garden as it was a beautiful evening. As Duane and a couple of his helpers laid out the refreshments, I saw a figure in black moving towards me. I did not at once recognise her. She was carrying a red Samian bowl piled with fresh bread. And she gave me a shy smile as she placed the bowl carefully on the stone table.

'Donata. You look so well!'

'Thank you sir.'

'Duane must be caring for you.'

''Tis his mother who has helped me sir.'

Duane's mother. The herbalist. Sometime, I must call on her and discuss her herbal remedies. Of late, and understandably, I had severely neglected my slaves – servants. I will not any longer call them by that demeaning term. And it's always somewhere in my mind, that Roman slavery will soon be at an end, at the same time as the army no doubt. If the time was right to leave Vectis, then alerting the servants and arranging duties would be a necessity. There was so much to consider. Under the management of Kendreague the farm would continue to thrive and employment of the men would be guaranteed. Despite my early doubts, Duane seemed to becoming adept at looking after the house.

I sipped my wine and thought about all the changes about to occur. The conversation, food and drink flowed without need for my involvement. Then I was interrupted.

'We have a surprise for you!'

Sassia fluttered before me as though she would leave the ground at any moment her little stick clattering to the grass.

What kind of surprise, I thought warily. A real surprise, or another bolt of thunder?

'Come!'

We all moved to the centre of the garden illuminated by flaring torches. There was a full moon, enormous and silver. I felt that it boded well both for my state of mind and the journey to Venta Bulgarum for my daughter's marriage. Laughter and happiness seemed infectious. I noticed Quinctia and the lad, staying close together, conversing quietly. But they were smiling too. Sassia showed me a stool on which to sit. There were other such seats arranged and Sassia, all in glittering yellow, sat herself beside me, her eyes starry beneath her feathery eyelashes.

'What is all this' I demanded of her.

'You will see, dearest Marcus.'

I gave vent to a (silent) groan.

The sound of a lyre sang through the garden, its plaintiff notes winding melodiously, as Marcia sailed into view, wearing a flowing tunica that enhanced her ample form. She played with such rhythmic perfection that everyone clapped as she took her position within the circle. She continued to play, achieving effortlessly professional notes on the instrument. I smiled to myself remembering the jarring notes that had resulted from Claudia's musical efforts.

There had been things to smile about then. My mind started wandering, mesmurised by the singing notes of the lyre.

I was being nudged in the ribs. Ouch! Sassia's elbows were sharp as bats wings.

I forced myself to focus on Marcia. And then I saw two Muses running gracefully through the stone archway. The musically accompanied dance held everyone captivated as Fannia and Claudia singing sweetly to the lyre, whirled and turned and kneeled and rose on their bare feet, sometimes linking arms, then drawing apart. They wore purest white tunics held at their tiny waists with golden plaits, their dark hair, bound on their heads with long strands left to flow in the breeze, swept by the passage of their graceful movements. I was transfixed. It was the most beautiful presentation I could recall seeing, anywhere, Roman festivals included. But this performance had a definite Grecian influence.

We all clapped and shouted our delight as they finished their dance and Fannia ran towards me.

‘Well Fannia – and Claudia – I am proud to have Muses singing and dancing in my garden. You have made me a very happy man.’

I meant it. We smiled at each other, Fannia and I; soon to be parted. But I could not think of that yet. Tonight was tonight; a unique episode in our lives. I hugged her. Then I remembered to praise Claudia for the choreography had been her design, and Marcia too, for her heavenly playing of her lyre.

Sassia twittered around delighted at her daughter’s success. And everyone else offered their own congratulations; except Laetorius sitting quietly with his wine bowl. Oh dear. He had neither heard the music not saw very much of the dance. And I had made a promise to help him. And I could not explain the reasons for my vacillation.

In was dark, the air had turned colder and everyone wandered, chatting towards the villa. I noticed Claudia and Finnius together, his head bending to catch something she was saying. There would be another marriage before too long.

A call from my daughter made me turn back. My eyes were drawn to the stone archway where so recently the two Muses had appeared to entrance us. Beyond the shadow thrown by the arch and illuminated by the bright full moon stood a female form. I moved towards her, at once perceiving the radiant familiarity of her dressed hair and her erect stature; her noble smile but a smile nonetheless.

The Big Fat Roman Wedding

Sol had sunk into the Styx. Far out to sea the sky was an iridescent blue, but in the harbour at Vectis, grey clouds spread their menacing veil over the ruffled waters. The seamen looked as negative as only sailors can. When you are in a hurry.

'Don't look too good.'

'My daughter is to be married. Surely you can make the crossing. It isn't raining.'

Not yet.

The men frowned disbelievingly. Fannia was in tears. Claudia and Marcia comforted her.

'It's good luck if it rains on the day before a marriage' ventured Marcia.

But Fannia would not be consoled.

Two boats were moored, waiting to transport my family and guests. That had taken some organising. Boat owners were uncooperative people, unless they had planned the journey for their own purposes. Kendreague had once more proved himself to possess excellent manipulative powers.

'If everyone gets aboard one boat, it will be more stable. Isn't that right darling?'

Laetorius hadn't heard Sassia's logical but untested argument of course and she redirected her question to me, including the endearment.

I asked the seamen the same question, excluding the endearment. They muttered unintelligibly to each other and the spokesman stepped forward.

'People in one boat, boxes in the other.'

What a relief, but not if the second boat were to capsize plunging wedding robes, presents and all to the fathomless depths. We nervously boarded the first boat and it heaved away immediately, sails tightly furled, the four oarsmen rowing as if their lives depended on it. Perhaps they knew it did. There was obviously no time to be lost, as a massive cloud frowned at us and the sea became more than merely ruffled. We sat or crouched in the bottom and held onto anything handy as the oarsmen veered the elegantly carved but inelegantly unstable vessel towards the mainland.

I watched the tumbling frothy waters and imagined I could see Melania Lupurca's calm countenance smiling at me through the green waves.

Melania Lupurca. The vision of her standing in the stone archway lit by the moon had taken away my breath and left me terrified that she was a shade to be snatched from my sight. But she was no ghost, as she and I moved in harmony to greet each other.

'Marcus Cassius' she said.

The exact timing of what happened next is unclear to me but I remember walking with her through the villa and we two sitting apart from the merry crowd, and Philippus's whines dominating conversation. But I didn't care any more. Not about Philippus, nor about my other guests.

'I never thought to see you again' I told Melania Lupurca.

'How could I not see dearest Fannia before she departs for her marriage?' she asked.

'You came to see Fannia.'

My heart sunk. She had not appeared unexpectedly at my villa in order to see me.

'I am very fond of Fannia, as you know. And she understands that I cannot be present at a Roman marriage ceremony. But she and I have talked and she knows that I am very happy for her and that is the important thing. And I am delighted that Claudia goes with her. Kendreague will look after you all.'

The lady's gracious thoughts were for all our welfares. Not mine more than any other.

As my disappointed heart plummeted to the weighty hem of my toga, she summoned Claudia and prepared to depart.

They moved towards the door, Fannia, Claudia escorting Melania Lupurca. I followed behind feeling awkward and uncertain. Was this brief encounter to be the last?

Melania Lupurca looked over her shoulder.

'Marcus Cassius …'

Probably exhibiting too much haste, as if I cared, I was at her side in a bound, or two, as she held out her fragile hand.

'Please call at my villa when you return. I wish to hear all about the wedding. I shall wait anxiously, Marcus Cassius.'

If I possessed a tuneful voice, which I do not, I would have dedicated a prayer in loud song to Neptune to bring me home safely, for one reason. To bask once again in the incomparable company of Melania Lupurca.

The uncomfortable little boat swung dizzily, its bows dipping to dark waters, its prow rising high towards the sky. The women screamed. We all thought the same thoughts; that Charon waited, ready to receive us. I held tightly to Fannia as she cried and trembled. How could the god be so unkind, in June, the special month dedicated to the high goddess Juno and my daughter's wedding in her honour? And almost immediately the sun god took over, smiling at us as though nothing had happened. As we glimped the mainland, the black clouds changed to fluffy white, the sea was calmed.

Two very fine carriages waited on the shabby sea front at Clausentum. Feeling far from steady after our unnerving maritime experience, I watched Finnius approach the drivers and speak with them. Fannia was at my side. Her cloak revealed the white tunic that she had donned the night before in accordance with tradition. The bright orange flammeum hid her hair but I could see her face, and she looked very pale.

'That was a nasty crossing' I commiserated but unfortunately the nasty crossing was not the cause of Fannia's distress.

'You have forgotten the spina alba!' she told me accusingly. 'You should have kindled it in the hearth at home so that we transported the charred branches to my wedding celebrations for good luck. It is such bad luck to have forgotten.'

I had forgotten what I should have remembered, which left a clear impression of bad memory to go with the bad luck. But all I recalled with any clarity from the previous evening was being in the company, no matter how briefly, of Melania Lupurca. I must have looked completely dazed.

'The hawthorn has to be distributed amongst the marriage guests!'

I bent to pat her cloaked shoulder and kiss her flammeum-shrouded head in an effort to becalm the distraught little bride.

'We will find some hawthorn and I will arrange for it to be made ready.'

It sounded better than 'burned'. Where did these ancient customs have their origins? It was to be hoped that on the approaches toVenta Bulgarum we spotted a hawthorn bush. Meantime I spotted Finnius.

'We must have the boxes loaded and mount the carriages and get on our way' he urged.

The convoy, it transpired, had been organised by my daughter's future husband. I was starting to relish being escorted here and there with no effort required on my part. But I was after all, father of the bride. I suddenly realised that I had no idea whether Aquilinus Drusus had parents living or whether they too would be at the ceremony. But my thoughts had to be concentrated, as it appeared that I was expected to organise the seating arrangements in the roomy coaches. An unnecessary task as Fannia sat determinedly with Claudia and Finnius in the first coach. My daughter was slipping away from me. I felt very sad. Laetorius and wife and daughter were in the second coach. Somehow in the general confusion, Sassia contrived to be next to me. I have not mentioned, because I was experiencing mixed emotions about the fact that Quinctia and Philippus were not in our party. Duane approached me as we were leaving through the gateway of my villa. He was stuttering badly, I wondered why, as he explained that Philippus had developed a fever and Quinctia decided he should not travel. Concerned for the child, I made to return to the villa when Duane positively resisted my intent, jabbering that Quinctia asked that I left them alone. The boy's malaise was not s-s-serious. Rightly or wrongly I let it go. She had made her decision. Time had been short. Fannia had either not noticed or was too agitated to be bothered by their absence. There might be awkward questions later.

Meanwhile, I experienced a slightly unnerving situation as Sassia slipped her scrawny arm into the folds of my cloak. She was feeling unwell after that terrifying boat ride she said in her funny cracked voice. She didn't have to say it quietly. Laetorius had turned his blind eye and deaf ears whether he chose to or not.

Our possessions and boxes were stowed. The horses were whipped into action and we headed out of Clausentum. And who should I see, as I shrunk back behind the inadequate curtain, hovering affably outside his unlovely Roman look-alike tavern, but Modestinus, confidently rubbing his big red hands in anticipation of custom, the broad hopeful grin fading as our vehicles rushed past. I made up my mind to stop there for refreshments on my return. I felt compassion for the brash ugly man alone in the forsaken *civitas,* tussling with his wretched acceptance of a future becoming bleaker as the Empire forgot to care for its emigrants.

The four horses made excellent progress. We were in the vicinity of Venta Bulgarum in what I imagined to be record time. Kendreague sat with the first driver. There were a couple of other men travelling with us, strong silent strangers, who I learned from Finnius were *foederati* – friendly natives, whose jobs were to accompany vehicles from place to place and also guard the *civitas* gates. Although their heavy presence gave an impression of safety, the obvious necessity for guards emphasized the increasing dangers accompanying travellers nowadays.

The long light evening fortunately ensured arrival before dusk. I confess to be relieved for my party, and myself. But fresh worries assailed me, as we approached the familiar gates with no clue as to our lodging or where the marriage was to be held, nor indeed the address of the house of Aquilinus Drusus. Again I need not have worried.

There he was, standing near the gatehouse talking with a poised well-dressed woman. Fannia's shrieks of horror emanated from her coach, and the curtains were pulled together with a rattle. She should not have seen her bridegroom until the ceremony. More bad luck.

Aquilinus Drusus advanced.

'Marcus Cassius! What a coincidence. I was just explaining to my mother that you should be arriving very soon. How good to see you. I hear you have brought my bride!'

He jerked his head, laughing, towards the closed carriage.

'Fannia fears bad luck if you see her' I explained but he obviously knew all about bad luck.

'I promise…' he said loudly enough for Fannia and everyone else in the street of Venta Bulgarum to hear '…that I will not peek at my beautiful bride – yet!'

'Did you receive my message?' I whispered urgently feeling foolish, under cover of a noisy vehicle passing.

'Message? I have received no messages from Vectis. But I can guess the reason. There have been attacks of late on the postal messengers and the post lost or destroyed.'

He saw my shocked face as I imagined the poor postal messengers upon whose fate he made no comment.

'I am afraid these things are happening. Roaming bands of ex-slaves are a common threat. We do not have the squadrons available for patrolling every road. They have for the most part been drafted to Gaul and such places.'

The old excuse of the diminishing Roman army. Drusus's earlier comments about Britannia being a safe haven were obviously no longer applicable.

I recalled sending away the terrified slave of Fronto, who would have to fight merely to exist in the hostile country that once was his. He probably wouldn't have taken much persuading to join a desperate gang.

'Were the messages important?'

What an idiotic question. Who would fuss with the painstaking task of scribing messages on wax tablets and the ensuing hassle of sending them, if they were not important? But I explained about needing somewhere to stay for myself and five guests. Drusus was unperturbed.

'My mother's house is large enough to accommodate all of you.'

He called the elegant lady who had been neatly trapped by Sassia, obviously making up for many years of lost conversation.

Aquilinus Drusus introduced his mother whose name was Valida. She was very pleasant and welcoming, but there was something I couldn't quite understand about her. But she was definitely not Roman. Aquilinus Drusus left her with us, waving cheekily at the twitching curtain of Fannia's raeda.

I cajoled Fannia out of hiding and Valida led us past citizens returning from the market as it was evening, all laden with fruit, vegetables and some swinging dead chickens. (Ugh!)

Valida's house was a fine example of a town house hewn from solid stone with a good tiled roof. I only noticed the fine workmanship but there was another, happier squeal from Fannia. She was pointing excitedly at the imposing wooden door. It was bedecked with laurel, wreaths of flowers and coloured ribbons; the signs of a wedding. All the earlier bad luck must have been eradicated. We all entered through the decorated doorway to what was indeed a very large house. The surroundings reflected architecture based on the atrium of a Roman villa. And all the pillars were decorated in laurel and flowers to reflect the door and the occasion. The mother of Aquilinus Drusus had clearly gone to a lot of trouble.

Wide stairs led to a first storey. Two female body slaves escorted the women to their *cubiculum.* Fannia and Claudia were anxious to have Fannia's hair plaited which took some time and Marcia went with them to rehearse, she explained importantly to Aquilinus's mother, for her role as *pronuba.* I thought I recalled that she had played the part twice before and hoped there was not much left in the way of improvement. However Sassia hobbled after them, which was a relief. My arm retained a bruise where her talons had clenched it for almost the entire journey. I turned my full attention to our hostess who had poured wine into a silver goblet, very welcome too, and indicated that we sat for a moment. Poor old Laetorius hovered near us, mopping his brow, utterly confused by the journey and the general upheaval. He was shown to a cushioned bench and also given wine that instantly revived him.

'My son is a fortunate man. Your daughter seems delightful.'

She is delightful I thought. And I hope he knows how fortunate he is.

'You have a noble son' I said dutifully, except that I was beginning to believe it myself against all my initial misgivings, and his mother was charming. And not Roman.

'My son's heart was broken when his betrothed left Britannia unexpectedly with her *pater familias* to take up residence in Africa of all places. But after he returned from his visit to you, all Aquilinus could think about, and talk about, was your daughter. He thought she bore a resemblence to his former love. But Fannia is far prettier. And looks far more intelligent.'

Intelligent? Oh yes. And she has a mind of her own. I sipped the wine and looked about.

'This is a splendid house.'

'My husband had it built for us, before he…died. But Aquilinus since moved to his own new house. It is not far from here. Near to the Provincial Governor, where he works, as you know.'

But what did Aquilinus actually do up at the Provincial Governor's establishment?

'I know not of his position.'

'My husband urged our son to follow him and rise to become master of the scrivia as he had. Aquilinus longed for an army life, but he was an obedient boy and I think now he is glad of his father's insistence.'

So he worked in the cabinet. Now I began to understand why Aquilinus seemed to have fingers in all sorts of ministerial pies. A useful chap. A useful husband for my darling daughter. But my curiosity about his mother had not been satisfied. I looked straight into unusual grey eyes, healthy eyes, bright all-encompassing eyes that had recognised my questioning gaze.

'I met my husband when he arrived in Venta Bulgarum as a young scribe for the Provincial Governor.' The eyes lowered for a moment. 'My mother wove cloth for hangings and chair cushions. She was working at the Governor's offices and I accompanied her one day, not that I was of much help.'

She smiled at the remembrance of being a young girl of not much help to her proficient mother.

'I was born here in Venta Bulgarum. I am not of Roman origin as I think you have gathered.'

I nodded encouragingly but gently. I found myself thinking that I was glad that Valida was not Roman. I didn't know why.

'I met Aquilinus's father. We were very much in love. His *familia* were in Rome. We married but he insisted that we had a Roman wedding. So I became a Roman wife. Some frowned on us, Britons and Romans too. But unlike the men of the Roman army who cannot marry natives of Britannia, no objection was raised to prevent our marriage. And when Aquilinus was born, my family were happy, and the Government seemed relaxed and presented us with a present of gold coins. My husband was very important to them. I remember him meeting Valentinian on a secret visit to Venta Bulgarum after crushing the barbarian hordes that swept through our country.'

I experienced a flash of remembrance of my own, Melania Lupurca had told me of the event.

'He was a wonderful leader, Valentinian, no-one since has matched him.'

'What happened to your husband.'

'He became ill and he died. The fate of us all. But I missed him greatly.'

In a moment she changed from her remembrances to the present, so quickly that I took a moment to catch up. The journey had tired me. I could see that Laetorius was nodding and threatening to slide off the narrow bench.

'I must tell you something more.'

My hostess trapped my hand in hers. The grey un-Roman eyes stared at me with a disarming candour. Her grey un-Roman eyes terrified me. What more was it that she had to tell me? She must know that I was a widower and she obviously liked me. Was this yet another scheming feminine mind leaping ahead to pastures new? Where was Sassia when I needed her? Laetorius let go his empty bowl and it clattered to the tiles and rocked noisily back and forth.

Valida was not deterred.

'At the marriage ceremony…'

I gulped, transfixed with fear.

'…You will see a man. His name is Chrysippus. He and I… wish to marry. But I have not yet told my son.'

When all was in place for the ceremony, my daughter descended the stairs as I and the guests waited below. I could have cried at the beauty of her appearance. The long white tunic that she had worn because of tradition (bad luck not to) since yesterday seemed had been smoothed and freshened, held at her waist by a belt with a special knot, the *nodus Herculeus*. Her long dark hair was expertly plaited under the orange veil. She looked pale and serene. There should have been an artist present to describe her beauty in mosaic work or a wall painting.

Marcia, suitably attired in a silken tunica, accompanied Fannia carefully on their descent. The choreography had been perfectly synchronised as ten witnesses chosen presumably by Valida, moved towards a table where my daughter took her place and from somewhere in the background, Aquilinus Drusus, elegant in a vestis cenatoria even more heavily embroidered than mine, joined her. The delightful images of the tall bridegroom and the small bride were already producing sniffles amongst the females.

The ceremony began with the signing of the *tabulae nuptiales*, the witnesses taking their task seriously; after which plump solemn Marcia took the right hands of the couple and placed them in each other's. My daughter and Aquilinus Drusus then exchanged silent vows, the *dextrarum junctio*. The hush during this important declaration, was unbroken except for Laetorius's quavering voice asking where his wine was, and Sassia, looking furious, escorting him outside. If there had been a young child crying, which would have been worse? I hoped that the minor inturruption wasn't bad luck in Fannia's eyes although her wrapt face betrayed nothing other than concentration on her own meditations.

The *cena nuptialis* is always a jolly affair and light relief after the heavy silence of the preceding rite and this banquet was no exception. No expense had been spared in the provision of many dishes of delicacies and extremely acceptable ever flowing wine. There was even a group of musicians playing drums, flutes and lyres, adding musical gaiety to the happy scene as everyone took their turn to congratulate the couple, and voices grew louder and louder.

I was uncomfortably aware that it was my responsibility to supply all this entertainment as if Fannia had married on the island of Vectis. As we milled about after the refreshments had been cleared, I spied Valida, or the elegant back of Valida in a long midnight blue tunica, her hair coiled and held with jewelled slides. I needed to speak privately to her, to be sure that she understood that I meant to contribute to if not foot the entire bill for this lavish party. As I approached, I saw that she was talking to a large man wearing the distinguished dress of a procurator. An important person indeed. My new son in law certainly had friends in high places. The procurator looked over the shoulder of Valida, not too difficult as his proportions were tall as well as fat. Valida turned to me.

'Marcus Cassius. Let me introduce you to Chrysippus. Darling, this is my son's father in law.'

The time for the procession to the house of the bridegroom had arrived. Night had fallen, soft warm air filtered into the house, as we all made our way outside, well fed and well supped with wine.

And then chaos as Aquilinus Drusus snatched up Fannia, kicking her legs in fear and emitting terrified screams as he started up the street carrying her over his immense shoulder. Passersby backed against windows and walls, children cried out, women shrieked and wailed, some louder than Fannia. And as suddenly as the alarming episode had started, it stopped. Everyone laughed and clapped as Fannia, unharmed, ran back towards our guests, joined by Claudia, both as happy as children playing a childish game. Fannia would revel in the drama to perpeptuate the memory of the ancient and not so childish game – the rape of the Sabine women. It was another old Roman marriage custom; one that fortunately I had remembered. A more orderly procession formed. Marcia ceremonially handed Fannia a spindle and distaff, which she accepted gracefully but I knew that she would never use. And then joy of joys, right on cue, three young children ran forward. Two of the boys took Fannia's hands as she beamed happily down at them. Valida had done it again. What a woman. But there is another woman and I thought of her. I wondered if she thought of me all those miles away alone on Vectis.

The third very small boy who announced that his name was Sage, held a charred hawthorn branch. The lucky spina alba. Was there anything else I had forgotten? Jupiter, what sort of father was I?

It was gloomy in Venta Bulgarum now that darkness had fallen. I recall that in Rome in the good old days, free lamps were distributed at night. But some people were carrying torches, their shadows making the buildings dance as the noisy procession moved off, everyone shouting 'Talassio!'

Up near the great Government building, as Valida had described, lay the house of Aquilinus Drusus. As imposing a property as his parents' home. Aquilinus Drusus had obviously scampered back and now stood outside, a giant in the doorway of his house, dwarfing Fannia as she shyly approached him. There followed more drama. Fannia, my little actress, must have adored her wedding day. Aquilinus asked her who she was, and I could not hear her answer as the accompanying throng lifted her and swung her into the house. For the bride to trip up would be bad luck, she had told me. If someone had tripped up carrying her, would surely mean even more bad luck. But we were all safely inside a lavish entrance hall, well lit and beautifully decorated with wall and ceiling paintings. I approved. And this was my daughter's new home. But the ceremonial activities were not yet over as Fannia was seated upon the *lectis genialis* and whispered a prayer to the god of her new house. Tomorrow she would make offerings to the Lares and Penates.

As the lucky spina alba was distributed, we all left the house of Aquilinus Drusus and his new bride. At the doorway, Fannia ran to me and stood on tiptoe to kiss my cheek. Hot tears blurred my vision as I stumbled in the darkness of the street. I felt strangely detached from the other guests making their way less raucously back to the house of Valida.

Vectis my home

Kendreague and I were the only people who seemed in a hurry to leave Venta Bulgarum. Sassia had talked over her ankle problem with Valida, women all love medical discussions, discovering that the lady knew of a surgeon specialising in bones. Consequently Sassia and Marcia and poor old Laetorius who didn't even know where he was, were staying on a few days. Sassia seemed undeterred by my dire warnings of the dangers on the roads.

'You must return soon, to visit your daughter. You will not be put off the journey by unpleasant rumours. And nor will I. My darling Marcia may find a husband here. I am quite excited at the prospect. Valida knows so many people here. She is arranging a dinner for everyone including the newly weds. And she has promised a surprise during the evening. What fun! I am in such a happy whirl. The city has spun me around! How will I ever settle again in Vectis? When we are all safely back, perhaps we should see more of each other. A companionable dinner or if you preferred, quiet conversation…'

It occurred to me that perhaps it was no bad thing that Sassia was staying on in Venta Bulgarum. And I assumed that Valida's 'surprise' was the revelation of her intended marriage. Sassia would no doubt be anxious to tell me that piece of news. One thing at a time.

Claudia and Finnius seemed very unwilling to leave. Claudia's first experience of a lively city environment, not to mention markets and bars, had also caught them up and spun them around, as Sassia put it. And there was more. When I regretfully said goodbye to Fannia who looked happier and prettier than I had ever seen her look, she handed me a message for Melania Lupurca requesting that Claudia be released to become Fannia's servant. But I had to insist that they returned with me. Anyway, I needed Finnius and Melania Lupurca needed Claudia.

'But I want Claudia to be here with me and she wishes to stay in Venta Bulgarum.'

'Claudia and Finnius would hate being separated not only by water but a long journey' I reminded her. The wrong thing to say.

'Oh Finnius would like to live in Venta Bulgarum too' she told me artlessly.

Oh would he now? Over my dead body. I wish I had not said that even silently to myself.

'And I suppose I must send my best wishes to Quinctia.'

That stopped me.

'Quinctia told me everything. The whole deceitful story. After our evening in the garden when Melania went home and you had gone to bed. I never believed that the boy was my brother.I never liked either of them. And I never really wanted them at my wedding. But I forgive you dearest father even thought you really should have told me.'

'I wanted to protect you from unnecessary stress before your wedding, Fannia.'

Women! Would I ever get it right?

'I know. But I am tougher than you think.'

That was certainly true. I had it in mind to tell her not to let her husband bosss her around. There was no need. Fannia would be the household boss with back-up from the household gods, no doubt already spoilt with a plethora of gifts. As long as she didn't lose sight of her precocious femininity. And somehow I knew that she wouldn't.

Everyone seemed subdued on the journey back. In a hired *raeda.* With extra *foederati.* I had to pay for something. Valida refused to accept any monetary payment towards the considerable wedding expenses.

'You have given me a lovely daughter and a happy son' she said simply, adding 'when Chrysippus and I arrange our wedding, I insist that you are my guest.'

‘What does Aquilinus think about your marriage?’ I ventured.

‘Oh I haven’t told him. Yet. But I will.’

Clausentum. Late evening, but a beautiful late evening. A pink sunset enhancing the rundown panorama, the sea a rosy hue and as calm as my nymphaeum. There was not a boat in sight. A drunken seaman rolled towards us as we prudently held our breaths. He jerked a filthy paw towards the lazily slopping tide, slurring unintelligibly as he tried to explain something.

‘Come along’ I said with a brightness I certainly didn’t feel to my dejected and weary party. I led them up the shingly path to the taverna, bedecked with its familiarly garish statues of Roman gods and smoky oil lamps. Finnius and Claudia looked a little shocked. But they were tired and it was open. Modestinus did a good job at hiding his surprise at four customers turning up. Perhaps he knew we’d be back. He wanted to know where we had been and what we had done and if we had suffered from gang attack on the way. I answered him as curtly as I could; to the city, for a wedding and, no. I quickly ordered refreshments to get rid of him, reminding the others that if they did not desperately have to use the facilities, then they were better off not to even think about it.

The lovers melted into shadows at the back of the establishment. Kendreague and I flicked fat flies and sipped cloudy beer.

‘I think those two young people want to move away from Vectis’ I said.

‘Yes’ he replied noncommittally.

‘I suppose I will have to let Finnius go sometime. Vectis is too quiet a place for young people.’

I rallied myself. I thought of my own wavering decisions. And I was not young any more.

‘What about you Kendreague? How do you see your future.’

He sipped the dubious beer, pushed it away and then looked intently at me. I saw a haunting apprehension that formed a haze across his dark eyes.

'I should like to give notice to leave your employment' he said.

We abandoned our beers and the flies and the tavern and walked down towards the sea; a mutual unspoken decision. The tide chuckled quietly to itself, gurgling to and fro over slimy pebbles and spikey sea weed.

'There is something I have to explain' he said.

There was no boat expected until morning Modestinus was pleased to inform me, rubbing his grubby hands even more gleefully. Finnius and Claudia went to their allocated rooms, but I would have been surprised if both were used. Kendreague had taken himself off somewhere. I sat with a cup of mulsum that Modestinus unexpectedly produced. But despite my intention to have a talk with the man, I did not. He sat opposite me, with his wine, glad of the company. Tonight his silence was shared. Horses and cattle shuffled and coughed in a pen nearby. The stench of their dung hung noisomely on the night air. I stared into the blackness. I thought about what Kendreague had told me.

Kendreague and Quinctia were lovers. I should have noticed the subtle indications because their liaison was immediately recognisable now that he had told me. Particularly when I recalled the day that Quinctia revealed the truth about Philippus. I had been surprised to see Kendreague lurking nearby, in the rain. I should not have been. He must have put her up to confessing. But I didn't ask. His love for Quinctia shone from eyes that were clearer now that he had revealed their secret. He intended to return to his village taking Quinctia and the boy with him. He was confident that after the length of time that had elapsed, he would be admitted back to his people and that his lover and her child would be accepted. I felt very doubtful and said so.

‘The child will be mine’ he told me firmly. ‘We are calling him Dag, after my brother. The family will understand that he knows only the Roman language because of the slavery of his mother.’

I flinched at the word ‘slavery’. But there were a lot of memories that made me flinch where Quinctia was concerned. Jupiter! We all needed a new start. I wondered how the child would react to fresh transitions surrounding his change of status. Loving parents, however, should smooth the rocky path for him.

‘I intend to trace his real father. He should be made to pay for the cruelty and suffering he inflicted on his son and his…’

Kendreague shook his head.

‘We would rather forget the past. We want to get on with our lives.’

Kendreague promised to make every attempt to keep me informed of their re-settlement and I in turn promised to give him funds to employ extra guards for their journey. Kendreague was determined to succeed in his brave mission. I sighed, with relief and tiredness, but mostly with relief. Life without Fannia had not really hit me yet. I swigged the last drop of the wine.

‘How long are you staying open Modestinus?’

It was relaxing to drop into Latin again. Talking in any depth with Kendreague was a halting business. Modestinus jerked out of his own reverie and peered at me through the flickering lamp light.

‘I don’t mean just tonight. Trade generally doesn’t look too lively in Clausentum.’

‘I’m not giving up yet. I don’t worry too much about the thieves outside the town except when they steal my provisions before they have even arrived here. It’s the pirates that scare me.’

I awoke refreshed from a sleep that only Somnus could have planned, and was greeted by Modestinus with news that a boat had arrived and that he, Modestinus, had instructed the owner to wait for my party to board. I gave the man a handsome tip and shook his horny hand. I wanted to leave on a positive note.

'You have some fine wall paintings' I told Modestinus as we went.

He grinned revealing several impressive gaps amongst his blackened teeth.

'And the pirates can't take them!'

A sobering thought.

Vectis, my home. As our boat neared land, the island presented a glorious green haven. A rustic symbol of peace and tranquillity. Nothing bad could happen here. The oarsmen hove to and we all scrambled ashore and stretched our cramped limbs. Transport to my villa proved the immediate problem. There wasn't any. Finnius and Claudia were keen to walk the long path to the villa on their own. Finnius would send a raeda back to collect me and our luggage. I was happy to wait here in the sunshine. Kendreague hesitated.

'Go' I said. Quinctia would be waiting, although I didn't say that. 'But don't forget to come back for me!'

As the three figures disappeared into the dust of the lane, I allowed my lazy imagination to wander exploring the unusual sensation of homelessness, alone surrounded by my possessions in boxes. Sitting under the caressing sunshine, the idea was almost pleasurable. I imagined freedom too, a life without responsibilities; a life bereft of decision-making. I smiled to myself for indulging in such aimless thoughts. Easing my aching limbs onto one of the larger boxes, I surveyed my world. The boat owner seemed to be arguing with someone, their voices floated harshly up from the harbour mingling with the screams of gulls. A carpet of small blue and yellow flowers nodded at my feet, their wild fragrance tickling my nose. The great Sun God had climbed amongst the white burgeoning clouds and he beamed down at me. What a life. What a place. But it wasn't going to last forever. I had responsibilities and I had to make decisions. This dreaming inactivity was not the real world.

And then I saw it. The newly arrived boat, manned by six oarsmen, was oiled in a dark colour that stood out sharply on the sea. The hull looked battered, but that could have been merely shadow. The high prow was unembellished and the sails were of animal skins roughly assembled. As I peered, one hand shading my eyes, the boat turned towards the shore. The arguing boat owners had vanished, the craft bobbing where he had anchored it. Everything was quiet. I wondered idly where this new vessel had come from and why it was pulling into Vectis. It was not the normal type of boat that we saw here, and bore no resemblance to a coracle that some natives used but mostly on the rivers.

The six men were scrambling ashore. I watched, transfixed with the fascination of observing an enactment in which I played no part, as they climbed into the boat I had so recently clambered from. They seemed to be looking for something. I wondered why the enraged owner did not appear and challenge them. One of the men yelled to the others as he held up what appeared from my vantage point, to be a flask containing oil or wine and he tipped the contents briefly to his mouth. I saw him smash the pot and I heard the strange phenomen of delayed sound. The contents spread like blood on the deck of their ugly boat. They seemed in a hurry as they turned their attention to the surrounding land shouting to each other in a strange tongue.

I threw myself heavily onto the ground and crawled behind a growth of thicket, in the fearful realisation that these men were pirates. I have never in my life maintained such a stillness as in that prickly ditch, listening to the marauders clambering up the bank near where I had sat contentedly only a short time ago, guarding my possessions, surveying my island. I inhaled unpleasant whiffs of unwashed bodies and dirty garments mingling with wine and bad breath. There were no wrenching sounds to indicate that they were opening our boxes, but I heard clumping feet and heavy grunting as they carried off their booty. I lay there for an unimaginable time. I wanted to sneeze, I wanted to scratch. Then everything was still. No voices, no sounds, only the birds singing and the gulls screaming. Nervously, I raised my head and peered through the foliage. I could see the men lifting our boxes aboard their disreputable boat. Then someone shouted. Very near. Too near. I looked up into a massive shadow shutting out the light of the sun. I recoiled at the disgusting smell of sweat. I remember an unshaven face and a pair of piercing eyes beneath bushy brows, before something hard descended on my head. A mist of darkness closed over both my eyes. Now I know what Homer meant.

The Future for Vectis

An experience I would recommend avoiding is to be hit over the head by a pirate with the strength of Titan who didn't care if you lived or died. The best result to emerge from my undesirable experience was regaining consciousness and seeing a vision of Melania Lupurca. She held my clammy hand and kissed my dry mouth. She was definitely not a vision.

I had slept, unnaturally, for two days, causing concern to all who dared look at me. The person who assisted me out of my unnatural sleep? The widow of Fidus was urgently summoned, by Melania. All she did, I was told later, was to place a white powder under my tongue. It was enough. And apart from an indescribable headache from an outrageous bump that deformed my otherwise neat skull, I gradually edged nearer to normality.

Our expensive garments, wedding clothes and shoes including those of the Laetorius familia, and a cloak belonging to Fannia that she asked me to bring back (obviously considered unsuitable for Venta Bulgarum and therefore no longer required) had been taken by the pirates. Claudia was distraught; she had possessed very few clothes to start with. Finnius was counting the cost furiously, of losing his best attire. Kendreague was angry with himself because he had not stayed with me. I was merely relieved that we had not all been ambushed and killed and I had escaped with a mere clump as an after-thought before the pirates made their quick getaway. Clothing could be replaced. I did not like to dwell on the consequences if Kendreague had attempted to wrestle with six desperate Gauls. The last laugh was ours. There was nothing in the boxes to suit marauding pirates unless they fancied themselves parading about in embroidered outfits and perhaps their long-suffering wives would enjoy wearing the ceremonial sandals or fighting amongst themselves for ownership of Fannia's abandoned cloak. I stopped being amused as I remembered that I had not given Aquilinus the set of beautiful silver wine cups securely wrapped at the bottom of a chest. So the rogues had got something of value after all. My familia were obviously not meant to keep those cups. But perhaps they were bad luck. I sounded like Fannia.

Rain fell relentlessly. One storm after another rolled inland from Gaul. My slow recovery was accompanied by the sounds of rushing water and violent winds. This was Summer Solstice Britannia style but at least the sea-going pirates would be prevented from even thinking about paying us another visit.

Someone who paid me constant visits was Melania Lupurca, braving the puddles and the gales to be with me. We sat in the triclinium, Duane serving refreshments including my favourite honeyed wine that I am certain aided my recovery. As I gained strength I discovered that I was missing my daughter. The villa seemed uncannily empty. Even the petulant screams of Philippus might have been welcome. But Kendreague had taken Quinctia and the boy two days earlier during a lull in the bad weather, on the journey to his tribe. He handed the overseeing of my farm to a keen, much younger Briton who Kendreague pronounced as a good manager of the men. I asked Melania to confirm his comments, her command of the language, I freely admit, being considerably broader than my own.

I sipped and savoured the soothing luxury of the golden wine and when Melania eventually spoke her words distressed me.

'I am not a cowardly woman. But I do not envisage a life cowering behind the walls of my villa, fearful that every sound might herald an attack. Therefore I have decided to close the villa and move to the safety of a fortressed civitas.'

'I understand your concerns dear lady. Before going to Venta Bulgarum, I was experiencing similar thoughts.'

I omitted to mention that Melania, or to be precise the absence of Melania was the central reason for my own resolution.

'With all the upheavals of the past year, staying longer in the villa has, for me, lost its appeal.'

We talked on, late into the night. We discussed the merits of Venta Bulgarum and Noviomagus. I hoped she favoured the former. I certainly did. For one thing, I would be nearer to my daughter. I hoped to raise the possibility of Melania and I forming a partnership, I wouldn't have dared suggest marriage though it was very much on my mind. I also hoped that she might stay tonight, but Melania decided that she would return home. She was right. I got extremely weary as the day crept on. I lay in my bed, trying to make sense of our separate comments upon our mutual decision to move away from Vectis. It was a terrible feeling to consider turning my back on the place I loved more than anywhere else that I had lived and that had occupied so much imaginative thought. The planning of improvements to the villa, the reconstruction of the bath house, the commissioning of paintings and mosaics as fine, in some instances finer than any I had seen elsewhere; the designing of the garden. The villa expressed my appreciation of so many aspects of life from animals and birds, and images of my favourite gods, to farming and the cycles of the horticultural year. I attempted to console myself with the belief that I could make the villa secure, and return to Vectis when life in Britannia became more stable, and the destructive law-breaking gang culture had been brought under control. For the life of me, I could not see how such a control could be implemented because the army personnel in Britannia was badly depleted, lately made up of undisciplined, disinterested recruits and operating on borrowed time.

The Roman Empire had succeeded, admittedly with greater success in the south than elsewhere, in conquering Britannia and it had shown the people the desirable advantages of a civilised culture and invited them to join in. It had wooed and won the cooperation of all but the most extreme groups of dissenters. But Britannia had proved herself to be too expensive a commodity for too little return. By retreating from the land they had conquered, the Roman Empire would leave an unfilled void. It had failed in its duty to create a control centre of experienced governors and consuls capable of organising the political and military future of Britannia in its absence. That was the frightening reality. However, men would always need to farm the land. Food supplies would always be of primary concern, therefore it should be possible to keep the farm running. I would talk to Finnius. I feared that Finnius was fast losing interest in Vectis. But while I paid him, he would work for his money and together we would find a way of keeping the farm alive, while making my villa safe for my return one day. And on that positive note, I slept.

One year sped by. I had no news of Kendreague. I had no qualms as to his safety and that of his mistress and the child. But I would like to have known.

Fannia, my darling daughter, was pregnant. The only two messages that I had safely received both spoke enthusiastically of her happiness in her new life. And the second tablet contained the most incredible news of all. Fannia had converted to Christianity. She had visited Christians who had become her friends and she attended the Christian church in Venta Bulgarum. She indicated, sounding just a touch condescending, that it was so much easier to assimilate modern ideas and beliefs in the challenging environment of a big city.

I glanced nervously at the Lar as I took a necessary break from deciphering Fannia's script that had never been particularly readable. I swear he had stopped smirking. Gods could be unpredictable especially if they weren't pleased about something and this one was dusty and devoid of recent offerings. But Fannia reported, with no reference to bad luck that she had abandoned the household gods in her home, although she had not yet told Aquilinus. (I wondered if the other lady in Aquilinus's life had revealed her secret. If not, then he had some shocks coming his way.)

Claudia was still working for Melania Lupurca. Easy to understand why. Finnius was still working for me. Fannia, undeterred, described the acquisition of a little local girl who she was training, she said, to look after her and eventually her baby too.

Melania and I spent a great deal of time in each other's company. There was a reason. I had made her an offer and she had accepted. It was during the dark days of the Winter Solstice around the time of the Festival of the Saturnalia (great time for receiving gifts from grateful clients), not that Vectis saw too much of it, no gifts, nothing at all. Melania had locked up her home and moved herself and many of her belongings, including Claudia, to my villa. The best gift. It worked very well. We treated each other carefully. I ensured that Melania had plenty of space to herself and she allowed me to invite her to join me for dinner. I felt happy again. And Melania presented me with a gift; the intricate water clock that I had admired. Its clever mechanism excited me because I had read about the first such clocks named 'water thief' by the Greeks. This Roman design was naturally more complicated than the Greeks could have envisaged and I derived great pleasure from watching the movement clicking down the ratchet and the dial ticking the hours. I had never been so fascinated by time, absolute accuracy had never been an important issue for Romans: 'It is easier for philosophers to agree than clocks'. Which profound comment by Seneca reminded me that the Greek tutor was still living or perhaps lurking would be a better description at the far end of the villa. The kitchen women fed him like a pet puppy. And on the odd occasions when our paths crossed he assured me that he was studying some obscure educational exercise. I reluctantly gave him my precious scrolls as I had promised. I am a man of my word, but that didn't stop me regretting it.

Melania gave me some coins that her husband had avidly collected. One perfect aureus depicted the invasion of Britannia by Claudius. On the reverse, the image of an arch celebrated his invasion. On the obverse was Claudius's head in profile. The coins were in pristine condition. They would only increase in value but she insisted that I accepted them.

The world outside remained obstinately oblivious to Claudius's former glory. I heard that Clausentum had been attacked by pirates. Poor old Modestinus. All one could hope was that he had managed to poison them with his out-of-date fast food. But as fierce storms raged, it seemed unlikely that another attack by sea would be forthcoming for the duration of the winter solstice.

Long after the passing of the Winter Solstice, The only other Roman *familia* hereabouts had still not returned to Vectis. I could only presume that they were staying indefinitely in Venta Bulgarum. Had Marcia found a husband? Had Sassia paused for breath between conversations? How was Laetorius coping? What pathetic times for a man once so important.

We talked, Melania and I. Sadly, the discussions were all about moving from Vectis. We interviewed Euan the young Briton who had been left in charge of the farm by Kendreague. We were impressed by his intelligence and his stature. He was enormous. And he had a brain to match beneath his fair hair. The concept of managing the farm held no fears for him. Nor the more ominous threats of invasion.

'I will recruit able men from the village near to the harbour. They will keep look out. Our farm is important and it will be well guarded.'

I told him that while I was absent, he was to ensure that everyone had enough to eat before selling the surplus after which all the earnings from produce were his to distribute as he saw fit. With Melania's assistance, we drew up the simple contract in the form of which I had spoken. Duane's final question dealt me an unexpectedly hurtful blow.

'When will you be leaving Vectis?'

I diverted the question to Melania later. 'When do we plan to leave Vectis?'

Melania did not hesitate.

'We have no need for any delay. Venta Bulgarum appeals to me. And you also I think. When did you say that Fannia's baby is to be born?'

I commenced packing immediately. Bearing in mind the very real chance of attempted robbery, Duane and I carefully wrapped and stowed away items I could not take with me. It was a heart-breaking exercise. But joy of joys we discovered the silver wine cups. Wrapped and forgotten before the last journey. It felt like a symbol of good luck, finding those silver cups. Aquilinus could have them after all. I fingered the delicate artistry of the incised patterns. They were of an excellent quality. And they meant a lot. I fingered the hard lump on my head that had never quite vanished.

I did not relish an imminent departure from my beloved villa. But I would return. It was the immediate future that concerned me. Duane would be caring for the villa. Euan had already taken control of the farm.

And a miracle happened. On a day when the sea was becalmed, and a blue sky and a smooth sea heralded a period of reliable weather, Kendreague strode in to my villa, without warning for which he apologised.

'No apologies necessary, Kendreague. Come and tell me all that has happened.'

We all make mistakes. But the elders of his tribe obviously needed him and knowing the excellent qualities that Kendreague possessed, I could understand why. He was immediately pardoned and welcomed him back. With open arms, it seemed, although Kendreague told me modestly of his gratitude. His family were the most respected members of the tribe he said, pausing. I knew he was recalling that he had let his family down. But he had returned to them and humbly asked and received their forgiveness.

He had been empowered with the important position of responsibility to the present elder, successor to the deceased father of Kendreague's mistress who had apparently within a very short time fled with another man. An unusually scandalous business for the tribe, but times move on. Quinctia was accepted as Kendreague's wife. The women loved her, he said. And little Dag absorbed his new name and the new social surroundings and quickly found his feet. A couple of fierce sibling battles, one started by bullies taunting him over his Latin language, had established Dag as leader of the pack. Everything had turned out for the best. So why had Kendreague returned to Vectis?

His reply was as straightforward as the man himself. His loyalty astounded me, combined with his fearlessness in making what was not an essential journey in order to tell me his news.

'Postal services are finished. You gave me a fresh start and enabled me to return to my people with useful knowledge of the outside world that I would not otherwise have found. And I wanted you to know that Quinctia is expecting our child.'

Splendid news after which Melania and I collected many objects as gifts, and gold coins too, to give to him and anyone in his tribe he chose. Always supposing we were not robbed on the journey back.

Kendreague remained in the villa for two more days during which time it was decided that Melania and I, and Finnius and Claudia would journey with Kendreague and the two heavyweight foederati who had accompanied him. My kind-hearted kitchen women had fed them too. Talking of which, I left the Greek tutor to his own salvation and his free meals. And a last minute bag of gold, a small one. I had enough responsibilities without a penniless academic tagging along.

As the raeda heavy with our precious boxes, pulled away down the stony lane I thought of all the journeys it had seen over the past years, and while some fleeting memories were good, I recalled scenes of violence and disaster that I would rather forget. I stared behind us, distraught at the sight of receding images. The tall dovecote was alive with white birds fluttering in and out of the tiny domed openings and swooping around the red tile pitched roofs. Hidden behind their wrought iron grilles, the villa's small windows, shuttered for the duration of my absence, seemed to have closed their eyes. The great oak door bolted against intruders, was a yawning black shadow. I caught a turquoise glimpse of a peacock's proud tail. But Duane had promised to care for them. Some of Fannia's cats playing by the hedgerows cringed in the dust as we rumbled past. They had caught a rabbit. They certainly wouldn't starve in this richly pastural province.

As our boat sailed away and the green vista of Vectis vanished in the early morning sea mist, I seemed to be caught in a strange dream that bore me unwillingly from my beloved villa, bolted and barred, left alone, clutching its hoard of treasures.

As Modestinus had so rightly remarked, no maurranding villains could snatch my paintings or my mosaics. Lycurgus would be held forever, strangled by Ambrosia's vine; the neriads and tritons were enternally proclaiming the power of the sea. The shepherd and the dainty water nymph would flirt forever. It was the only badly executed mosaic in the villa, but charming in its own way. Perseus had slain the terrible Medusa and gallantly rescued Andromeda.

Staring into the waves below the boat, I again pictured the dancing images of the Four Seasons, and the Medusa herself flashing her dangerous eyes, her snake hair writhing amongst the disturbed waters. Brought over from Rome, kept in wrappings during my ten years in Durovernum and painstakingly inserted into the tesserae in my villa on Vectis, the Medusa was the only one of my irreplaceable treasures created in paint, stone or pottery that I had brought with me. I wondered when I would see them again? The murmuring breeze caught against the flapping sails whispering the unwanted answer to my question. 'Never, never, never'. But I didn't believe the deceptive wind.

There were no disappointing delays when the boat moored at Clausentum. A large armed coach had arrived to deliver much needed food supplies. The nervous driver and his even more scared looking bodyslave were returning immediately to Venta Bulgarum. We flew from Clausentum as though the horses had wings. I kept my eyes averted from the tavern, frightened of seeing signs of attack or destruction. Melania and I hid behind closed curtains, and opposite us Claudia and Finnius whispered to each other. They made an idyllic picture of young lovers. I told Claudia about Fannia's new girl, but Claudia seemed to have forgotten her urgency to become servant to her friend.

'Actually, I do not like babies' she had told me without any shame, reinforcing what I had heard about modern Roman women and their dislike of the ties of motherhood, except that Claudia was not Roman. What was happening to women these days? At least my darling Fannia did not follow the undesirable fashion.

'…And my mistress will need me when we are in our new house.'

That was fortunate for Claudia. I was not sure about the future for Finnius. There would not be a great deal to occupy him in the way of bookkeeping. But while there was a Roman presence in Britannia, I would need to keep up a semblance of attention to business. I would continue to run the farm, if only on wax. I tried to envisage what happened to us if and when the Roman presence finally disintregrated and how we would be regarded, as former citizens of the Empire. We were surely not seen as a threat. But there was nothing to do but wait and see, and in the meantime try to create a comfortable existence behind the protective walls of a *civitas*.

Melania seemed as calm as always and I wondered what she thought about in her more vulnerable moments. There were facets of Melania that remained a mystery. The day was unusually warm and I opened the curtains and peered outside, just as the carriage pulled to an unexpected halt. Kendreague was standing a short way off, his back turned away from our vehicle. His height and stature made an impressive sight as he poised, like a god, his bow bent for action. As he loosened the arrow, my eyes moved on, not so fast as the arrow but in time to see a large buck deer slumping to the ferny ground with a deadly thud. Kendreague ran forward to examine the beast and shouted back to one of the other men for help. Together they hauled the deer by its fine antlers and we waited within the raeda whilst it was lashed to the top. Kendreague climbed into the crowded interior and Claudia and Finnius shifted for him to be seated.

Melania was extremely displeased.

'Was that killing necessary? We are not in urgent need of sustenance.'

Kendreague did not reply. His strong features were set with impenetrable firmness. I said nothing. Kendreague obviously had his own reasons. I turned my attention to the changing scenery as though I were seeing it for the first time. We were passing through a valley of lush vegetation and then the road climbed between dark, heavy woodland, dipping again where the banks rose high on either side and bushes clung precariously to overhanging rock. I was almost dozing despite the uncomfortable jolting motion of the carriage. Claudia's head rested on Finnius's shoulder and they both had their eyes shut. I occasionally detected a nodding movement from Melania next to me. Only Kendreague remained alert with an animal intentness as he stared out at the passing landscape.

Then it happened. We were violently thrown about as the raeda jolted to a halt. Amidst the neighing of horses and shouting men, the road surface rang with the clamour of hooves and boots. Kendreague leapt out as the commotion grew with a terrifying intensity and I knew that we were under attack. Amidst the confusion outside, there was a shriek of pain from Finnius and a scream from Claudia and at first I couldn't understand why. And then I saw. An arrow had pierced the side of the raeda and embedded itself in Finnius's cloak, from which garment bright blood spread with alarming speed. Melania grabbed Claudia's arms, pulling her away as I lunged across to where she had sat and ripped open Finnius's clothes. He was groaning and clawing at his thigh but I saw that the arrow had been slowed by its passage through the wicker wall of the raeda so that the tip only pierced muscle and was easily removable. Melania had already torn a strip of hem from her long tunica and passed it to me to stem the blood flow as I hastily pulled away the arrow point amidst yells from Finnius and more screams from Claudia. Outside, the shouting and scuffling continued. I decided that I had no choice other than to put aside my fear and I climbed down, my hands bloodied from Finnius's wound. The sight outside was like no tableau I had ever seen.

I was confronted by a Roman soldier in a crimson cloak and a brass helmet. He carried a shining shield that he wielded awkwardly. In his right hand he held a spear that looked too heavy for him. Behind him, five others, wearing ragged tunics, and animal skins that any animal would be ashamed of, were brandishing clubs hewn from knotted wood in an undecided way as if waiting for a command. These rough men should have aroused fear, in me if not in Kendreague. But they were betrayed by their white faces. Their terrified eyes flickered between our three bodyguards balanced on the raeda holding their bows taut and Kendreague who had obviously implemented his own bow and was looking at the body lying face down in the dust. Without considering the obvious dangers, as I staggered forward and half-kneeled by the prone form. A spent bow lay at his side. An arrow shaft protruded from his back above the heart. A pool of blood had seeped into the dust. I rubbed my blood smeared hands on the moss and climbed more slowly than I had knelt, to my feet, imitating a frail old man, and stayed prudently behind Kendreague who had bent his bow again, his intentions aimed at the motley collection of marauders. I peered more closely at the Roman soldier. He looked extremely un-Roman despite his dress and equipment. He couldn't deceive anyone for long. Someone had obviously killed a soldier in order to acquire the uniform and the trappings. He was the leader of the gang. But he looked beaten, his pale face pinched beneath the helmet.

'You have killed my brother' he said slowly. Even I could interpret those few devastating words.

'He killed one of my passengers' Kendreague reminded him.

I kept quiet. I saw a clipped ear on the bared heads of the defeated warriors; the cruel branding. These then were escapees from slavery, a few of many that were purported to be roaming Britannia. They looked more desperate than dangerous, those poor absconders, but desperation creates a breeding ground for danger. I wondered at what moment the first of the men would lunge forward and fullscale slaughter would begin. But I had a feeling of being outside the grim tableau as I watched and waited. And then rain began falling heavily, pattering through the trees. The sweet smell of freshened foliage rose to our nostrils. The pathetic Roman soldier lowered his spear and his shield clattered noisily to the hard road. He sobbed and I simultaneously heard Claudia crying quietly in the depths of the raeda as the rain gathered momentum bouncing off the road, deflecting the grasses along the verges, drenching the motionless group of men.

'Do you have a settlement in this area?' Kendreague asked him harshly. To show a sign of remorse would have inferred a sign of weakness. He remained in charge of an unpredictable situation that could change without warning.

The men nodded and one pointed a filthy hand clutching his club towards the distant hills.

'Go back to your camp' Kendreague told him. 'We have nothing on board to give you. That is why I took that…' He jerked his hand up towards the deer.

'Where did you get it?' one of the men marvelled speaking out bravely. 'We are starving. We have seen nothing worth killing to eat for days.'

At Kendreague's gesture, two of our foederati who had kept very quiet during the confrontation, unloaded the animal and dropped it, the antlers clattering as it hit the road.

'Hunt harder, by night' Kendreague told them grimly. 'Go!'

He shouted the last instruction with such force that the men turned away, their animal skins dripping with water, two carrying the blood soaked body of their comrade, the others hauling the deer.

The Roman soldier turned back again, rain dribbling down his helmet and onto his nose.

'If you are a Briton, how is it that you have a fine carriage?'

'I stole it. I am cleverer and faster than you will ever be. Go. Bury your brother and recover your strength! I might be back! Oh and do not forget to pick up your shield. And as for you, Roman scum!'

He grabbed me very roughly and I was about to protest when I recognised the need for dramatic skills of my own.

'Please don't hurt me - again!' I cried as Kendreague bundled me into the raeda. Fannia would have been proud of me.

Kendreague had proved himself as our salvation. Those men may have been cowardly but we were no match for their starving desperation. And the foederati had seemed as scared as the rest of us. No wonder the driver looked so frightened when we boarded at Clausentum.

‘It that why you killed the deer? In case we were attacked?’ I asked Kendreague as we gathered speed along the road from the gloomy area of the confrontation. Kendreague smiled grimly.

‘I seize the moment’ he replied.

Finnius was in a lot of pain, but it was lucky for him that the wound had been no deeper or no higher. I reminded him of that, but he was not consoled. Finnius might be an excellent book keeper but his threshhold of pain was not up to Roman standards. I hoped for his sake that it was not tested again.

The Future for all of us

The men guarding the gates of Venta Bulgarum took a lot of convincing that they should let us inside the city walls. It was dark and they strongly resisted opening up after nightfall.

'Come on' I said in my most persuasive and least irritated voice 'we have already been attacked on our journey. Look at the damage to the carriage not to mention to my servant's leg.'

They did not seem too keen to look at Finnius's leg although one of them shone his oil lamp near to the raeda disregarding the risk of setting it on fire whilst they discussed the damage with each other in their rough unintelligible language.

Not surprisingly the hotel had closed down. It might have paid its way in Italy or Gaul. Not in this tiny province. Some enterprising person had lost a lot of money. Grudgingly the guards interrupted my conjectures, and let us through the gates into the city. Despite the inconvenient delay, it was encouraging that they carried out their duties to protect the citizens of Venta Bulgarum, if not quite so encouraging that they didn't automatically let a Roman citizen through. By now, it was very late. Everyone waited by the raeda under the light of a torch near the gates, for my decision on the next move. I did not feel inclined to scare my pregnant daughter by hammering on the door at this hour.

Just when I was despairing of knowing what to do, a familiar figure appeared out of the blackness. A shabby woman, wiping rattails of hair from her face, carrying a smoky taper. I saw a wide toothless grin. It was Birkita. She remembered me. We laughed at our recognition of each other and Aine came very nimbly from the shadows across the street to join in. A reunion indeed. Not what I would have wished for my first night here. But as on that earlier occasion of our meeting returning exhausted from Londinium, we were all grateful for their hospitality. It only needed Kendreague to go and purchase pies… But it was far too late for that. Instead he unpacked the boxes and stored them inside Birkita's cottage. We helped the suffering Finnius to limp inside too, but I gently refused Aine's offer of her special remedy for arrow wounds, explaining that my own skills were sufficient.

'Aine is a mystic' said Birkita. 'You should pay attention to her. We saw the weddin…' she added, pouring out beer that I remembered was pretty good stuff.

'Oh you should have made yourself known' I told them, secretly relieved that they had not. They had watched from a distance and seemed satisfied with that.

'How are things here in Venta Bulgarum?' I asked them.

They told me everything was as it always was, which wasn't much help and they seemed surprised at the question. When I said we were here to stay they were even more surprised. There's a lovely house up the top of the forum, Birkita said, large enough for you all. I kept my eyes averted from Melania's. As I said, I was not able to read her thoughts yet.

Aine grabbed Kendreague by his shoulder because he was sitting down and she could reach.

'My brother, did you see him?'

'Tegan is well, working hard on the farm, and his wife too when it's harvest.'

'His wife! I don't want to know about Her! What of the children?'

But Kendreague had no news of the children, which disappointed Aine.

We all dispersed to sleep. Claudia and the badly limping Finnius went off with Aine the mystic. Mystic indeed. What funny old dears the two were, her and Birkita. But I was exhausted, as we all were after our fearful escapade on the journey. I prayed to Jupiter, that next time that I travelled that road, the problems would be sorted out so that people could travel without fear. I wondered about the large property beyond the forum that the crones had mentioned. I was feeling very excited at the prospect of seeing my darling daughter. There was someone snoring over the far side of the cottage. I was too tired to be curious. I slept.

I woke to early morning sounds that were never experienced on the island of Vectis, carriages rumbling past, men at the gates shouting at each other, footsteps passing close to the cottage, all the realities of city life that I certainly had not missed but would soon become part of my own everyday life.

There was no sound from anyone in the cottage except Birkita who I do not think ever retired to bed for fear of missing something, as I crept outside, blinking like a cat in the sunshine. She followed me.

'I hope that your daughter is well' she croaked at me making it sound like a foreboding.

As I hastened up to the house my apprehension quickened and I cursed myself for my stupid fears. Aquilinus himself opened the door. Not having seen him for over one year I was instantly shocked at his unkempt and weary appearance. This was not the swarve, elegant man my daughter had married. His own amazement at seeing me standing outside his house hid something else. He grasped my arms, shaking them until they hurt.

'Marcus Cassius! By the gods, I did not expect you!'

'Well here I am. Are you going to let your father-in-law in.'

He led the way through his palatial entrance hall, where a new marble embellishment was displayed; an immense heroic Achilles attempting to pluck the deadly arrow from his heel. The statue had to be Fannia's innovation, she had always loved Homer's heroes. We passed to the triclinium, where I was not altogether surprised, recalling her last message, to see a painting depicting the God of the Christians enduring the agony of His crucifixion. Not a very tranquil sight to look upon especially while having dinner. I turned to look at Aquilinus who was shaking his head in a despairing manner. Perhaps he did not like the painting either.

'The physician is with Fannia now.'

'Physician? What in Jupiter's name is wrong? I must go to her.'

Shocked out of my disrespectful musing I made for the broad stairs but he caught my arm.

'Wait. He will be with us soon. Fannia is very sick.'

'Why? What is wrong?'

'She gave birth early in the morning of yesterday. We have a son. All is well with him. A fine big boy. But Fannia…'

'Why?'

'We think due to the loss of blood. And she no longer knows us or her child.'

'Jupiter! I have to see her!'

The physician was descending the staircase. As he mopped his brow and looked at us, I recognised him.

'By the gods! Crispinus! You here! Am I so relieved that you are attending my daughter. She could not be in better hands. How is she?'

'Marcus, it is so good to see you, but I regret that the circumstances are grim. Fannia is very weak. I cannot encourage her to recognise anything in her surroundings, not even the babe. Not even when he cries.'

He turned to Aquilinus. 'Find a wet nurse without delay.'

But Aquilinus stood like a statue himself, seeming unable to move.

'She will die?' I said.

'If there is no improvement during the coming day and night, I fear she will slip from us.'

I bounded up the stairs, breathless with shock, entered the room darkend by closed shutters. Fannia lay upon a wide bed, a pathetically white and motionless form. Her eyes closed. She looked peaceful. But her inertia was the most unnatural condition for a newly delivered mother. The baby mewled softly in a crib. I only glanced at the child. His head turned to seek the comfort of his mother. He was indeed a strong child, in need of sustenence. I returned to Fannia. I whispered in her ear that I was with her, pleading her to open her eyes. There seemed to be no reaction but her eyelids fluttered almost imperceptibly.

A tall fair woman, a Briton, entered the room interrupting my attempted communication. She set about checking Fannia, carrying out her task gently and quickly. I returned to the father and the physician.

'She seems peaceful. But I saw her eyelids move when I spoke.'

Crispinus shook his head. How I was beginning to hate the hopelessness of that movement.

'We need a stronger sign of returning strength' he said gravely.

We walked slowly back towards the Forum, through the commotion of the crowds, in despondent silence until Crispinus asked me where I was staying and for how long.

'I heard you had retired and moved to an island on the south coast.'

'That is true and we have been very happy there. But communication and travel is proving a problem that I fear will escalate. The island is vulnerable to attacks. I intend to settle in Venta Bulgarum, to be near my daughter and my…'

My voice tailed away into a heavy sob that shamed me and racked me. But the man sensibly took up my comments about the city.

'Venta Bulgarum! A wise choice. I have been living here for nearly six years. Securely guarded city walls count for peace of mind these days. We experience no lawlessness problems in Venta Bulgarum. I know of a large house up beyond the forum…'

'Yes I have heard of it. Perhaps I will look at it – sometime…'

The fame of the house seemed to have spread all over the city. But now was not the time.

We agreed to meet again early next day for his further examination of Fannia. When I returned to Birkita's cottage, Melania immediately recognised my despair. I slumped onto one of Birkita's hard benches as she put her arm upon my shoulder. Birkita bustled in, demanding to know about my daughter. Melania shook her head.

'We shall go and see her when Marcus has rested a while' Melania told the woman.

'I will fetch Aine' said Birkita firmly.

I groaned when she had gone.

'I have already turned down that wretched woman's so called medicine for arrow injuries. My daughter is beyond the help of a mystic.'

'I will deal with her' said Melania, patting my arm, as she followed Birkita's route.

My head in my hands, I heard the sounds of energetic activity outside that filled me with despair as I thought of my darling daughter, lying unmoving, weakened beyond help. The liveliest person I had ever known seemed to have resigned herself to leave us forever.

There was a loud click of the latch and I looked up to see Finnius and Claudia.

'Melania has told us' said Claudia sadly.

Finnius strode over to me, which was something of a surprise. He was not limping.

'How is your injury?'

'The pain was terrible during the night. I was burning up. Aine talked with me. She gave me one of her potions. I slept.'

'And today the inflammation has gone away' said Claudia.

'And the pain too' added Finnius.

'Like magic' contributed Claudia again.

'I am very pleased for you' I said puzzled, because logical Finnius was the least likely person to believe in the curative powers of a potion administered by an old hag.

'Melania has told Aine of Fannia's sickness. Aine has a cure for Fannia too.'

So that is how Melania, myself and Aine presented ourselves at the house of my son in law, who looked in silent horror at the old hag.

'I shall watch her with care' I whispered. 'But I have seen for myself that she has achieved an amazing result with a badly infected injury. Don't worry' I added because he did not look convinced. 'We have to try to save my daughter - your wife. Have you found a woman to nurse the infant?'

He shook his head dismally. Why did everyone do that?

But Melania and Aine were already at the door to Fannia's room and I rushed up the stairs, two at a time, out of breath before I reached the top. My state of fitness was at an all time low.

Fannia had not moved since I left her. Of that I was certain. Her eyes remained closed, concealed by transparent eyelids laced with delicate blue veins. Aine opened the shutters and sunlight streamed in while she stood at the bed, looking silently at my daughter, turning her tatty head this way and that.

'What are you proposing to do?' I nervously asked the hag. But she was delving into her capacious bag, carefully extracting a small stone phial.

'Open her mouth' she commanded Melania. She shook a tiny quantity of greyish powder underneath my darling child's tongue. That was all.

'And now?' I said.

'Now? Nothing now.'

'What are these potions that you use? I am a surgeon as you know and they interest me greatly.'

'What's that?'

'Your potions. What are they?' I remembered her deafness.

She cackled and started to talk again, more of an inarticulate mutter. I turned despairingly to Melania.

'Please…'

Melania nodded and quietly translated as the woman spoke not seeming to mind, but she might not have heard.

'None of your fancy medicaments' she translated as Aine cackled.

'Her remedies act with the patient's own vital force. Her grandmother, her mother too, taught her and the remedies are always successful. She says she has made some assumptions about your daughter.'

'What do you mean? She cannot speak. What can you possibly know about her?'

'The way she is resting, the expression on her pretty face, the condition of her hair, her skin…'

'She is weak through loss of blood! What in Jupiter's name has the condition of her hair got to do with that?'

'Yes she has lost a lot of blood but her body is making up the loss. It is her own vitality that is her enemy. She is very hot and wet, which Aine thought would be the case, so she gave her substances that are cold and dry…She needs salt too and other remedies. But that comes later, after she has regained the desire to open her eyes and she wants to get better and nurse her baby.'

That remark made me angry.

'Of course she wants to nurse her baby. Her unconscious state cannot dictate how she feels and thinks.'

'The hidden part of her mind is controlling her strength. I am acting on assumptions I have made' Aine apparently repeated stubbornly.

'Aine will return tonight and administer some more remedies and says we shall see an improvement by morning. Oh and we must not let a wet nurse feed the child. She has instructed the woman to release the milk from your daughter's breasts and hold the babe's mouth close. The action will help your daughter and the first milk is needed for the babe's health.'

I knew the importance of that of course. But I had known of no great harm coming to a child who did not receive the first milk. Or perhaps I had just not continued to observe such a child. I confess to not understanding Aine and her strange mystical philosophy. But Fannia was dying. If a surgeon as highly respected as Crispinus could not save her, I would willingly try another way.

Melania was translating for me again.

'She will need water when she opens her eyes. Plenty of sweet water.'

The old woman's sharp eyes saw my quizzical expression.

'Not honeyed water. Sweet water means good and fresh.'

Aine shuffled away. Melania closed the shutters and sat down on the bed and took Fannia's inert little hand in her own.

'There is nothing we can do but to wait. And I will sit with her. Go.'

Melania inclined her head. It was a positive nod, for a change.

I went.

Venta Bulgarum

The sounds, and smells too, of daily life in a regional capital, for such was Venta Bulgarum, mercifully could not be discerned from within the splendid house that was soon to be mine. I wandered around, imagining myself in occupation, for the second time. The solid brick and stone exterior, the high quality of the glass in the windows, had all prepared me for expectancies of the rooms within. I was not disappointed. In fact I was delighted. Mosaic floors throughout with geometric and floral designs; most walls painted with murals of urns and floral decorations, none so intricate as those in my villa, but nervertheless pleasing to behold. There were enough items of good furniture so that one could feel at home immediately. The previous owner, a man of obvious good taste, who must also have been a high ranking official, had moved by order of the Government to Noviomagus.

The best news of all was that Melania Lupurca graciously accepted my offer to reside here. One visit had been enough to persuade her. With so many rooms, and the pleasant spaciousness of its location for a town house, we both felt that the gods had been with us. Or I did. I was always careful not to mention the old gods when Melania Lupurca was around.

Closing the door to my new home, at that moment my raeda clattered to a halt outside, and Kendreague and a couple of men commenced unloading the boxes. Now it was really my new home. And I spied Melania and Claudia and Finnius walking out of the Forum towards me. They were smiling too. It was a smiling day and Sol contributed to it, releasing glorious bright warmth.

Melania approached me.

'We must go and see Fannia' she reminded me.

Oh yes, Fannia. In the three days during which, together with my son-in-law, I went through the formalities to obtain ownership of the house, she gradually recovered. Whatever strange substances Aine had administered took effect quickly, that very night in fact. It seemed like a miracle. Melania had no doubts that it was. For had not Fannia converted to the Christian faith? I said nothing. But neither Crispinus nor I could supply medical answers. The nearest to a solution was Fannia's telling of a strange dream in which her baby spoke and told her that he loved her. She looked as perfect as I have ever seen her look. Radiant, in fact. Propped up, nursing her son. My grandson. I liked saying that to myself. My grandson. He had a red face and startlingly black hair. Very much like his father in fact. But he was my grandson. He was to be named Lucius, after my father, his great grandfather. I felt almost like an intruder, watching the mother and babe absorbed in each other. I made my excuses.

My son in law cornered me as I departed.

'I am very glad you have decided to settle here in Venta Bulgarum' he said unnecessarily. He had told me so a few times recently. His mother also. But did he yet know of her intention to marry and give him yet another relative in the form of a step-father?

'Come and see my house.'

'When I am not so busy. Marcus Cassius, your name has been brought up recently at the Government meeting.'

That was quick. I had only arrived recently. But I was not sure I liked the way he said it. Suddenly he was the official and not the relation. He saw my surprise.

'It was my duty to report your arrival. Everyone who comes to settle here has to be entered on the register. There is some concern that you do not have an occupation. I explained about the farm on Vectis, but I was rightly reminded that you cannot be responsible for the farm so far away.'

'It is still my farm. I have left good men in charge.'

'Yes yes, I appreciate that. I would not have thought it could be otherwise. But we are talking about here in Venta Bulgarum. The question of taxes has been raised.'

I groaned inwardly. Not again. I had earned my money and paid taxes on it too, and I wanted nothing from the Government.

'I tried to explain that you are a self-sufficient man and told them of your profession.'

'Oh no!'

'I am so sorry Marcus, but if I had not spoken out they would have sent someone to investigate which might not have been pleasant.'

He paused and we both remembered the last occasion when I had been 'investigated'.

'So what happens now?' I asked helplessly.

'Venta Bulgarum has no resident eye surgeon. It has been suggested that I approach you to request that you commence your profession here. Crispinus would help you to start up your business in the correct manner for physicians by the laws that govern this civitas. You have a large house that would easily accommodate your surgery. I will ask Crispinus and you to dinner and you can talk freely together and find out all you wish to know.'

I had come full circle. I had left Durovernum to escape life in a *civitas* and the pressures of my profession. For ten years I had enjoyed well-earned freedom in beautiful surroundings on my beloved island. And now I had returned to life in a *civitas* with its accompanying stresses, forced unwillingly back into the repressive bounds of bureaucracy. I felt deflated. But I knew that I had no choice.

Just as I had no choice but to say farewell to Kendreague. Quinctia would soon be giving birth. And fair to say his value to me had been fulfilled many times over.

I grasped his arm warmly.

'You have been a true servant and a good friend' I told him. 'I hope that our paths cross again.'

Especially if the Roman army ever left Britannia.

He nodded, almost as thought he read my thoughts.

'I too hope we see each other again. To be your servant was an honour.'

I purchased a horse for Kendreague. From a rather dubious character who seemed to frequent the wooden shack of Birkita very regularly. He had no further need of the animal, he told me. No. Not now he had taken up residence. He was asleep curled up in a corner the night we arrived, but I was too tired to think anything of it. Birkita seemed happy, her toothless grin wider than ever. Buying the horse was the least I could do. Because I would never cease to be grateful that Kendreague had been my reliable and strong protector, and had fallen in love with the woman who could have blighted my future chances of equanimity. And now he was impatient to return his people, to Quinctia, and to Dag the toughest little character in the Belgae tribe, to listen to his proud stepfather.

I watched at the city gates as Kendreague, his bow always ready at his side, his possessions including our gifts tied in panniers, rode the draggletailed but impressively large beast through the archway and out of our lives. I watched until the flying dust concealed his passage. A little of my love and a lot of my admiration went with him. Without Kendreague, I doubted that I would be standing here, in my new environment, near to my new grandson (here I go again), and with Melania Lupurca ensconced in my enviably impressive town house.

It had been a busy morning. And among my new patients there had been a familiar one. Old Laetorius accompanied of course by Sassia talking excitedly as soon as she approached the door.

'We were so pleased when we met Fannia in the market and she told us that you are here.'

'So you stayed in Venta Bulgarum. How is your daughter?'

'Marcia is betrothed. Such a lovely man. You must come to dinner and meet Rutilius and his mater. Rutilius's father was an army casualty. Rutilius has a house on the other side of the Forum. Such a lovely house. Marcia and Rutilius make a lovely couple.'

So everything was lovely then, except Laetorius's unlovely eye.

'What of your villa on Vectis?'

'We will go back – some time…'

Sassia faltered, not seeming too sure about her answer. While she paused, unusually for Sassia, to take breath, I made my examination and talked Laetorius through the procedure so that he understood exactly what I needed to do to clear his sight. I do not believe however that he understood. They would return tomorrow by which time Sassia would have made a date for dinner. I did not mention my house guest. And neither did Sassia. She had probably chosen to forget.

Almost three years had passed since I moved to Venta Bulgarum. With guidance from Crispinus, my practice was quickly established. Finnius had some paper work to do for me again. He and Claudia were planning to be wed in June, the favourite month for Roman girls, despite the popularity of Christianity that precluded obedience to Juno. My own household gods haad been firmly locked away in the villa on Vectis and I wondered occasionally if my least favourite Lar was plotting revenge. Here, in the house at Venta Bulgarum, I insisted that Melania displayed her most precious ornamentation. But Melania was very discreet over her religion. Unlike Fannia, she displayed no iconic decoration anywhere in the public areas of the house, although I cannot speak for her cubiculum. I had not yet been invited there. The two women went to the Christian church every week but Melania never invited me there either. Perhaps one day I would invite myself to the church. That would surprise them, both of them.

Melania and I were each other's constant companions at dinner, and when we called to see Fannia and my grandson, little Lucius. What a precocious lad he was. Into everything, toddling too fast until his chubby legs let him down and his screams echoed around the high elegant rooms. Fannia was in her element as a mother. Her devoted care filled me with pride.

Not much news of the outside world filtered through to Venta Bulgarum. I regularly questioned my son in law as to the state of the Empire and more importantly of Britannia but perhaps he genuinely did not know anything. Or perhaps he was sworn not to reveal anything.

I lay back on my couch, groaning with the pleasure of stretching out my limbs. I often indulged in this welcome relaxation, following the exit of the last of my morning patients. It reminded me of Rome, where everyone tended to have a quiet couple of horae before the welcome cool of the evening woke us again. I never gave much thought to Rome nowadays, but I was sleepily receptive, comfortable to let the memories wash over me, wave upon wave of images that I thought were long forgotten. Alas I have no memories of my mother, she died giving birth to me, but the affection my father always invoked, brought about a reassuring vision of her shade, when I was ill or haunted by bad dreams. More ominously, I felt my father's despair for our great Rome, the seat of our Empire, renowned all over the world, forsaken by its emperors.

Lying on my couch, I watched dreamily, my father taking me along the Via Sacra that ran through the great Forum, the route of the religious processions, pointing out the temple of Venus and Rome at the eastern end and the Portico of the consenting Gods and the Temple of Vespasian on the slope adjoining the Forum. I can recall the building of the Circular shrine the Temple of Romulus, but my favourite of the temples was the Temple of Saturn because it was the most sacred location in the Forum, where Hercules himself dedicated an altar.

I could still envisage the Capitol and the golden Rome holding the world in her hand. She encapsulated my image of Rome. The undefeated conqueror. I saw again the immense Circus Maximus, the emperors' palaces looking north towards the formidable Colosseum and the building that intrigued me more than any other. The Pantheon, the huge domed rotunda almost concealed behind traditional pillars conceived by the Greeks, replicated by the Romans.

My father was always impressed by ingenious craftsmen. He took as much time to describe the Aqueducts, perfection in hydraulic engineering, as when he explained the height of the Pantheon dome having the identical dimension as the diameter of the floor level, going on to describe the whole structure from its foundation on a ring beam, not that his technical descriptions meant much to me then or now. The most fascinating feature of the Pantheon was the central oculus throwing the only light downwards within the building. Around its dark edges there always seemed to be huddles of men whispering ominously or so it seemed to me as a child. I was torn, wanting to stay and gaze up at the bright circle of sky, but fearful of the mysterious murmuring conversations below.

Fleeting pictures of my wife and her onerous family appeared, too distasteful to contemplate but of course I am human, recognising human curiosity over Flaccilla's whereabouts and the identity of the mysterious medical person she had disappeared with. And I remembered Egnatius. Now I would very much like to know his whereabouts, despite Kendreague's insistence to leave the past behind. I heard myself growling restively, half in and half out of sleep. I allowed my meandering thoughts to settle in Vectis. If everything continued to go well, I had said to Duane, I shall accept your silence as good news. Duane had promised faithfully that he would find a way to convey any occurrence of bad news to me. But I feared that breakdown in communications in Britannia had already happened. It was the only piece of news that my son-in-law seemed willing to tell me. Once when he and I were drinking falernian together without the women, he said firmly that it would be folly to think of returning to Vectis and that he feared for the safety of my villa and my property. He didn't mention anxieties for the men and women and children, the natives of Vectis. I wondered what information he had not divulged. But he would not be pressed further.

However nothing prevented my conviction that my villa on Vectis waited for me. One day I would return, travelling on safe roads and crossing to the island on a calm sea. And I could visualise the dovecote alive with white birds and my blue and gold peacocks strutting on the green grass. I had to hold onto my dream. And to the hope that Melania would be in the dream with me.

And what of the future?

A loud knock on my door broke up the already disjointed reveries. I knew it was an emergency. Venta Bulgarum's new iron foundry was too often the scene of terrible accidents. Only the other day a slave was brought to me with sand embedded in his eyes. 'When we pour the hot metal into the mould of wet sand, the mould sometimes flies apart' I was told by the man that accompanied him. The risks went with the job, but the poor man was blinded in his left eye and a doubtful prognosis remained for the other. And I doubted that would I receive any payment from his master.

As I straightened my tunic, the door admitted Melania. She seemed so disturbed that I sat her down and held her hands. I liked to do that even when there was no excuse.

'The gossip is all over Venta Bulgarum. A party of auxiliaries have arrived from Londinium. The last of the army are preparing to leave.'

She gasped the last words so that she choked and coughed.

'Londinium… will have no protection. What terrible news. What of our friends? I cannot bear to think of it.'

It was some moments before I could question her, as her beautiful eyes filled with tears. I gently patted her back.

'Who told you this?'

'Fannia called. She is waiting to see you, Marcus.'

'Why the gods did you not tell me?'

It was the first occasion I could remember that I had raised my voice to Melania. But I think she understood or perhaps it brought back memories of her irrascible deceased husband because she seemed to vanish away. I went to find my daughter. Fannia had been given the news by Aquilinus dashing home for a quick bite of bread, cheese and a honey cake between a heavy work programme brought about by the unexpected arrival of the squadron.

‘Melania is terribly upset because you have friends in Londinium.’

I remembered Paulus and his wife Statilia desperately hoping to remain in Londinium. I recalled telling Paulus to flee to Venta Silarum if things looked bad. But I wondered how much better it would be over in the west of the province. They will stay in Londinium, I predicted silently. Life will go on with or without the Roman army. Everyone needed to survive. More to Paulus’s point, everyone needed bread and fast food.

‘I think Melania worries too much’ I shouted to Fannia over the noise of the screaming Lucius. It was easy not to call him my grandson when he made such an ear-splitting din. Fannia picked him up and rocked him back and forth hugging him to her lately ample bosom.

‘He’s hungry’ she explained.

No consolation. I needed some peace. I needed some fresh air.

‘I have to go out’ I said to the surprised young matron.

I located my son in law. He was standing in the centre of the square before the Government building. He was talking to a man in centurian’s dress uniform. Since my confrontation with the desperate band of ex-slaves, I was unwilling to take anybody at face value. But this fellow sported a short sword that he was obviously comfortable with. He wore a red army cloak and his face hugging, plumed helmet kept his face straight and distorted his words. And I immediately recognised him at the same instance that he sighted me.

‘Well, if it isn’t Marcus Cassius!’

‘Fabatus!’

It could have been awkward. It wasn’t. The man laughed, Aquilinus laughed.

‘You are still alive then after all the chances you took?’

‘I had a good servant’ I reminded him.

‘Your slave! I remember him. Built like a gladiator. My men had it in for him, I remember that too. Where is he?’

‘Returned to his tribe.’

‘You freed him?’

‘I did.’

‘Why in the name of Mithras did you do that? You could have got many more years’ work out of him before he was brought to his knees. Slaves of his quality are not easy to come by. But of course there is an untapped wealth of slave material here in Britannia. More are caught every day. Do you need another slave? I know of a good dealer.’

I did not want to encourage this diatribe.

‘When you have ended your discussion, I would like a word with you, Aquilinus.’

I walked away from them. Why did I always recall Seneca and his appropriate comments on life? But the words of Seneca would not have impressed the likes of Fabatus. I thought of them anyway.

‘Please reflect that the man you call your slave was born of the same seed, has the same good sky above him, breathes air you do, lives as you do, dies as you do…Treat your slaves with kindness, with courtesy too; let him share your conversation, your deliberations and your company.’

I watched the unconcerned comings and goings of the citizens of Venta Bulgarum, and a few slaves too who were running instead of walking, some carrying heavy loads on their backs and probably in their hearts as well. My son in law stood beside me.

‘I have not much time to talk, Marcus.’

‘What is this news I hear about Londinium? What civitas will be the next to be abandoned by the Roman army?’

‘This civitas is well protected. It would take a heavily disciplined army to break through, and most of the lawless roaming bands are small in numbers and badly armed - as I believe you know only too well. Do not worry Marcus. I am not. How amusing that you met with Fabatus!’

He smiled at my straight face.

‘Well Fabatus found it amusing. I think he secretly admires your determination. And he admired Kendreague too. I think our Fabatus is always on the lookout for a slave like Kendreague to add to his collection.’

I ignored this.

‘Why is Fabatus here in Venta Bulgarum?’

‘Oh he comes here from time to time. On this occasion, he was in charge of the auxiliaries from Londinium. An important officer has arrived here also. But I do not think he would interest you. It is army business. If you will excuse me, I have to return.’

I spent a restless evening pacing the house. There were changes afoot. If the Roman army were starting to pull out, how safe were we, the Roman citizens? I had asked myself these questions before. Now they seemed more urgent. But Aquilinus would not jeopardise the safety of his little familia. He knew how the land lay better than me. Or did he?

Dinner with Melania was a silent process. Neither of us ate very much, although the cook we had employed produced excellent food. She had successfully disguised the chicken so well with a delicate sweet sauce so that I did not recognise it until the fourth mouthful. I replaced the platter on the dainty repositorium together with my slender silver spoon. The set of spoons, and the repositorium had been here on my arrival. I was beginning to wonder if the previous owner had left in a hurry, so many valuable items seemed to have been left behind.

‘Everything seems to be very uncertain since the arrival of the army from Londinium. It is extremely worrying’ commented Melania.

‘It is only a few auxiliaries’ I corrected her. Women never got it right when they gossiped.

‘No my dear Marcus. Fannia told me that the entire barracks have been emptied. Londinium is on its own.’

Since long ago on Vectis on the night before she had left for Londinium, Melania and I stayed together. Our togetherness was unquestionable. We were moulded into our togetherness. The bright morning was unwelcome, because we had to part, and talks had to resume. About our futures. All of our futures.

Venta Bulgarum was seething with soldiers. Red cloaks and shining helmets coloured the normally drab street and the Forum and the market. We fought our way through the unyielding armed bodies, Melania, myself, Claudia and Finnius, to reach the house of my family before Aquilinus departed for work.

Aquilinus did not look amused at seeing us in force, so early, or at all. Fannia absored in feeding Lucius looked mildly surprised.

'What is the problem?' said Aquilinus as though there could not possible be one.

'We have a right to know what will happen to Roman citizens once the army are removed from the civitas.'

Finnius had spoken out. Good for him, although I was surprised because I thought it should have been my prerogative.

'The place is full of soldiers. How long are they here? And when they go, will our squadrons go also?'

My grandson wriggled determinedly off Fannia's lap. He staggered towards me on his funny fat legs, and grabbed my knee with a podgy sticky hand. Whatever had he been eating? I refrained from touching him but I gave him an encouraging smile, while trying not to panic about the state of my tunic.

'Ga ga ga' said Lucius. It was a linguistic start.

'We are completely safe' said Aquilinus not fully addressing the question.

'We will be outnumbered' said Finnius the accountant.

I took over.

'You are prepared to stay here, with your family. You are not concerned by the future lack of professional armed support for the civitas.'

I could see Aquilinus wanting unsuccessfully to duck the issue. He blinked rapidly. He was nervous after all.

'At present, we are safe here. There is a possibility some time in the future…'

He paused and I knew he was about to divulge information that should have been secret.

'I may be relocated to New Rome.'

Fannia uttered a little scream. I could not tell if it was excitement, fear or surprise.

'Ah' I said.

'I must go' said my son in law.

We all sat round the triclinium and waited while Fannia adoringly cleaned up her squirming son and handed him over to her servant, who had meantime taken a sponge to my tunic without success.

'Whatever was he eating?'

I got no reply. Fannia was in another world.

'I may go to New Rome!'

'Is it the first you have heard?' asked Melania.

Fannia nodded.

'Aquilinus is not allowed to give out information. So you must say nothing to anyone.'

We were all very quiet.

'What about Finn and me?' wailed Claudia presently.

'Come to New Rome. Melania, you would love it there. Everything revolves around the Christian faith. It will be wonderful.'

'And if Rome is vanquished?' This from Finnius. 'There have been rumours for a long time.'

'But that will never be allowed to happen. The Roman Empire rules the whole world.'

She sounded like me at eight years old, standing in the Forum in Rome, believing that the world belonged to Rome, for ever. But already Rome was relaxing her grip on a tiny outpost of her Empire that she had never really conquered completely.

I stood up. I wanted to go back to my new house. I had to think.

Two evenings later, a messenger called to invite Melania and I to dinner, with the Laetorius family. It was a sumptuous affair, in an exceedingly sumptuous house, the renting of which had been arranged by Sassia in the early days of their stay in Venta Bulgarum. The days had turned into years and they were still in residence. The vast dining room held us all easily. I have never seen so many couches. Laetorius lay with his wine cup, comfortable if vague. I was gratified that he could see much better, even if he could hear even less. I was introduced to Rutilius, Marcia's betrothed, a handsome Roman with a nose to match. His mother had not accepted the invitation. She doesn't go out at all since her dear husband was killed, explained incredulous Sassia, carelessly in the hearing of Rutilius. He seemed to weather it, he should be getting used to Sassia and her disarming statements. Sassia gave Melania a passing smile that faded as soon as it had began. Fannia must have told her about Melania and me. I don't think Sassia was very amused. But Sassia was the perfect hostess and she did have countless dining room slaves to oversee. Aquilinus and Fannia looked as perfect a couple as ever although Fannia concealed her once girlish figure under a suitably voluminous robe interwoven with golden threads.

The surprise guests were Aquilinus's mother Valida and her distinguished army partner, Chrysippus. Aquilinus showed not a little surprise at seeing them together. He and Chrysippus obviously knew each other only slightly. I saw him raise his eyebrows inquiringly at his mother who looked delightfully calm, wearing the blue dress I recalled from Fannia's wedding. In fact the evening was graced by three beautiful mature women. Tiny vivid Sassia, in red of course. Valida, elegantly tall as female Britons so often are. And my own magnificent Melania, wearing the silver robe with golden threads that I remembered from Vectis days. How sweet the memories were and how fortunate I was that Melania was still at my side.

As we rose replete from our couches, we all wandered amiably, except Laetorius who seemed to be peacefully sleeping, through to a wide hall successfully designed as an atrium, even to a central pool with a stone ledge wide enough to sit upon. The ceiling above had been painted to represent blue skies and white clouds and supported by pillars delineated in gold paint. Aquilinus, not interested like everyone else in the impressive surroundings, almost bounded to his mother's side, unspoken questions bursting from his head. But it was the military man Chrysippus, who commanded our attention.

'Ahem!'

The animated buzz of conversation died away.

'I am honoured to be invited to such a splendid dinner' he said in his booming voice well used to being projected. 'My thanks to our hostess Sassia.'

There was a gentle murmur of appreciation and a patter of applause.

'I am also honoured in a more personal way. This charming lady, Valida, has done me the greatest honour by accepting my offer of marriage.'

Chrysippus and I found ourselves standing together later in the evening, after congratulations had been offered to the couple, and after Aquilinus had recovered from the shock and taken it quite well. People ventured into the night air for there was a small garden attached to the house, a rare luxury for a town house. For the sake of conversation, I could not resist mentioning to this eminent man, about the presence of the military in Venta Bulgarum, displaying an ignorant surprise that he obviously enjoyed.

'It is the final residue of men from Londinium. They leave for Gaul in two days.'

'So Londinium is on its own now.'

'Sadly yes. Have you ever been there? It is a place of great charm, a magnificent forum, and some temples well worth a visit. Too late now though. I fear for its future.'

‘Why do you say that? I have been to Londinium and met people who want to stay and make the place work.’

‘Oh it is not the citizens. The marauders from the north, and from abroad too, see it as a prime site to capture and use for their own devices. It will be looted and raised to the ground I fear.’

‘Why did the Empire desert Londinium?’

‘Too expensive old chap. That’s the bottom line. No industry to speak of. Nothing to export. Too expensive to import. That ridiculous channel of water has cost the Empire dearly in men and ships. The whole of Britannia has cost too much for too little return. The Roman Empire should never have bothered with it!’

I had heard a similar comment somewhere before. It made the pronouncement no more palatable.

‘It seems terrible to conquer native territory, modernise it and then simply abandon it.’

‘More to it than that old boy. The Goths, Visigoths and the Alans and all the other marauders are scavenging across the Northern Empire. The army is needed to protect areas that have far more use to the Empire.’

I took the bull by the horns.

‘Are you involved in these military activities?’

‘No. Thankfully, I am retired, old boy.’

I persisted, hating his condescending manner.

‘What of New Rome? Is it safe?’

‘I do not class anywhere in the Empire as safe nowadays. But it should be safer than anywhere else, if that makes any sense.’

It did and it didn’t. But I wasn’t going to get much further. I decided to find Melania but Chrysippus had decided he hadn’t done with me.

‘You are a surgeon, I believe Valida told me.’

‘That is correct.’ I looked around desperately for Melania, or Fannia, or even Sassia.

‘I suppose you haven’t heard of Constantine?’

I hadn’t. Not since the original Great Constantine anyway. I was bored now. I needed a cup of wine.

'He is actually, or was until recently, an obscure army officer. But he is taking over more and more power, and fast. Impressive fellow. He has the makings of a great leader. He is here at the moment.'

'In Venta Bulgarum?'

I knew that Chrysippus didn't mean he was here at Sassia's party.

'In fact, Constantine has engaged Aquilinus's services to perform some paperwork for him. Aquilinus will soon be my stepson. We will be almost family you and I.'

I laughed too. But it didn't seem that funny.

'You should meet Constantine. Ask Aquilinus for an introduction.'

And thankfully the eminent man moved on to bore someone else. I hate name-dropping even though I had not heard of the name. Why should I, a surgeon, want to meet an army officer, up and coming or not?

Melania sidled shimmeringly up to me. She whispered seductively. Melania did not ever whisper seductively. It was charming to hear.

'Please take me home' she said.

We were roused when it was scarsely light by sounds of marching, musical instrument blowing, swords and shields clattering. I staggered to the window and drew back amazed.

As far as the Forum, I could see solders. Seething squadrons of red and gold. The noise of their boots was deafening. I flung on my tunic and thundered down the stairs. Finnius was already at the door.

'There go the first of them.'

'Leaving Venta Bulgarum?'

Finnius did not bother to answer such a stupid question but I was hardly awake. He left the house and I followed, behind the marching army, until it reached the city gates. Beyond we could hear horses snorting. As the gates were thrown wide, we could see huge carriages of equipment and supplies. The army moved untidily outside, jostling with each other in a very un-military way. A crowd of citizens had joined the spectators. Everyone was very quiet. Beyond the city walls, the squadrons re-formed untidily, these were not well-drilled soldiers. As they moved thunderously away, a hush fell over the entire civitas. I knew what every single person was thinking. Soon enough, we too will be on our own.

My son in law called at the sixth hour. Melania offered him refreshment but he declined. He had something on his mind. Finnius who happened to be passing, stopped, sensing the atmosphere as Aquilinus spoke.

'In two days time, I am leaving Venta Bulgarum. I am being sent to New Rome. Of course…' he added hastily '…my familia also go with me. There will be places for all of you. Finn, you and Claudia may also travel with us.'

'So Venta Bulgarum is being abandoned.'

'No Marcus. There are no imminent plans. This is a call of duty to me. And half a century of soldiers will be leaving at that time, so it is obviously prudent to make the journey in safety.'

Melania and I sipped our wine thoughtfully, after a light repast of fresh bread and a vegetable potage, typically Britannic, of which I had become fond. I mentioned that we have a very good cook. But for how much longer?

'How do you view this sudden exodus to New Rome?'

Melania sighed.

'I hate the thought. I know I should welcome the chance to live in New Rome again. But…I feel that we are being dragged along, unable to make a decision for ourselves. For the young people, the move is right. Finnius and Claudia will marry and have a fresh start. Valida called to see me, she is very excited. She of course has never travelled outside Britannia. But I am nevertheless surprised at her eagerness to forsake her homeland. I wonder how she will be accepted. But of course she has the eminent Chrysippus to protect her.'

'We forsook our homeland' I reminded her.

Melania nodded.

'Remember, it was against my will that I left Rome. Your spirit of adventure led you to seek other places to use your skills. But now, what lies ahead? Will we sink into retirement like Laetorius. I am not ready. I failed in my efforts to help the people of Londinium, but despite my disappointment in my own ability, I do not now want to settle back and let others run my life while I do nothing.'

I reached out and took her hand.

'It is very strange, but you have voiced exactly my own thoughts. I do not relish tagging along on the back of Aquilinus either.'

And who would come to visit us, once we were settled comfortably, uselessly, within the grandeur of New Rome? Chrysippus, bored, with no one to impress? Fannia, towing my noisy grandson, when she had nothing better to do? I felt a strange mixture of emotions towards my familia. They had to get on with their lives. But I did not envisage being a part of it.

'We have not long to decide' I reminded her again.

'We do not have to leave' Melania said. 'Aquilinus told us, there is no immediate danger.'

She has made up her mind, I thought.

Once again I watched the red and gold noisy confusion of the army leaving Venta Bulgarum. And with them, the colourful flurry of my departing familia. It was with mixed feelings of relief and sorrow that I saw Fannia so excited. Fannia, who had always wanted to see Rome. The place she would see was presumably somewhat different, geographically and logistically. It would be interesting to learn how much of Rome had been re-created.

'Try to send messages to us' I said. What else could I say?

She promised, smothering me with kisses, holding up chubby Lucius who slobbered obligingly over me. I had not been a particularly attentive grandfather but then he wasn't particularly critical.

Valida, and Chrysippus who I thought looked a little apprehensive, perhaps he was experiencing the same reflections on his future role as Melania and I had, bade us fond farewells.

Finnius, correct as ever, reminded me where my paperwork was. He knew as well as I, that it was unlikely ever to be required by the Roman Government who had more pressing matters to deal with, or not. He did, however, make a request, that for Finnius seemed out of character.

'If you should see Kendreague, say that I think of him. He is a fine man.'

Melania and Claudia hugged each other and whispered women's secrets. Claudia was crying. Melania was as controlled as only Melania can achieve when the occasion demands.

And lastly, Aquilinus, smart and alert to his role as important member of the Government and as head of his own familia. He grasped my arms.

'We will get messages through as often as we are able' he lied, being as aware as I about the unlikelihood of any messages getting through, often or ever. But I appreciated his concern. Aquilinus hesitated. So he was obviously not feeling at his most efficient.

'I was supposed to arrange a meeting for you with our new officer Constantine. In the confusion of the last hours, I did not.'

'Has he a problem with his eyes?' I was surprised to hear the name again. A medical consultation was the obvious reason for the meeting that had escaped Aquilinus' attention.

'No no. But when you next go to the Government offices, be sure to make yourself known…'

He added 'If you change your mind and wish to leave Venta Bulgarum, you know there is always room for you with my familia in our home at New Rome.'

Melania and I watched and waved from the gatehouse, waving at the receding cloud of dust, although it was unlikely that anyone could see us to wave back.

'Safe journey' said Melania quietly. Then her self-control dropped as she sobbed and clung to me. We turned and I escorted her through the gates that closed with a ringing clang behind us.

'Have we done the right thing?'

I was sure we had, particularly after Aquilinus's last well meaning but lofty comment about 'his' familia. I knew that I could never become beholden to Aquilinus in his fustian role.

Venta Bulgarum settled down again. Except for the arrival of yet another great number of soldiers, two days after the departure of my daughter and my grandson.

Melania invited the Laetorius crowd over for dinner. Melania has a great sense of reciprical manners. Sassia was talking about returning to Vectis.

'Laetorius wants his garden' she explained. 'The one here is so small, no room for much more than a few small urns of flowers.'

How could I tell her that Laetorius's home probably no longer existed let alone her garden. One part of me believed that Vectis had been over run with pirates and the life crushed out of it. One part of me believed that everything was how we left it. I had never heard from Duane. But if I was honest I could imagine the sinister reason for that.

Rutilius and Marcia persuasively explained to Sassia how much safer we were here in Venta Bulgarum.

'The roads are too dangerous without an army escort and now that the army is not available…' This sensible argument from Rutilius as he lifted his wine bowl, and it was then that I noticed his right hand. The two first fingers were missing as tidily as if they had never been there. My curiousity as to why he had not followed his father into the army was satisfied. Or perhaps he had been injured in the army. Either way I could not bring myself to enquire and Fannia was not here now, because she could have asked Marcia.

Sassia shrugged.

'Everyone is scared.' She threw me an accusing look. She knew I was scared. Sassia was obviously getting bored. She was much more mobile having recently had an operation on her knee, about which I was not going to ask either.

The evening was successful to a point. Our cook had triumphed again. But Melania agreed with me as we waved the Laetorius lot off the premises, that everyone was edgy, quick to snap back, and most of all, uncertain as to the future here or anywhere. Sassia regretted that she never said goodbye to Valida, and Chrysippus where her emphasis lay. 'Such a handsome man, that lovely uniform!' I wondered derisively if he was still entitled to wear the lovely uniform seeing that he was retired. It did not matter now. I wondered what did matter now.

Unusually, I had no patients, so I was going to the market, an unfamiliar occupation for me. I walked briskly, as not unusually it was raining. And I needed some exercise, not that I ever took much but at least on Vectis, I could wander at will. Here, confined within high thick stone city walls, exercise was severely curbed. I wondered where my familia were. At the precise moment when a heavy hand upon my shoulder pulled me up.

Fabatus smiled down at me, his smile was a grimace but a friendly one. He had better not ask me if I needed a slave.

'Marcus Cassius. You are alone in Venta Bulgarum nowadays.'

A very obvious comment. I grimaced back at him. I had a question for him.

'What happens to the furniture and effects at my son in law's house now that he has left Britannia?'

‘If the Government needs the property, the furniture and everything else will be left for the incoming family, as in the case of your own house.’

Everyone knew everything about everyone. I felt irritation coming on and I was getting wetter without a thick cloak.

‘Those going abroad permanently can only take minimum possessions with them, restrictions on space and weight you will understand.’

Why had I asked? I remembered why I had asked.

‘I just wondered if there was anything that my daughter left behind, which perhaps I could look after for her.’

‘The keys to the house are up at the Government office. It will not be a problem. By the way, while you are there…’

‘Yes?’

What was hidden in the centurian’s cloak? I never trusted him.

‘Have you met Constantine?’

Heroic Achilles, elegantly enduring his death throes, seemed to watch me as I went from room to room. Searching through my daughter’s and Aquilinus’s house was a depressing business. The silence was oppressive, as I recalled the screams of my grandson and the other household noises one takes for granted. Until they are no longer there. It reminded me of when I did the same for my deceased father. I felt as though they were all dead. I searched on, hating myself for my thoughts, but Fannia had been very thorough considering she had only two days’ notice to leave the civitas. A pair of pretty sandals in a long wooden cupboard caught my attention and I picked them up sorrowfully. I would take them anyway. Beneath the shoes I saw a waxed notebook, the pages bound neatly with leather thongs. Untying it, I was amazed to see many pages of notes. They were scrawled in her difficult to decipher hand, around the time I went to

Londinium. It was Fannia's diary and it had been fashioned for her by dear old Fidus.

Returning the keys up to the Government offices on the hill was as much exercise as I could manage for one day and possibly the rest of the week. My legs ached, echoing my depression, as I trudged the steep incline. But at least the rain had lifted away. Fabatus was not about, I was glad to note. Another centurian, the one to whom I returned the huge key from the impressive metal lock, stared at me with interest as I signed my name on the tablet of visitors.

'Marcus Cassius. Would you wait.'

He disappeared, as a great clap of thunder echoed outside. I could almost feel the building shake. I hadn't recovered from the startling effect, when two men approached me. An energetic, stocky man possibly in his thirties held out his arm from beneath a swirl of scarlet cloak. He smiled winningly, confidently.

'Marcus Cassius. I am pleased to make your acquaintance. I am Constantine.'

It was late in the evening, before I could speak to Melania. She knew, of course, that I had something weighing heavily on my mind. She knew me so well.

'I went to the Government today.'

'Oh.'

'I met an extremely important soldier.'

'You were waylaid by Fabatus?'

It wasn't often that Melania joked. But I was impatient to tell my story.

'The soldier is an Officer. His name is Constantine.'

Melania showed no sign of recognition and taking heed of my serious expression, did not indulge in comments about Constantine the Great.

'Constantine engaged me in an extremely interesting discussion. He has offered me a position in his army.'

'Oh.'

Melania patiently refilled our goblets, the silver cups with the particularly unusual history. I had at last presented them to Aquilinus. But they had been left behind in the house. I retrieved them, along with Fannia's diary and sandals. The silver cups were back with me again. And I liked drinking from them again.

'The man has vision. He is clearly a strong leader of men.'

'He must be a leader and persuasive too, if he has offered you an army career that you are obviously considering seriously, at your age. Marcus, you have no experience of fighting. Oh really!'

'No, Melania. I am not invited to fight in his army, which as you say would be ridiculous.'

'Then please tell me!'

She was becoming impatient. We were all fractious these days. Venta Bulgarum had ceased to dispense calm reassurance to the citizens within its walls.

'Constantine is preparing his forces to depart for Gaul. He is assembling a large army, some from here in Britannia, others waiting overseas. Once in Gaul, he intends to establish a garrison and a fortified civitas or whatever they are called over there. The place, called Arelate, is already in existence and in the hands of the Roman army. Constantine has plans to create the new Gallic Empire, and Arlelate will be its stronghold with Constantine in full control. He has the support and backing of the centre at New Rome. Gaul is important to the Empire, and Constantine, I am convinced from talking with him and examining his plans. By the way, some were dictated to Aquilinus and are in his hand! Constantine is the man for the job. And there is more. He is already being hailed as the new Emperor, by the Roman garrison here in Britannia.'

Melania had been listening patiently.

'But where is your part in these great plans, Marcus?'

'Surely you can guess my darling. I am to be Surgeon at Arelate.'

I spent a busy time, revising forgotten knowledge concerning disease and injuries, with much help from Crispinus. Being a lot older than me and not too strong of late, he was glad to impart knowledge and loan me his books and scrolls, though only the gods knew when I would return them. Melania also sat in on some of my instruction, as she is eager to be my assistant and to advise people on health matters. She is very enthusiastic about the project. Like me, Melania is happiest when there are fresh exciting challenges.

It is our turn to leave the walled civitas of Venta Bulgarum. For myself and Melania, there are few regrets. Gaul, with Arelate as its centre of power, will provide a new life for us both. It is a long journey, over the sea, down to the south of Gaul. We plan to marry as soon as we are established over there. Our love for each other flourishes daily.

The muffled clopping of the horses' feet, the grinding of the wheels, the boots of the soldiers ringing on the solid Roman built roads, take us away from everything we know. On to the coast of Britannia, skirting the pathetic burned out ruins of Clausentum. Somewhere in the distance, beyond that narrow, treacherous strip of water lies the island of Vectis the place I will always hold tightly in my heart. Our ships will pass quite close to the island, but I shall not look. I have to remember Vectis as it was and perhaps still is, but inaccessible at this time, in the new daunting scheme of things.

One day, I know I shall return; perhaps as a shade drifting through the gardens; pausing at my nymphaeum, disturbing the white doves, hearing the rural activities from my farm. As I wander through my beloved villa I will make not so much as a mark or a shadow on the exquisite patterned floors, nor utter a sound in the silent warm air. If my ghostly return is thousands of years distant, I will have never abandoned the villa on Vectis where I lived and loved. I and my darling daughter Fannia and my adorable companion Melania, and all the many others that shared our world, loyal, good or corrupt and bad, for such is the essence of humans.

I will always be there amongst the waving grasses and the ancient stones and the calling sea.

By 411 AD the Roman Empire had fallen apart.

Notes by the author

The places:

Vectis – The Isle of Wight
Calleva (Atrebatum) - Silchester
Clausentum – Southampton
Londinium - London
Noviomagus – Chichester
Tamesis – River Thames
Venta Belgarum –Winchester
Venta Silarum – Caerwent

The people:

Domina	Female head of household
Foederati	Friendly natives
Ordinari	Slaves specialising in specific skill(s)
Pater familia	Male head of household
Patria potestas	Women and children subject to power of the *pater familia*
Praetorian	High ranking army official
Procurator	High ranking official in top household (i.e. Emperor)
Univira	Matron married only once

The clothes:

Armilae	Bracelets
Endromida	Heavy cloak
Flammeum	Orange wedding veil
Focale	Scarf
Monilia	Women's jewellery
Stolla	Women's long simple belted robe

The architecture:

Atrium	Reception area usually with rooms grouped around
Impluvium	Central pool in Atrium with wide opening in roof
Cubiculum	Bedroom

Caldarium,tepidarium,	The baths: room with hot bath, middle temperature,
frigidarium	cold bath
Hypocausis	Stoking area for heating water and baths
Nymphaeum	Pool usually in garden
Peristylium	Garden surrounded by colonnades
Suspensurae	Floor supported on small brick columns for circulation of hot air beneath
Tesserae	small mosaics forming patterns
Triclinicum	Dining room

The furniture:

Cathedra	High backed chair often particularly for women
Cagoena	Wine holder
Orbis	Table top
Repositorium	Table for holding food placed near dining couch
Trapezophorus	Central table support

Miscellaneous:

Panis candidus	Best or top quality bread
Mulsum	Honeyed wine
Raeda	Four wheeled carriage

Weddings:

spina alba	Hawthorn torch (distributed at weddings as good luck)
tabulae nuptials	Marriage contract
dextrarum junctio	Silent exchange of vows
cena nuptialis	Wedding banquet
lectis geniali	Position where bride sits facing door of her new home and offers prayers to the household god

Funerals

Ustrinae	Site of funeral pyre
'hominem mortuum in urbe ne sepelito neve urito...'	Last rites
Gods and Goddesses: Jupiter and Juno	Two principal Roman gods, brother and sister, husband and wife, Juno goddess of women and marriage, Jupiter responsible for weather, storms.
Sol	Sun god who appears and vanishes daily
Somnus	God of sleep
Charon	Ferries the dead across the river styx
Mithras	God of soldiers
Lares	Spirits of departed ancestors, protected family. Almost every household owned an altar to the Lares
Boudicca	Heroine widow of King of the Iceni tribe, flogged, daughters raped, when Roman army plundered
Horace	Roman Poet 65-8 BC. Keen observor of contemporary life in his poetry. Influenced by early Greek poetry.
Seneca	Roman philosopher and celebrated Stoic
Constantine	In 407AD, in Britain, hailed as new Emperor – his later departure heralded the end of the Roman Empire

Lightning Source UK Ltd.
Milton Keynes UK
UKOW02f2023050516

273615UK00002B/11/P